LIES & ILLUSIONS

HEAVEN'S REJECTS MC #4

WALL STREET JOURNAL AND USA TODAY BESTSELLING AUTHOR

AVELYN PAIGE

BLURB

She ran from life with the MC. The MC is the only life he wants.

Presley Sanders was once the princess of the Heaven's Rejects MC. But that life was never one she wanted. That's why she ran the first chance she got. But now Presley has a target on her back, and the club is her only hope. Even if it means sacrificing everything, she's worked so hard to forget.

Beau "Voodoo" Martin has loved Presley since the moment he laid eyes on her. Even when she ran, he followed her, making little connections wherever he could. But now she's back and she's in danger, and Voodoo is determined to protect her, no matter the cost.

But when love mixes with lies, lives can be ruined, and souls can be shattered.

Dedication

Dad,

I miss you every single day.

Happy Birthday in Heaven.

I love you.

MPD#792

Chapter 1

FOUR YEARS AGO

PRESLEY

"THERE'S no fucking way that I'm letting you leave," my brother, Mikey, orders from the doorway of my room. Not this crap again.

"Well, I hate to break it to you, big brother, but I'm an adult. I can come and go as I please *without* your permission."

Mikey shoves off from the doorframe and stomps his large feet toward me in a huff. His anger flows off of him in heated waves that might be able to melt the polar ice caps had they been in this room. Most wouldn't challenge him when he's like this, but I'm not going to back down. He can yell and roar, but that will not change my mind.

"You are my little sister, and I will be damned if I

let you cut and run out of state without so much as an explanation."

"This isn't up for discussion. You and your one-man committee can just move on."

Leaving the shirt I was tucking into my bag, I spin on my heels and go face to face with my seething brother. His height looms over me, and for a split second, I feel dwarfed by his giant presence. He's like the heavyweight prizefighter breathing down the neck of his underdog opponent, even though I'm the underdog in this card, he'll be the first to fall to the mat in defeat.

You made this deal, Presley. Don't let his anger make you second guess the decision. This is your chance to leave, and you are taking it.

I cross my arms over my chest, standing my ground. He huffs his disapproval loudly. His cold blue eyes reflect the image of my father who died long ago, yet still lives in the darkest part of my mind. A piece of me that I will continually fight from coming to the surface. My brother may have fallen in line with my father's version of life, but that's not my destiny. I will never live that life.

Mikey's coldness brings a haunting thought hurtling to the forefront of my mind. *Just how much has my brother embraced the dark side of our father in my absence?*

Mikey has a wife and a family now, but just how much has he followed in my father's dark footsteps on a dangerous path? We both have a piece of that bastard inside of us. While my brother seems to have embraced it with open arms, I fought it.

It's been nine years since I spent more than a few days back in this town, and today would be the last time I set foot back here for the next few years. That was not a coincidence. Every trip back home from school was like a knife to the heart. My family life wasn't picturesque. Not by a long shot. It was dark, unhappy, and filled with death and destruction. My father's club is a far cry from a family, and even though I was treated well, I saw what they didn't want me to see. Even after my father's death, the Heaven's Rejects are still a group of men who make the devil look like a child acting out to seek attention. Wherever they are, death follows.

"You are not going. End of story," my brother declares in his matter-of-fact tone. Too bad for him that tone has never worked on me like it did with his brothers.

"I *am* going," I retort back, narrowing my eyes. His argumentative retorts remind me so much of how we argued as children. Is that what we are going to resort to in adulthood? What more can I do to show him that I don't give a shit about his opinion?

He growls in a rage, and to further my point, I turn my back on him and continue to pack. He will not intimidate me into staying. Mikey's large hand reaches out, grips my shoulder, and spins me back to face him.

"I gave you four years at that expensive fucking school. Then when you asked to go to graduate school, I relented and paid for five more years. You've gotten that degree, and it's high time you come home."

He's not wrong. Without his help, and the small life insurance policy my dad had left in my name, I would have never even been able to afford the tuition for Stanford University. I was grateful for what he did for me. He equipped me to pursue my dreams, and deep down, I know he had intended for me to come back well-educated and ready to stay home. But I didn't want to stay here, and honestly, I don't know if I ever would.

The time I spent away from the Heaven's Rejects MC was a peaceful leave of absence that only reassured me that distance was the best thing for me. I had spent years living as the crowned princess, under my father's rule and then my brother's. It was less than bearable. Every second I lived under this roof, fear ruled my life. Between the messes that my father had clearly left behind for my brother to deal with, to the change in the culture Mikey had tried to instill here, I was out of my comfort zone. I had tasted freedom, and that was a feeling that I was never going to give up. No amount of guilt over my brother's support would change my mind when so much was at stake.

"Yes, I'm aware of who paid my tuition, but you can't seem to accept that I'm not like you," I hiss back at him. "You're happy here living as the king. I never was. After dad died, I thought that would change, but it hasn't. You're becoming *him*. Just like he wanted. If I'm going to survive in this world, it has to be away from here. Away from this club. And away from *your* influence."

The words that just left my mouth cut him deep, as I had intended them to do because, for a split second, I see a momentary flutter of sadness cross his face. He needs to understand, and this is the only way to do it. If I didn't do this now, he would continue to fight me tooth and nail, until the bitter end where I would end up a prisoner in my own house. I had to hurt him or he'd never let go.

"Will you at least tell me where you're going?"

"The east coast," I shortly answer, before turning my back on him once again.

"Jesus," he utters while pinching the bridge of his

nose between two fingers. "That's all you are going to give me, isn't it?"

I sigh internally, knowing that this is going to hurt me much more than it will him. Mikey is cold and calculated like my father, and moments like this remind me how truly different the two of us really are now.

"What about Mom?" he adds in, delivering a low blow.

"Mom understands. Unlike you."

And she did, even if I had lied to her about getting an internship with the biggest psychology group in the country. It was an internship of sorts. That's what I was clinging to as the real reason, but it was much more than an internship. It was a chance to become something. A chance to get away from here and further my career. One that I was taking with open arms despite the consequences that would come with it. Another opportunity like this would never come again, and I had to seize it. This was my chance to forge my own destiny, even if I was trading one devil for another with a laundry list of demands that I was required to meet. Sacrifices had to be made, lies had to be told, and secrecy of the highest level kept.

As much as I despised this club, Mom was my only reason for short trips home. Just thinking about leaving her makes my heart die a little bit inside. But it isn't up for negotiation. She's the sacrifice that I had to make to get what I wanted in my life without furthering my debt to my brother and his club. She's the price I had to pay for freedom.

It's just a few years. You do your job, and then you're free.

No family ties, no visits, and no locations. The devil, who now owned me, wanted me to cut off ties from pretty much the whole world. When they dangled everything that I had ever wanted professionally on a gilded string, I pawed at it like a playful kitten hoping to be adopted. I was desperate for something more in my life, and they were willing to give it to me on their terms. They wouldn't relent on me making calls home to my mom, but I had already ensured another way to make that happen. I guess it's the only good thing about being the daughter of an evil incarnate because I knew how to think outside of the box. My mother was the only bright spot left in my life, and I needed her, even if it was only to hear her voice.

Mikey rubs his hand over his brow in a feeble attempt of trying to come to terms with what I'm telling him. His skull is thick and filled to the brim with stubbornness. Just like me. We were cut from the same genetic cloth. Even with so many years between us, I knew him better than he knew himself. He was the protective big brother, and I was the doting little sister who idolized him when we were closer as kids. Until all that changed the moment he joined the club. The playfulness inside of him was replaced by a man I hardly knew, and that is who is standing in front of me. Mikey was now Raze, Club President. He was a man that did what he wanted, and everyone would fall in line behind him. The club came first, and everything else came in a distant second.

Except for me. I grew up while he wasn't watching.

"Mikey," I start. "You know that I don't belong here. I'm not the little girl that used to follow you around all the time. I'm a grown woman with a doctorate in psychology. This internship is the opportunity of a lifetime, and despite what you say, I'm taking it."

He looks away briefly before returning his gaze back to me. The sorrowful look on his face gives me the answer I know is about to leave his lips.

"Fine," he grumbles. "But I want you to come home when you can. Mom will miss you."

"I'll try," I lie. "This program is really intense, and I don't know how much downtime I'll have."

"I guess I can accept a try," he disappointedly concedes.

Before I can even respond, his large arms wrap around me and bring me into the tightest hug that he's given me in years. The familiarity of his embrace momentarily brings me back to the good days of our childhood, before it snaps me back to reality. This was a fleeting moment of weakness that would disappear the minute he left my room; when his guard would go back up.

"Mikey," I squeak. "There's a car waiting outside for me. I really need to finish packing. My plane leaves in a few hours, and I'm not even remotely ready to go."

He reluctantly releases me and walks out of the room without another word, in defeat. Even with playing the ace in his hand by using mom as an excuse, I trumped him in the end. I look around my small room at my mom's house. It's an odd feeling knowing that this may be the last time I'm in this room. My walls are lined with photographs from my brief stint playing softball, academic club competitions, and a news article about my acceptance to Stanford. A dusty shelf next to them houses my trophies and medals that are reminders of my high school days that are long gone. My heart hurts as I scan the room as memories come crashing back.

Shake it off. You know what will happen if you stay. Leave the memories behind.

My brother's muffled voice coming from down the hall instantly brings me back from my trip down haunted memory lane, as a reminder for my flight pings on my phone next to the opened and half-packed suitcase. I quickly grab the few mementos I decided to bring along and top it off with the rest of my clothes before zipping it closed. I grab my phone and slide it into my back pocket before moving the heavy suitcase off the bed to the door-way. It's sad to think that so much of my life currently resides in those three bags. It's pretty pathetic.

Mikey's voice grows louder, as I hear him arguing with my mother about me leaving. He doesn't realize that Mom has always wanted what was best for us. He took Dad's road, and I'm following Mom's new path. Dad's death freed us all, but for her, this was a chance at another life. She didn't have to worry about being a single mother or being homeless. She was well cared for and enjoying life for the first time in a long time, even if she was under the watchful eye of my brother from a distance.

I look around the room one more time before hoisting one of my bags over my shoulder, grabbing the other two, and leaving my old room behind.

Mikey and Mom pause at the sight of me. Tears begin to well in my mother's eyes.

"I wish you would let me drive you to the airport," she offers. Leaving her behind on the curb in tears would break me, and I can't take that chance. I must do this. It's my only way out.

"I know, Mom," I reassure her. "But the internship paid for that expensive car outside, and I don't want to get off on the wrong foot with them."

"I know, baby," she relents.

Another ping sounds from my phone. It's time to go.

"I love you, Mom," I softly cry as I reach out. Her small body wraps around mine and shakes from sobs.

"I love you," she cries against my shoulder. After a few minutes, she pulls her tear-streaked face away from mine and rubs her hand across my face. "Be safe, baby."

"I will."

I look to my brother, who stands next to her, and he doesn't budge. His stubbornness is apparently unwilling to give up control long enough to say goodbye. But it's for the best. He would only try to convince me to stay again, and I'd rather leave this place without another argument. I nod to him as I pass by. His silence remains as I head out of the door.

Before I get two steps outside, a man in a black suit quickly grabs my bags and loads them into the back of the car. He ushers me into the open door. I slide into the warmed leather interior of the black town car. The sound of the door shutting behind me sends a shiver down my spine, and again when he climbs into the driver's side. The car jolts as it begins to pull away, while I watch my childhood shrinking in the distance through dark-tinted windows.

As the view of my mother's house disappears, I turn around as my own tears begin to drip down my face. I sob for miles until there's absolutely nothing left inside of me. The wet circular stains from the tears are now my badges of courage. The tears leaving my body represent the fear of the unknowns and loneliness of being secluded from my family. There's only one thing left inside of me now, and that's the resolve to see this through.

This was my decision, and it's one that I will have to live with for the rest of my life. I just hope that it was the right one.

Chapter 2

VOODOO

"OLD BUSINESS?" My club president asks to the crowded Church room. My brothers look around at each other, watching for anyone to add additional information into our daily club meeting.

Hero, our VP, clears his throat, and I suddenly get the sense that I'm not going to like what I'm about to hear.

"I'd like to bring up Slider's patch vote."

I stifle a groan. The kid has stepped up when he's been asked, but his cocky attitude has started to wear on me. In his mind, he's already earned his patch. The reality is that he still has so much to learn about what it means to take the oath and join our brotherhood. He fared well in our more violent moments.

That I can't deny. He just needs to learn that not everything is going to end in a bloodbath. The delicate balance between peace and violence was fast becoming the new normal for us. He just had to accept that, instead of looking for another fight.

"Do you really think now is a good time?" Tyson retorts with a questioning look plastered on his face.

"I think we need to make our decision soon," Hero fires back. "It's not like he hasn't gotten his required time in. We need the numbers. The latest run in with Rex should be proof enough of that."

"I agree, but I'm with Tyson on this. He's put his time in, but I have some reservations about the kid. He needs more time to mature, before we give him full status. We shouldn't jump to add in new members just because our numbers are down. If we need help, we can call in the other chapters," Raze offers as a suggestion to the table discussion.

Raze shifts in his chair, pulling his hands up to the gray, stumbled beard that whips around his chin. The last few years has visibly aged him, despite the resurgence of his more youthful pursuits with Darcy as his old lady. He is almost chipper on occasion with her around. I should send her flowers for that one of these days or would that be weird? A card with "Thanks for fucking my Prez" might just send the wrong impression. I scratch the gift idea and pay more attention to the conversation going on around me.

Hero scowls, but doesn't say anything more. He doesn't always agree with Raze, and I get it. We're stubborn fucking bastards who think with our dicks most of the time, but Raze is right on this one. There's no threat lingering on the horizon to warrant such a rapid-fire response. The suggestion that Hero made is something else entirely. I just need to find out what.

Raze adjourns the meeting, and as I'm leaving, I spot Hero heading into his office. Now's my chance to find out what's really going on in his head without the audience of our brothers. We might share just about everything, including the club pussy, but something is off about him. I haven't seen him like this since Dani's kidnapping by her stepbrother from hell.

I don't even bother knocking, when I shuffle into his office and close the door behind me. His elbows are firmly planted on his desk, and his head hangs low in his hands. Hero doesn't even hear me enter or shut the door behind me. Oh yeah, something is definitely up. He'd be halfway across his office with a knife at my throat, if he thought I was an intruder.

"What's up your ass today?" I question him.

His head shoots up like someone screamed "FIRE!" in the clubhouse.

"Jesus, V. I didn't even hear you come in," he quips with a startled look on his face. "You need a damn bell around your neck."

"You just wish you had my stealthy ninja skills," I tease him back, and that elicits an eye roll from him.

Plopping down in the chair across from him, I prop my feet up on his desk and take a sip of my coffee that I brought to the meeting with me. Extra dark with a shot of extra espresso. Just the jolt of holy fucking shit I need in the morning to get these batteries going. It's like drinking motor oil, but hey, it does the trick.

"Get your fucking feet off my desk, dude," he orders.

"What? It's fucking oak, not mahogany, Effie," I fire back, as I comply with his wishes. He cocks an eyebrow at me, and I just shake my head.

"You really need to get out more. How did you not catch *The Hunger Games* reference?"

Hero just stares right at me without showing any emotion on his face, while shaking his head in return.

"In case you haven't noticed, I've been a little fucking busy with club shit on top of having twins and a pregnant wife at home."

I smirk back at him. He really has changed so

much from the resident VP asshole extraordinaire into a semi-domestic family man. He used to be such a hard ass. Now, he's just a pissy little pussycat with a ring on his finger. Dani tamed the beast incarnate and gave him twin girls to terrorize him the rest of his life. He tries to act all big and bad, but with a future filled with pink tutus and Barbie dolls, he is getting softer by the day. It's fucking priceless.

"Is Dani the problem?" I ask gingerly.

"Don't let her hear you say that. Pregnancy hormones mixed with my woman is about as easy as trying to fucking find a needle in the damn haystack. If it's not In-N-Out cravings at three in the morning, it's a specific kind of ice cream that only one place seems to carry and they're never open when she wants it. I have a fucking stockpile of that shit hidden in a freezer just in case. That's how bad it is."

"She's pregnant?" I tease him, as I jump out of my chair and do a fake celebratory dance. He scowls back at me. You'd have to be an idiot to not notice that Dani is pregnant again. It's just not polite to say that in public or to her face. I do have manners after all. Some days.

"Shut up, asshole."

"I see someone's hormones are raging. What? Does Dani want you to get your shit fixed after this one?"

Please be another girl. He deserves it at the rate he's going.

Hero growls at me, and then gets a very serious look on his face. I move at a glacial pace just to fuck with him. After years of knowing the guy, I know how to push his buttons to just above the explosion point. It's a skill, and it comes in handy, when I want to annoy the piss out of him.

"No, but I have more at stake than ever before. What happens if Dani is in labor and shit comes knocking on our door? I want my family safe, and I think the best way to deal with that is bringing in more guys. We may be out of the shit business, but it doesn't mean it's done with us."

I consider his side and nearly agree with him before I stop myself. He knew the risks when he came into this club, and maybe Jagger's death has rattled his brain more than I first assumed. Sure, it was a direct hit with all of us, but we've made the best of what happened and fixed it from happening again. Rex's resurgence was a bit out of left field, but again, that problem is dead and buried. Our threats were dwindling like an old maid's chance of ever getting a man. So why is he worried about this now?

"I get it, Hero. Having a family is scary shit. You and Raze have the most to lose out of all of us, but your brothers have your back. If you are worried, I can beef up some of the security at your house. Maybe even put up more cameras if you want. You know, I could even get you a copy of anything I record in that bedroom of yours," I wink trying to ease the tension.

"Stay out of my fucking bedroom, V," he growls. "But I'll take you up on the security offer."

"Fine," I huff. "But sex tapes are so last year. You could live stream that shit now."

"No," he growls louder. I pop up from the chair, and extend out my hand to him. He stares at it, before reaching out his own and shaking.

"Happy to do business with you. I'll be over later to install those sex cams for you."

"Not in my bedroom, fucker," he yells out the door as I leave, heading across the hall to my own domain.

"Good morning, girls," I call out to my computers along the north wall of my office, as I flick on the light switch. "Did you behave last night?"

Of course, silence is all I get in the return, other than the soft hum of fans running internally and the echoes of my footsteps on the linoleum floor. I'd be crazy to think that they would respond back. Well, until I get the chance to figure out a way for that to happen, and I have a few ideas. But that is neither here nor there. I have bigger fish to fry.

"Alexa, play my get shit done mix," I request to my Amazon Echo that sits on my desk, as I set my metric fuck ton size coffee and phone down. The cup begins to tip, but I save it from ruining the paperwork littering my desk from a previous case from the security group our club runs. Just another case of a cheating spouse and the wife that cat-fished him into confessing. It was an open and shut case that required very little of my technical wizardry, as Ratchet calls it.

"Playing get shit done playlist," her electronic voice repeats. Within a few seconds, the sounds of Five Finger Death Punch blare out of the speakers that are perfectly Bluetoothed to my Echo.

My ass moves to the beat, as I walk over to the computer consoles and touch the screens like Vanna White to wake each of them up. The screen on the left blinks off the Anime Marvel porn screensaver of Wonder Woman and Agent Romanov getting down and dirty. I don't know what horny Asian kid drew and designed it, but I fucking love the Internet for giving it to me.

Lines of computer codes scroll and flash across the screen, as the search program I had running last night is still going. Which is surprising because you wouldn't think that finding a hole in the State of California Government family services department would be that hard. They had to be working with outdated technology because finding a back door should be child's play. Maybe my hacker extraordinaire skills were becoming obsolete.

Nah. That's not possible unless we're talking about some punk North Korean hacker. They'd be the ones who would give me a run for my money.

I watch the screen flick through the codes of the government's database for a few more minutes before I shrug my shoulders and turn my focus to my other task for the day. Sliding over to the other computer monitor, I swipe my finger across the screen. *Good Morning, Boss Man* comes flashing up, and I swipe my finger on the scanner to unlock my more secured of the two consoles. The dossier of my target pops up, and I refresh my memory on the case, finding out more information about Ricca's therapist, Dr. Matthews.

She may hold the key to getting my brother's ass back to his club where he belongs. With her counseling Ricca, Ratchet is concerned that she might have gotten Ricca to spill about her time here. She was a wild card, and I only like to deal in absolutes. In her case, I needed to know more about her and find a way into her life to monitor her activities a few thousand miles away. Mixing business and pleasure wasn't something that I liked to do as a refined professional. However, this one would be filed among the special cases.

The fact I had come up short was driving me crazy. I was lying awake at night trying to figure out another angle or re-creating a crazy backstory about why she was eluding me. Everyone had an Internet footprint, and other than an account on a dating site that I had found, she was a ghost. Ghosts are suspicious, and something wasn't jiving with me about her.

Casper or not, she had to have information out there, and I was forced to think outside the box. This case called for the highest level of discretion. It required looking at every angle with kid gloves, in order to not disturb the case currently going against my own brother and the old lady he hopes to have on his arm, when he returns. Yet, it didn't stop me from contacting her through the dating site. It was the last resort and likely the only way to connect with her on a personal level. In order to get into the mind of someone with so much pull over Ratchet's situation, I'm pulling out all the stops.

I just didn't expect to find her so interesting.

Call it a curiosity, but I couldn't help myself, when her profile popped up so perfectly on my first web search. The profile read like a doctoral dissertation. It was just the facts. No funny quips. No sexual innuendos. If this woman was looking for love, she was doing it all wrong. Even her photo was generic. Her face was obscured by her long, dark hair, and a single brown eye was exposed. It was so boring that it was somehow turning me the fuck on with the mystery of what was hidden beneath her hair. Was she just too shy? Was she ugly? Was it an embarrassing mole like in *Austin Powers*? The suspense was killing me so to speak.

I'm weird. Sue me.

I did complete my due diligence, by searching her mystery photo against stock photo databases and Google Images. Nothing came up. So, either the photo was real, or she was a magician with Photoshop. Either way, she's piqued my interest on a level that may or may not be completely professional in nature.

The biggest surprise came when she messaged me back within a few days. Well, not me-me, but the computer start-up CEO me who lived in San Diego. Creating an alternative reality of myself was almost fun. The man she thought was on the other side of the screen was a suave bugger. The one with all kinds of features that made the ladies yell woo-woo. Not that I wasn't good looking because well, I think I am, but I still had to be careful. If I fucked up, while looking into her personal life, my photo might lead her back to the club. The guilt of lying to her via a fake profile picture, as I got to know her more, was nagging at me. The photo was a necessity for the club and the country, you could say. She could be the crazy stalker type of girl. Not that I wouldn't mind a few more stalkers in my life, but that's beside the point.

Our first few conversations were the basic getting to know you questions. Kids (hell no), jobs, and relationship statuses were all checked off the list. The beginning was a delicate dance of re-con. And when I was satisfied that I had both found the right person and that she seemed to be interested in furthering our conversations, I put the ball back into her court with giving her my phone number. Well, a burner phone number because again safety first. Crazy stalkers might be fun, but now isn't the time to bring that shit into the club, so soon after the issues we had with a former colleague of the club. But he was dead and the other club that came riding into our territory was sent on their merry way back down the yellow brick freeway. Everyone's adrenaline was still running on high alert, and disturbing the balance between sanity and rage was still wavering on a day-to-day basis with Ratchet so far away. He was needed here, but without some closure with Ricca, he wouldn't be fit for duty.

The sound of a light saber rings from my phone, and I slide in my wheelie chair rolling back over to my desk. Pressing my fingerprint to the home button of my iPhone, I unlock the screen and find that the good head doctor had finally replied to my message.

How's the tech world today?

Ah, small talk. My favorite kind. I smile as I type out my reply.

It's all code to me. How's the brain business? Did you send any patients to the loony bin?

The terrorizing three dots of agony flash on my screen as she replies.

Not today. You know I couldn't really tell you, even if I did.

She's playing the small talk card, but she's also playing hard to get, and I'm starting to like it.

Ah. The hippo law.

The dots show up immediately, and I already know she's going to correct me.

It's HIPAA. Any plans for the
weekend?

I pause for a moment, before I respond.

Oh, maybe a jaunt on my yacht in the
Pacific or a trip into the heart of
Vegas. You could come with me. I
bet you'd look beautiful on my deck.

Smooth, dumbass. I wonder if she'll even pick up on my play on words.

The dots flash off and on for several minutes, before her reply finally pings back. I flustered her. Score one for me. As a therapist she should be seeing this song and dance from a mile away, but I get the distinct feeling that she's not exactly knee deep in social interaction with the way she's responded to me.

Your deck? That doesn't sound dirty
at all. Besides, you don't even know
what I look like. How do you know if
I'm beautiful?

Hook, line, and sinker. It's time to go in for the kill.

Well, your profile picture was a little mysterious, but that brown eye of yours is pretty beautiful. You should send me a real picture of yourself, so I can prove to you that I'm right.

Play your cards. Come on. Give me what I need.

I stare at my phone for an eternity. No dots. No pings. Fucking nothing. Did I overdo it? Did I push too soon? Jesus, a month of talking to this woman, and I may have fucked it up with a photo request. This actually seems like a reverse dick pic kind of reaction.

Tossing my phone on my desk, I slide back to my computer screens. The scan of the code is still working, and I space out watching it as a distraction. But even the clock ticking on the wall is taunting me.

Tick. Tock. You. Fucked. Up.

I shove away from my computer monitors with an audible huff, while I internally berate myself, but a ping brings me my salvation.

I bolt for my discarded phone, dropping it in the process.

"Motherfucker," I exclaim, chasing after it. I drop to my hands and knees under my desk. Finally, my fingers grasp it from the dark, depths of the underside of my desk along with a long lost Cheeto. I look at it for a second, considering whether or not to take a bite, before tossing it over my shoulder and unlocking my phone. It would probably be the start of the newest plague if I had eaten it anyway.

My finger shakes, when I click on her name, and my breath is sucked right out of me, when her photo pops up on my screen. Her heart-shaped face is framed by long, dark hair from her profile picture. Her lips are pursed, but it's her eyes that draw me in and won't let go. Two of them are definitely better than one.

I stare at her photo far longer than I should, and send a copy of it to my personal e-mail account. I will search it like I planned, but I didn't want to take the chance that it would self-destruct and disappear. There's something about this woman, and this photo only makes me want to know more.

> You are the most beautiful woman that I have ever seen.

The dots return again, and I get lost in texting her for nearly two hours, until my code search program comes through with my way into the government website. I had hacking to do, but it wouldn't be the only thing on my mind.

This might be a game of cat and mouse, but the lines of which part I was playing, were beginning to blur.

Chapter 3

PRESLEY

"THIS IS SUCH A BAD IDEA," my patient, Ginny, says to me as I make the final turn of our journey.

And she isn't wrong in the least bit. This *is* a bad idea. In fact, this is the worst idea that I have ever had, and believe me, I've made some questionable decisions over the course of my life. Decisions that usually involved a man or my brother's motorcycle club somehow. It wasn't easy growing up as their little princess, and the first time that I ever felt free, was the day I kissed that part of my life goodbye. Fate had another plan for me, and I've never looked back, until now when I really need them in my hour of desperate despair. I just hope that my brother won't put us out on our asses to fend for ourselves, after how I left this life behind.

"You're right. It's not the most logical direction that we should take," I tell her with a sigh exiting my lips, right after the words leave my mouth. "But it's not like we have any other options at this point."

"I know," Ginny mutters. "I just hate the idea of dragging them into my mess. I've already done that to you, and I feel so guilty."

I try not to laugh at her insinuation this club would be going out of their way to do some dastardly and illegal deed. She feels guilty for involving a band of men who have done more nefarious things in their lives, than the average human being could even dream about. The things I've witnessed as a childhood bystander, still makes my skin crawl. My father was a sick and twisted bastard who enjoyed torturing those around him and their families. While he never once subjected me to that kind of thing, I still knew about it despite my mother and brother's feeble attempt to shield me from that part of the club life. He was pure evil, and it didn't take years of graduate school to figure out that my father was a homegrown sociopath with a penchant for loose women and illegal activities.

I reach across the console, and give her hand a quick, reassuring squeeze. Ginny didn't deserve this kind of life, and despite her past, I can see the scared, little girl inside of her. She may have entered my life as a patient, but after years of privately treating her, she'd become more of a friend. Something that I desperately needed in my life when secrecy and a past of misery lay at my feet.

"We're in this together whether we like it or not. This is our only chance to survive."

"I know," she nearly whispers. "I just don't want to face him again. It wasn't supposed to be like this. When it was safe, I was supposed to come back."

"Safety is never something that is guaranteed in this world. Dangers lurk around every corner, and right now, danger is shoving us back to a place we both ran from. Give it time," I tell her. "My brother won't hang us out to dry." Hopefully.

Ginny's face drops at the mention of my brother, and I know the reason in an instant. Her own brother, that I hadn't until recently learned, was a part of the same club. He was also seeing one of my other patients. Why do all things seem to point right back to this damn place? I run, and it just follows me. It's ridiculous.

"Don't worry about him. He'll be happy to see you."

"At first. Then he'll be pissed."

Something that I couldn't fault him for because again his kid sister faked her own death, but that issue is between them, unless they want me to mediate their reunion in a professional manner. Other than that, my nose would stick to my own business with my own brother who might be a little pissed. Ginny needs to face him, if she is ever going to get past the guilt she holds over how they left things. This could be her first test towards finding herself again. Well, and taking care of our little issue that is currently hunting us down.

A familiar sight comes across the horizon, and my heart thumps like a drumline within my chest. It was a place that held so many hurtful memories of my childhood, and mostly of my father.

Don't think of him. Not now. He's dead. Put him in the past and move on.

As the parking lot entrance comes closer into view, my mind begins second guessing this decision. Like Ginny, my brother and I's relationship was estranged at best. Growing up, we were thick as thieves, but when my father died, something changed in him. The kindness that I once knew slipped away to something darker. He became the shadow of my father. I just had to hope that in the years we've spent apart that my brother hadn't become the proverbial apple that fell from my father's crazy tree, because I didn't exactly leave on the best of terms.

The parking lot is fuller than I expected when I

turn in. Sundays were usually the lighter days at the Heaven's Rejects Clubhouse because everyone was either still drunk, passed out, or dragged home by their old ladies. To say that I was surprised by the number of cars and bikes still here is an understatement. The club must have partied late last night for this many people to still be lingering around.

"There goes my plan for a quiet entrance," I mutter under my breath. I sneak a look over to Ginny, and her face is a coiled mess of anxiety and fear.

I quickly find an open space, pull in, and kill the engine to the car I bought with cash back in Oklahoma. I unlock my seatbelt, and stare at the entrance of my former home. The weathered look of the building that I remember has faded away into a more modern architectural style with dark new siding, and a far less scary vibe ebbing from it.

At least my brother invested more into this place than my father did. It doesn't look half bad I begrudgingly have to admit. I had honestly expected to find it a crumbled heap of rumble with some haphazardly built shelter to replace it.

Maybe he has changed.

Ginny looks over to me with fear registering in her eyes that plead for me to find another way out of our situation. I plaster on a smile trying to ease her.

"It'll be alright, Ginny."

"I hope so."

Taking one last deep breath, I pop the handle on the door and step into the hot California sun for the first time in years. The rays beat down on my skin, and the sting of it feels almost comforting, after living in the Midwest for so long.

"Welcome home, Presley," I mutter to myself, before shutting the door of the car behind me, as I begin taking my last steps of freedom.

Home sweet home never terrified me more.

Ginny slides from the car behind me, and jogs up to my left side.

"Last chance to turn around," I whisper to myself, as I pull open the door.

I step into the room and shock registers immediately. So much has changed, and so many women and children now fill the main room of the club-house, and every one of them has fallen silent. Face after face turns to look at me, and likely there are a few hidden guns ready to be drawn from the few men seated at the bar in the far corner. Not a single face looks familiar.

Shit. I should have called first. I just walked us both in the viper pit without a single weapon to protect either of us or a way back out for us to escape.

Ginny presses tightly against me, and I can feel the shiver from her body rattle against my own.

Rushing into a clubhouse with guns and trigger-happy men may have been the stupidest mistake of all, despite having once been a part of the family here. I take a deep breath and try to center myself. It doesn't work.

"Can I help you, doll face?" one of the men from the bar says, as he slides from the barstool with his beer still in hand. "You two lovely ladies looking for a job?" he asks with a curious cocked brow. His eyes rake over our bodies; sizing us up most likely thinking we are club whores. He stops just one step of being uncomfortably close. He's tall and looks like a damn Viking with his blond beard and longer hair. I get the sudden feeling that I'm a little fish in a predator-filled pond.

You should have called. You're being stupid, Presley.

"Looks like the cat has your tongue, doll face," he teases and those within ear shot laugh.

"I'm here to see Mikey. I mean, Michael," I stammer out. Ginny's hand reaches for mine, and when she finds it, she squeezes hard.

"The Prez is a little tied up at the moment, which you could be too if you say the word," he continues with a cocky smile. "Can I take a message?"

"Tell him his sister is here to see him," I demand.

"The Prez doesn't have a sister," he laughs. "Nice try."

I guess my brother really hasn't changed much since the last time I've seen him, if his club brother doesn't know about me. Just great. This will be harder than I imagined.

"Why don't you go ask him yourself?" I insist, standing my ground. "Or better yet, ask Maj."

He hisses at the sound of my sister in law's name.

"That bitch doesn't breathe here anymore."

Something has definitely happened there. Thanks for telling me, Mom. I never liked the woman, but she should have at least told me that my brother had split from his wife.

"Darcy!" the man yells over his shoulder.

"Jesus, Slider," a feminine voice rings out from one of the hallways. "This better not be a summons to judge another gun show between you and Ratchet again. I just got Roxie down for a nap."

"Got a woman here who says she's Raze's sister. Do you know anything about that?"

Shuffled footsteps come quickly from behind him.

"Move your ass out of the way, Slider," she orders from behind the man blocking my entry. A petite woman with dark hair sidesteps him and gasps at the sight of me. "Presley? Is that really you?"

"Um, hi." I declare with a slight wave.

"You idiot," the woman I now know as Darcy

scolds the great wall of man in front of me. "Let her and her friend in the damn room."

I look to both of them with confusion clear on my face.

"I know we haven't met, but I'm Darcy, your brother's fiancée. Your mom has told me so much about you."

Woah, wait. Did she just say fiancée? That explains the reaction I got when I mentioned Maj. He's divorced or she's dead. There's no telling with this club, which way she walked or crawled out this door.

"Nice to meet you," I automatically respond. I don't mean to be so cold, but our little problem is a bit more pressing than introductions. "Can I see my brother?"

The woman flinches slightly at my lack of warmth towards her, but she's a stranger to me. This entire place is filled with strangers. I honestly don't know why I was expecting to see familiar faces knowing how much of a revolving door this kind of place has.

"Sure," Darcy affirms. "I'll take you back to his office. Follow me."

She turns on her heels, and we fall in line behind her. Ginny stays close, as we cross the room with all eyes still on us. I notice out of the corner of my eye that the man who stopped us has returned to the bar, and that's when I notice his prospect cut. He's not a full member, which explains his overreaction to our presence in the club. He's still trying to get his foot in the door to become a full member, and he took this opportunity to assert his authority over someone for once. Too bad for him, that I can see his act a mile away. My father had numerous prospects during my childhood, and he taught me that they were here to pay their dues and do the members bidding. They were the lowest rung on the MC food chain, and the least of my worries.

Darcy leads us to my father's old office, and an odd sense of nostalgia hits me hard. I spent many days sitting on my father's lap in the room that my brother now occupies. He loved me in his own way during the early years of my life, and inside this room, was one of the few happy memories that I did have of my father, before his world turned to darkness, drugs, and death.

We stop short of the door, and Darcy knocks. My brother's gruff voice echoes off the walls from inside, as she twists open the door.

Mikey sits inside behind the desk. His head is shaven now, and his beard is nearly all gray with a few patches of his dark hair flecked amongst the stubble across his chin. His face remains focused on his work before he notices me. He pushes away from his desk and in three large strides, he engulfs my body in a hug.

"I thought you'd never come back," he mutters against the top of my head.

I relax against his familiar embrace, forgetting for a split second why we are here in the first place. He releases me, and his eyes catch Ginny behind me.

"Is that?" he asks, looking between the two of us.

"Yes," I respond.

"I take it this isn't a social call then," he declares gruffly.

"No, it's not. We need your help."

Chapter 4

VOODOO

I'M SO FUCKING DEAD.

The woman that I have been secretly texting and e-mailing for Ratchet is not only Ricca's former therapist, but my club president's sister. The woman who has consumed my every spare second thought, daydream, and nightmare is here, and she doesn't have a clue as to who I really am. The man that is standing here in shock and awe at her presence is nothing more than a creeper staring at her like a fan stares at a celebrity on the red carpet.

The minute she walked into our clubhouse I knew I was royally fucked. Not like I-might-die kind of fucked. Not like I'm dead as in cease to breathe or live, but six feet under with maggots eating my entrails while my club president, Raze, pisses on my grave and laughs kind of dead. This is the worst kind of fucked up situation that a man could find himself in.

It can't be that simple at all. Not in my life. If you looked up the word fucked in the dictionary, you would find some wordy definition of the word that graces my vocabulary far more often than any civilized person should use it, and also my photograph.

Pretty bad, right? Well, take that image and multiple it times a million because that's the situation I'm in right now. All in all, it could be worse, but not by much more. After months of living under the guise of a wealthy tech guru, the woman that started creeping into my life one text at a time is just inches away from me. While I had planned to eventually meet her in person and explain myself, this wasn't what I expected at all. Every goddamn inch of me was screaming on the inside of my body. I was in pure shock and completely ecstatic to finally be so close to her, but the minute it was revealed to me that she was Raze's sister, I shoved every feeling I had for her back into the not going to fucking happen box. If Obi-Wan Kenobi was here right now, he'd be waving his hand in my face and declaring that this isn't the woman I have been looking for.

"V?" Raze says, as he steps out from behind his sister, and the girl I now know as Ratchet's once thought to be dead sister Ginny, who is currently wrapped up tightly in her own brother's arms. "You okay?"

"Yup," I squeak out, like a teenage boy in between his voice change. "Just wanted to know what all the commotion was," I lie.

"Long story," Raze mumbles. "Get the guys into Church. Now."

"Sure thing, Prez," I respond, before turning on my heels.

Don't look back, dumbass. Don't do it.

My head turns, and I look at Presley's tiny stature that is dwarfed, behind her brother's large frame. Her eyes catch mine, and I avert them immediately. This isn't the time or place for this shit.

"Church!" I yell out to the crowded main room of our clubhouse. My brothers respond immediately moving away from their wives and kids, filing into our meeting room. Darcy, Raze's fiancée, leans against the bar top with observant eyes, as she watches the commotion of the room simmer. She already knows something is wrong. The other ladies look to her and begin gathering around her, as I turn on my heels walking towards the meeting room and stepping inside.

The large table in the center of the room is nearing maximum capacity with every seat taken, except for Raze's head chair. Several of the newer brothers are leaning against the walls surrounding the table. In the recent months, our club has seen an influx of transfers from former chapters that had disbanded, thanks to Raze's ex-wife's betrayal of her husband's club for the interest of her own cartel family's desires. But Maj and her goddamn Mexican Manson family aren't our problem anymore, after our little jaunt to Mexico. The sun set on their bullet ridden bodies, and we never turned back. Our club changed after that, and for the better. We are all still getting use to the newer brothers, which is why Hero wanted to patch Slider in, but the relationships and trust are slowly starting to build. Trust takes time, and unfortunately, that hasn't exactly been in abundance around here until recently. Our club was making far larger strides to becoming independent from the shit shows of our past. Peace would never be easy. It is painstakingly slow, but in the end, it would benefit all of us. We just had to get there first.

But with Raze's reaction to his sister's return, I knew that it was all about to end.

So close yet so fucking far away.

"Did you catch that little spitfire of a woman giving me the business end of a tongue lashing?" Slider asks. "Shit, she was fine as fuck. I wonder how good that tongue of hers would feel wrapped around my dick."

"She's none of your concern, prospect," I hiss. "Show some respect, motherfucker."

"Jesus, V. Who pissed in your cereal this morning? She's a good-looking woman. Since when is commenting on a beautiful woman a crime?"

"Just don't," I order him. Slider starts to say something else, but a familiar sound echoes off the wall from the office area making the entire room go quiet.

Raze's heavy footsteps stomp through the door with Ratchet on his heels. Raze reaches back and closes the door behind him, before stalking to his place at the head of the table. Ratchet stops just beside him, and places himself at Raze's left side, but remains standing.

"Brothers, we have a situation," he declares.

My stomach drops. He knows what I did. I can see my obituary now. There will be some mumbo jumbo about my life, listing my few legally acceptable accomplishments just before my surviving family member's names. But the part that I know will seal my fate will be at the very bottom. Followed by the next part that will list my transgressions for the entire world to see. That I screwed with my club president's sister, and he disemboweled me as a warning to the other men in his club to not follow suit. I will be the example on Raze's wall of what not to do in an MC.

"We have a situation that involves my kid sister and her friend."

"Old man trouble?" Thor teases from the back of the room.

"Who's the other chick?"

"I wish it were that simple. The young woman with her is Ginny Azzo, Ratchet's sister."

I let out a silent sigh that maybe, just maybe, Raze doesn't know about Presley and I just yet. Ginny's return may have spared me from Ratchet spilling the beans, and my life ending on the floor of Church.

Not today, Satan. My soul is still free.

Silence echoes against the walls of the room. Every man stands quiet as the grave, except for Slider and his uncontrollable mouth. The guy needs a permanent brain to mouth filter installed on a good day, and I have a feeling the shit about to come out of it is going to end in his ass being kicked. It was a privilege that we allowed him to attend Church, as a prospect on rare occasions. Something he was about to abuse for the millionth time.

"Sister?" he whispers to Hot Shot, who hushes him in return. "She single?"

"I thought your sister was dead," Hero questions, looking to both Ratchet and Raze.

"Obviously not, asshole," Ratchet barks back. "Watch it, Slider." His tone is dark and angry. I don't even have to ask because I know that her reappearance has re-opened a wound for him. In the few times he would even talk about his sister, you could hear the pain in his voice, over not being able to save her from the fate she found. I thought that he might be happier than he currently stands now knowing that she's still alive, but he clearly isn't at that point yet. I make a mental note, that until he calms down, to steer clear of him. Even though I consider him one of my best friends in this club, this is a side of him that I want to avoid. One false move, and he'll explode in rage. It's one of the reasons that he's our club's enforcer, cleaner, and death dealer.

"How is that even possible?" Tyson gently nudges.

"Witness protection. Apparently, Ginny has been in the program for a few years now."

"Okay, but how does that explain Presley's involvement?" Hero asks. "What is Ginny to her?"

"Presley was recruited by the FBI as Ginny's therapist."

"How is whatever this is our problem?" Slider asks. "I didn't think we cared about the outside shit anymore." Ratchet glares at him, and even at this distance, I can see him mentally dismembering Slider just at the insistence that neither of them or their problems should matter to us. If he keeps this up, I may help Ratchet kill him.

"It's our problem, prospect, because they are our family," Raze begins to yell as he moves around the table, coming nose to nose with Slider. "We protect our fucking family," he spits. "If you feel differently, leave your prospect cut on the table and you can take your ass right out of that door. You're in this room because I allow it, and if you can't follow the rules of my fucking club, you're done here. Do you understand?"

"Yes, Prez," he mumbles, falling back into his chair with a slump. For a man who was an inch away from his vote and patch party, he sure knows how to fuck his chances up. If we had taken the vote today, he'd be out on his ass or a prospect for life, because of his utter lack of respect for this club and our rules, when shit hits the fan.

Raze moves away from him and looks to all of us.

"My sister and Ratchet's sister are in deep. As in deep enough that this might be worse than Mexico. Ginny is involved in one of the largest organized crime trials of the century. She is the key witness for the FBI's case, and without her, everything is fucked."

"I take it her cover was blown?" I ask respectfully.

"Yes," Ratchet interrupts Raze. "Both she and Presley have been made by the crime family, and if we don't protect them, they'll be as good as dead."

Tyson looks around the room, and asks the one question that is on all of our minds. "Which family?"

"The Zezza's," Raze flatly answers.

The room erupts in yells, protests, and shock.

"Are you crazy?" someone in the back of the room exclaims. "The Zezza's are the largest organized crime family in the entire country. Hell, maybe even the world."

"I know it's bad, but we're the only fucking chance they have. They're dead if we turn them away."

I look to my concerned brothers, and push away from the table and stand. Hero follows suit, and addresses the room, while I look on.

"When we patched in, we vowed to protect and serve this club. That includes family. If this were any of your sisters, wives, daughters, or fucking cousins once removed, we'd stand by you. Your club president is asking you to stand by him and weather the storm."

"I'm with you," I declare.

One by one, all of my brothers, and even Slider, stand with us.

"Thank you, my brothers," Raze commends.

"What's the plan, Prez?" Thor, our newest recruit, requests.

"For the time being, Ginny and Presley will be secured here. I'm calling for an immediate lockdown of the clubhouse. If you feel the need to send your old ladies or children away, I will not stop you. Our priority is protecting them, and I will be assigning round the clock guards on them at all times. This means that the security business will be light handed, so we will need to bring in a few guys from the other chapters to cover the load and keep watch on the clubhouse. Ratchet and I spoke prior to the meeting, and we both feel it's best that he takes Ginny."

"What do you need me to do, Prez?" I ask, knowing that with Presley here, I'm going to need a good distraction. She has no idea that I'm the man she's been talking to for months, and that isn't exactly knowledge that I want to share to the world yet. So, the busier I am, the less likely that I will try to act on the feelings I've developed for her, while helping Ratchet and Ricca gain custody of her brother.

"I need you to get all the information you can about these Zezza fuckers, V. I want to know where they call home, their ranks from top to bottom, every single meal they eat, and even when they take a dump. If the rumors I've heard about these guys are remotely true, we'll be fighting an uphill battle. For now, we are assuming that they don't know Ginny and Presley are here, but that can change at any minute. Any information you can get will help us prepare."

"You got it, Prez," I reassure him. "Likewise goes for any information Ginny can provide me about the case and what she knows about them from a personal standpoint would be great. I could hack the federal database, but that's the last resort."

"We'll get the information you need, V," Ratchet offers. I nod in return. "Raze and I have agreed to allow both girls to speak to the entire club. Information needs to move at real time speed."

"And what about Presley?" Slider asks with a sly tone. "I can watch her."

Slider's insistence of inserting himself into Presley's path grates even more on my paper-thin nerves. His choice of continuing to think with his cock and not his big boy brain is about to get him into trouble. The old adage of, if I can't have her neither can you, is about to go into effect, if I have my way. Raze should be enough to scare him off, but Slider is a special kind of fucking dumbass, when it comes to pussy.

"I appreciate your change of attitude, Slider, but Voodoo will be the one in charge of guarding her. He will keep his hands to himself unlike you."

My heart stops, and I look on in shock. Raze has just delivered me like a prized sheep to a slaughterhouse sale. Staying away from her will be nearly impossible now, and I get the sinking suspicion that Ratchet volunteered me for the job.

Bastard.

Chapter 5

PRESLEY

"THIS WAY," my brother's emotionless voice calls, as he ushers Ginny and I into the room that I have known my entire life to be the secret sanctum of nefarious men. The fact that Ginny and I are likely the first two women to ever break the threshold of this space should intrigue me, but it doesn't. Being invited into this room isn't a privilege. These men are going to ogle at us both like prized canaries in gilded cages begging for crackers for party tricks. A sentiment that only reminds me more of why I left this hell hole in the first place. Women mean nothing more than a warm hole to stick their dick in and to bear their pack of unruly children. We're property to be owned, taken advantage of, and then dumped when the next young piece of ass walks into the room and willingly opens her legs.

No, this rare occurrence can only mean one thing. They're willing to take us in, but the problem lies with whether or not that protection comes with a price. Being the younger sister of the current club president and the daughter of the former, I can only hope that Mikey goes easy on us.

Stepping through the door, the idle chatter of the men seated around the table, extinguishes to utter silence. Each pair of eyes are locked onto the two of us, and the uneasiness of being on display, sends a shiver down my spine. Ginny must sense it as well because she inches closer to me. My brother sidesteps around us, stalking over to two open seats near the head of the table. He gestures with his hand for us to take them, and we both comply. The worn leather of the chair squeaks, as I lower myself into it, and the back awkwardly tilts.

"Shit," I exclaim, as the momentum shifts my equilibrium, and I feel my body falling backwards to the floor. A pair of large hands suddenly appears on either side of my shoulders and stops the motion from continuing.

I peer up from under my lashes to see a man with bright blue eyes and dark hair, peering down on me. His eyes are so piercing that I can feel myself being crushed under the weight of their intensity the longer I stare into them. He remains silent, as he flicks a switch under the chair and returns to his own seat. I shift my gaze to my brother, and notice his quick nod of thanks to the man who saved me from going ass over head in front of the entire club. I don't think my pride can take that kind of embarrassing exposure, especially when I'm already here begging for help as it is.

"Why are we in here?" Ginny quietly asks, breaking the silence. Her bewildered eyes lock onto her brother across the table, looking for a sign of hope.

"We need information about the men who are after you, and also how you were discovered," my brother curtly declares.

"Does that mean you're taking us in?" I ask, returning his coolness back at him.

"Yes," he replies sharply. "This club doesn't turn away family, even if that family turned their back on us."

I hiss at his rude implication of my disloyalty to this club. For years, he's tried to convince me to come home via my calls with my mom. But I had Ginny, and I couldn't leave, even if I had wanted to return to this den of nightmares.

"You really want to do this now, Mikey?" I scold him. "In front of your entire club?"

One of the men to my brother's right abruptly stands, staring me down.

"You will address our President correctly. Family or not. You will show him respect in this room," the man orders me.

I stow the urge to roll my eyes at the insinuation of this man requesting that I bow to my brother's reign. His entire club is delusional, and all of them are in desperate need of psychiatric help. I bet that I could make a killing with sessions with each of them, including my own brother. I stow that thought away and return to the conversation at hand before it goes off the rails even further.

"You must be under the impression that I allow him to rule over me," I hiss back at the man. "If me falling in line is part of the requirements of your protection, I think I will take my chances outside."

The man across from me sneers his disgust at my lack of groveling at my brother's feet. If I wanted to kiss his ass, I would have done it by now. Sure, it's probably not a good idea to challenge my brother's authority in front of his men, but I will not be a fucking doormat to his egotistical rule. I'm not a member of his club, and I will never be. He just needs to understand that fact for what it is.

"Enough!" My brother bellows. "Hero, don't

fucking talk to my sister like that again. She's my family."

The man straightens up, nods, and re-takes his seat in silence.

I internally fist pump in celebration to my W in the win column, but the joy is short lived, when my brother turns his attention back to me.

"Slow your roll, Presley. You hate the club, we get it, but I will not tolerate disrespect of any kind from you and your smart-ass mouth. These men are willing to protect you, and they will not be treated like the gum on the bottom of your shoe because you have a superiority complex. Am I understood?"

Knowing that there isn't a clear way out of this, I just nod in agreement.

"Now that the pissing match is over. Let's get started."

I swivel in my chair and look to Ginny. Her terrified eyes scream for me to go first, but Mikey has other plans.

"Ginny, I know that you're scared, but I need you to tell us why you were in protective custody in the first place."

"Because of my ex-boyfriend, Gio Zezza. I saw him kill someone, and I ran to the police."

"And the police shipped you off to the FBI?" he softly questions. While Ginny was in the restroom, I warned my brother of her fragile state. Thankfully, he is respecting my request of not pushing her too hard. This is a lot for her to deal with in a short period of time.

"Yes, they wanted me to testify against him."

"Did Gio know of your connection to the club or who I am?" her brother inquires.

"No, I hated you and the club for shipping me off to that old woman as a keeper, so I used a fake name," she says a bit too harshly.

Ratchet flinches at his sister's sharp words, and I can't blame him for the reaction. Ginny's anxiety and upbringing explains her knee-jerk reactions to stressful situations. Unlike others who would consider acting out so abruptly, she makes split second decisions, which lands her in situations like this. We had made progress on this over the last few years, but she still had her flight over fight moments.

"And it was the FBI that faked your death, correct?" Mikey asks.

"Yes," she whispers with her head hanging low against her chest. I watch her for a few seconds, and when she looks to her brother, tears begin forming on her olive-colored cheeks. The guilt she has suffered knowing that her brother thought she was dead has been staggering. It was easy to see she loved him more than life itself, and it ate at her from the inside out.

"Too much," I mouth to my brother, effectively urging him to switch his attentions onto me. Her brother notices my request, and smirks a silent thank you for sparing her from further interrogation. As much as I want to hate the guy for the men he associates himself with, I can't. When Ricca was in my care, she lit up, when he came back into her life, and his gentle tenderness with his sister now in front of his brothers is unexpected. There's much more to this man than what lays on the surface it seems, and as a therapist, that fascinates me.

I shake the professional curiosity from my mind when the line of questioning is switched to me.

"And how did you become involved in this?" a man asks from behind me.

"I guess starting at the beginning is best," I sigh, shifting in my seat in preparation of this story.

"Four years ago, I was approached by the FBI to treat a patient in their custody, after her current therapist quit. They offered to move me to a remote location where I could meet with their patient, as well as start my own practice between sessions. It was a paid internship of sorts," I recall.

"And that patient was Ginny?" her brother asks.

"Yes. The agents protecting her gave me a false

name, but after a few sessions, Ginny opened up to me about her real first name. I continued treating her for the next few years."

I notice the man who saved me from the chair incident earlier eyes are locked on me, as he scribbles down notes. He pauses when he notices me watching and instantly diverts his eyes from me.

"My last session with Ginny was an emergency call."

"An emergency?" The man scribbling notes questions. "What type of emergency?" I watch him, as he writes furiously. His hand flies over the paper at light speed. He peeks up from time to time watching me, and it unsettles me just a little bit. His focus seems to solely be on me, even when Ginny is talking.

I turn to Ginny, seeking permission to continue further because what I'm about to say would breach just about every portion of HIPAA.

"It's okay," she whispers.

"Ginny has a severe form of episodic anxiety. Periods of prolong stress or sudden excitement can trigger her symptoms. After our last session, Ginny confessed to me that she felt an impending sense of doom, and that she didn't feel comfortable in her current safe house. She had an episode two days after our last session, and I was called back in to treat her further."

Her brother's eyes soften, as he looks at his sister. Knowing only bits and pieces of their childhood story from what Ginny has told me, I can now clearly see the bond between them. Their life had been rough, and her disappearance and faked death couldn't have helped their fractured past memories. Maybe time together now would help heal those wounds. I remind myself to offer and help them through those feelings, should they wish after the dust settles.

"And that's when it happened?" my brother asks.

"As many details as you can give would be helpful," the man with the notes adds.

"Mid-way through my session with Ginny, a loud bang came from the front room of her safe house. Several more came after it, before I realized that they were gunshots. Ginny began to panic, and I quickly covered her mouth to hide our whereabouts. I shoved us both into a closet and barricaded it the best I could."

As the memory floats back to me, I close my eyes and force myself back into the situation again.

"Heavy footsteps came into the room, and it wasn't long, before a tall man with dark hair threw open the doors and dragged us out into the living room. Another man grabbed Ginny, and shoved her away from me. I tried to get to her, but the man above me shoved his gun into my face. I thought we were both dead, until another shot rang out and hit the man standing above me. I bolted from the ground and bull rushed the man who had Ginny, while he was distracted. Once he was down, we ran out the back door. We got into my car and just drove."

Ginny noticeably shivers next to me when I open my eyes again. She reaches out for my hand, and her sweaty palms grasp mine tightly.

"Ginny, I know this might be overwhelming for you, but did you recognize either of the men there?" Mikey asks.

"No." she quietly answers. "But they were Zezza goons."

"How do you know that? Did they have any distinguishing marks, emblems, or anything to ID them as a part of the crime family?" the man with the pad asks, while twirling his pencil in his hand.

"They both had on a silver pendant around their necks that all Zezza family members wear. It's Saint Jude, the patron saint of lost souls. Gio wore his like you wear your vests. He never took it off."

Mikey looks to the man who is furiously scribbling again on his notepad, waiting for him to finish his thoughts. I watch him, and I can't help, but wonder what his place is in this club. Unlike the other men, he doesn't really fit the bill. He's leaner, and much shorter than his self-proclaimed brothers. I notice his tattoos peeking out of the cuff of his Henley shirt.

"That enough to start with V?" my brother asks the man.

"Yeah, it's the best kind of start you've ever given me for a job, Prez. I'll be stalking those bastards like sitting ducks. They won't even see me coming."

My brother narrows his eyes at the man I now know as V, and just shakes his head. Ginny's brother sneers at him.

"That's enough for today I think," my brother declares. All of the men stand up, and exit the room, except for Mikey, Ginny's brother, and V.

"For the time being, Presley, we are going to set you up here in the clubhouse. We've got the room to spare, and you'll be more protected here."

"You're kidding, right?" I chide him. He knows how I feel about this place.

"It's for the best, LeeLee," he says, using the nickname that I once loved hearing come out of his mouth. "We've got the numbers here, and we control the environment."

"And let me guess, I can't leave."

"You got it. Each of you will have someone with you at all times. Ratchet will be with Ginny, and V will be with you," he says, motioning to the man beside him.

"Prisoner in my old house with someone tailing me. Just what I wanted for a coming home present."

I roll my eyes, knowing I have to accept my fate. I came here for help, and this is the price I will have to pay. My freedom now lies in the hands of the club that broke my family apart.

Chapter 6

VOODOO

AS SOON AS the meeting adjourns, Ratchet whisks Ginny away and disappears into the living quarters. Presley sits in her chair for a few minutes looking like she just lost a battle before she finally gets up and exits the room. It's plain to see that she's out of her comfort zone here. It's a sentiment that I understand completely. She's a stranger in her old home and on the run. Nothing about that is easy to deal with.

I scribble down a few more notes that cross my mind from the meeting, as Raze moves to stand next to me. I can feel his eyes scanning the pages, before I lay down my pen and close the pad of paper. Shoving it into my back pocket, I slide from my chair and head towards the door without saying a word to him. My brain is firing on all cylinders as I process the information given to me today. The angles of attack are endless possibilities to find the right path. I just had to choose the right avenue to pursue.

"You know what to do, V," Raze declares, stopping me in my tracks. "Protect her with your life."

I swallow hard knowing that if I screw up that my club will kick my ass. I had to keep my mind on the prize and not let myself get distracted by Presley. I had to protect her despite the flourishing feelings that were growing inside of me.

I spin on my heels looking back towards him. Raze's face is hard and serious.

"Yeah," I offer up because it's the only thing that I can say that won't end with my head on a pike outside of his office. I doubt spilling my secret as an excuse for keeping her safe would do the trick right now. "You want the works?"

Raze thinks for a few seconds, before answering me back. Every decision will require careful consideration because this is the first time that we're going into the fight as the underdog. The Zezza's have more people, connections, and likely better tech than I could ever dream of. I almost lick my lips just thinking about getting my hands on some of their sick new toys if we make it out alive.

Not the time, asshole. Bros before toys.

"I definitely want cameras on the entire clubhouse, real time access via my phone and computer, and breach sensors on all the doors and windows."

"You got it, boss," I concur, while ticking away at my mental shopping checklist. While I would normally go to my supplier on my own, someone else is going to have to take over picking up my order. Slider perhaps. Making him a little errand boy and getting him away from Presley sounds pretty fucking good right now.

"Money is not an option, V. Top of the line all the way. Should have done it a long time ago to be honest," he replies, with regret dripping from his voice.

"You could have never guessed this was coming to our doorstep, and that your sister or Ratchet's would be the harbingers, Prez," I offer, placing my hand on his shoulders.

"Had things been different years ago, I doubt this would have ever happened."

Pain is clear across Raze's face, and I know he's internally blaming himself for his father's demented issues. Though I wasn't around back then, the history his father left tainted everything in this clubhouse. The stories of the members long gone were carved into the foundation, and it was never something any member new or old could forget. The only thing we can do is go forward and not go back to the way things were.

"You calling up guys from down south?" I ask.

"Not until we have a full assessment. Thor knows a couple of guys that would be interested in helping, since he's still recovering if we need them."

Thor recently found himself smack dab in the middle of a scuffle with Rex, after he nabbed another club member's girl. He ended up injured in the firefight, and he has been on light duty since. Not that he's complaining, since the new girl is nursing him back to good health. She's a pretty little thing, but she really needs to work on her people skills, since two of our club girls are now gone for fucking with her. Thick skin is almost a requirement around here, and some girls just can't hack it with club whores around all the time.

Would Presley fit that same mold, or would she be different since she's seen it firsthand before?

My mind wanders for a split second before I snap back to the current conversation and not the internal one continuously going on in my head.

"He's a good fit around here. I hope he stays on permanently."

"Me too. He's the kind of guy we need with some of the upcoming security work that is being negotiated."

"His big ass better be good for something, after eating us out of house and home the last few weeks."

Raze laughs just as Presley's voice reverberates from the clubhouse main room. We both look to each other and run towards the sound. Has shit hit the fan already?

I skid around the corner and screech to an abrupt halt. Raze and I stand in awe, as we find Presley and one of the club girls nose to nose. For fucks sake, it's day one and she's already riling up the natives. Just what I need on top of everything else. I start toward the ensuing chaos, but Raze throws his arm out and stops me. He just shakes his head no when I look up at him.

"Let it play out."

"Past issue?"

"Oh yeah," Raze reveals, with a telling look on his face.

"North and South Korea, bad?"

"Worse."

Great. She's got a crime family after her and beef with a club whore. She is really going to make this bodyguard thing interesting without adding in the whole online relationship aspect. What have I done to piss off someone upstairs to deserve this? Maybe my head on a pike would be easier at this point after all.

Raze refocuses back to the two women locked in a heated battle of words and possibly a battle of wills. Presley's body tenses to counter Ruby's defensive stance. I have to hand it to Ruby. She's willing to take someone on who not only is bigger than her, but is also pretty much the princess of this club.

"I distinctly remember that club whores don't run the place. Now move, Ruby," Presley orders, as her brother would.

Ruby's fists ball at her hips. We're about to be in def-con one if this continues, and my body is itching to defuse the situation, before it gets there. A catfight would normally peak attention both above and below the belt, but this is different. This isn't the time for this. Maybe Raze is right to let this just play out. We might be better for it in the long run, if they can clear the air now rather than later.

"I don't have to do shit, your highness. The last time I checked your pull around here died when you left. You being here means absolutely nothing to anyone, especially me."

"I get it. I left. I left the perfect little club that you idolize for saving your life, but it ruined mine," Presley starts to yell. "That is something that you'll never understand."

Ruby starts to say something else just as Darcy comes into the room with Roxie on her hip.

"Are you ready to meet your Aunt Presley, baby?" she coos, without looking up at the scene playing out in front of her. Her eyes look away from Roxie and her smile fades. She flicks her gaze between the two women about to face off in the main room, and she stops dead in her tracks.

"What in the actual fudge are you doing?" she yells. "Ruby, back down. Now!"

Darcy starts towards them, baby still in tow, and shoves her way between the two of them.

"I'll stop when she fucking leaves," Ruby demands.

"Language around the baby, Ruby."

She winces, as she offers up an apology. After Roxie repeated a few choice words, Darcy enacted a no swearing rule, when she is at the clubhouse. The amount of fudges, flipping, and freakings that have come out of my brother's mouths since could land us on our own reality show. I even have a title for it. The Nucking Futs MC Show. Pretty catchy if I say so myself.

"I–," she stutters, before Darcy hushes her again.

"You two obviously have history, but it's just that. Move on."

Presley looks on, pleased with herself that she's

winning the argument. I have to admit that smug is not a good look on her.

Roxie babbles on her hip, throwing in the few random words she knows, including the word fucker that makes her mother wince and me smile. Darcy's fight against her learning bad words is already failing miserably. Roxie is the daughter of one of the greatest men I have ever known, and he had the dirtiest damn mouth on the planet. Jagger's genes paired with her adoptive father's own mouth has doomed her. She'll be swearing like a sailor in no time.

Raze slides from his spot, and I follow along behind him.

"Dah," Roxie screams, when she sees him and outstretches her little arms out for him. Raze smiles, as he takes her from Darcy and kisses her little cheek, causing her to giggle.

"Hey baby girl," he tells her, and I swear I hear just about every pair of ovaries cry out in the room. Why these damn women melt over a man with a baby is lost on me. The only thing that I can compare it to is when I hold a new iPhone for the first time. It just doesn't get a collective aw from the peanut gallery in response. Their loss.

Presley watches the scene in front of her, but says nothing. A flash of shock crosses her face before she returns to the task at hand.

"Mikey, why is she still here?" she starts, before Raze cuts her off.

"Just stop, Presley. You don't like her. I know," he tells her. "Say hello to your niece, Roxie."

Presley softens, as Raze passes Roxie to her. Her tiny little bottom lip wavers once, as she looks with wide eyes at her aunt. It might not have been Raze's most brilliant move to hand over the baby to a complete stranger.

"Hi Roxie," Presley softly says, as the water works begin to pour from Roxie's eyes. Presley tries to soothe her, but ends up just passing her back to Raze. Even I know it was too soon, and I don't have any kids. Smooth move, Prez.

"She'll get used to you," Darcy says noticing the hurt in Presley's face. "In the meantime, let's get you settled into your room."

Presley nods, and looks back to Raze and Roxie, before following Darcy back to the guest rooms near the back of the clubhouse. I start to go after them, but a sharp look from Raze tells me otherwise. Like Roxie, Presley needs time to acclimate, and maybe get to know her future sister-in-law in the process. It's been a trying day for sure, and the dust definitely needs to settle.

Raze stalks away from me and towards one of the couches, and I turn heading back to my office.

I work for a few hours getting the list of things I need for the security overhaul, and send Slider on his merry little way to fetch them for me. To say he was thrilled was an understatement. His attitude was in serious need of adjusting.

He reappears in my office an hour later with the supplies. I take each one of them out of their box, inspecting that they are all intact and function properly. Gathering the few things that I need for Presley's room, I tuck the box and my tools under my arm, before heading her way.

Each step closer to her room seems like an eternity. This will be the first time that I have been alone with her, and I'm fucking terrified I'll spill my guts in a verbal word vomit. I'm usually the guy that is calm, cool, and cracking jokes during the bad shit. Not today, and definitely not around her. My feet stop just outside of the guest room door like they are stuck in quicksand. My hand quivers, as I reach up to her door and rap a few times. The room remains silent.

Be cool, fucker. Don't screw this up. First impressions are the most important, even if this technically isn't the first time you've met.

"Come in," her voice calls out through the door. I take one last breath and open it, entering into her new domain and my new living hell of battered emotions.

If I were a praying man, I might have just asked for some patron saint of dumbasses to give me strength, but even I know no one would answer them.

Chapter 7

PRESLEY

MUCH LIKE THE OUTSIDE, my brother had invested money in renovations on the inside of the clubhouse. What once would have been a simple room with just a bed and a nightstand is now nearly a full suite. I was shocked, when I discovered that he'd even had a private bathroom and a flat screen television installed in the guest room. I could see him doing it in the brother's rooms' maybe, but definitely not a guest room. Those were usually reserved for someone who probably wasn't going to walk out of the place alive, got themselves into a bit of trouble, or a visiting club member. It wasn't extravagant by any means, yet it was comfortable. Settling in took mere seconds, since I had nothing to my name, except for what I was wearing. Darcy stood awkwardly in the room with me for a few minutes, making small talk.

Days without sleep had worn my body out beyond normal functionality. I owe her an apology later, since I know that I likely came off as a bitch to her. She is my future sister-in-law, and I need to get to know her better. Apologetic niceties would be reserved for tomorrow. All I wanted was a hot shower, new clothes, and the longest night of sleep in my life.

Just as I was about to get started with my trifecta of relaxation, I hear a knock at the door.

Fucking great. What now.

"Come in." I call out to the person on the other side, and the door swings wide. The man who was ferociously taking notes during the earlier meeting steps through the threshold. His eyes are wide, when he sees me curled up on the small couch in the room and quickly diverts them away. I look down to what I'm wearing. Nothing about the clothes I have on screams indecently appareled, so I have no clue why he refuses to make eye contact.

"I take it that you are the bodyguard?" I ask the man, who has darkened my doorstep with a box tucked under his arm.

"Yeah," he murmurs, while fumbling the box free and trying to outstretch his hand.

The patch on the back of his vest clearly indicates that he's a full member, but his uneasy demeanor is that of a prospect. Is it him or me? It could possibly be my relationship to his president or the fact that he's the sole person in charge of me. Maybe this is his first solo assignment. He doesn't look young enough to have just patched in, but it's so hard to judge anymore. This man could be twenty-one, and I would be none the wiser to it without checking his I.D.

I have to admit that his nervousness intrigues me, since usually the caliber of men in this club are nothing more than a walking hard on, meatheads, or grunting instead of talking. Maybe he's just a man of few words. God, I hope he was because living with him as my shadow for the next few weeks or even years was going to wear on me. I love my privacy, and having to invite a complete stranger in, goes against every one of my life rules.

He fumbles the rattling box twice more, before finally setting it down and approaching me. His long, lean fingers brush against mine in an awkward handshake.

"I'm Voodoo, but you can call me V," he rattles off. He stiffens at my touch, and I see a slight smile crack on his face. My eyes connect with his nearly silver-blue pools, and a rush of familiarity hits me, when his hand fully engulfs mine. His eyes suck me in, but it's his touch that's intoxicating. My skin buzzes as the connection between us continues, like little ripples of electric currents zipping from hair to hair.

Did he feel that too?

He jerks his hand away a little too quickly, and turns his focus back to the box on the table.

Yeah, he definitely felt that.

Have I met this man before? What if he's a legacy patch member of someone I knew once? If I had met him before, then he was a void in my mind, and those were the most dangerous kinds of lack of recognition.

As he fumbles around inside the box, I notice wires peeking out of it.

Lord. This is the guy my brother thinks is going to protect me. He's a nervous wreck. I think I might have a better chance protecting myself at this point.

"I didn't know the club hired blue collar guys these days," I remark. "I guess skill sets of all kinds are useful around here, when you have to keep everything in house." His confused look in return almost makes me laugh.

"The wires," I say pointing at them.

"Oh," he chuckles. "Raze, I mean your brother, wanted me to upgrade the security in the clubhouse."

"I see."

I watch silently, as he pulls a few small cameras from the box and sets them down on the table in a systematic approach. He checks each one carefully, before turning around again and noticing that I'm watching him. This man definitely has a mild form of Obsessive-Compulsive Disorder.

Stop analyzing him. His mental health isn't any of your concern, as long as he's stable enough to keep you safe.

"Cameras?"

"For your protection. These will detect changes in temperature, motion, and sound over a certain decibel range."

"Like screams for help?" I inquire, with a knowing look on my face.

"Or for pleasure."

I cock an eyebrow at him, and his face quickly flushes because he realizes what he just said, and where my mind just went.

"Oh shit. Did I really just say that?" he back peddles. "Sorry. Not exactly used to having a lady around here."

"I can tell," I smile.

"So, my brother plans to monitor me from afar or am I to be on display for the entire club's viewing pleasure?" I sharply question him. Just the idea that my brother wants cameras on me begins to infuriate me. It may all be in the name of protection, but this seems like overkill. The Zezza's have no idea of my connection to the club, and as far as I know, Ginny never revealed to Gio her real name. This place should be the Fort Knox of safety as it is, but it's like my brother doesn't trust his own men. Maybe things aren't as great as I thought around here.

"The only two people who will have access to these cameras are your brother and myself, but just as the security expert," he back peddles.

"I see," I offer back coolly.

Oh yeah. My brother will be hearing about this. I may be a prisoner here, but I refuse to live as a real live version of a show pony in a ring. Safety is one thing, but this is more than that. He wants to keep an eye on me, so I don't bolt again.

"It won't take me long," he assures me. "If you want to hang out in the main room, I should be done in about thirty minutes or so."

I consider his proposal, but dismiss it almost immediately. Being out there would mean facing Ruby again, something that I'm not exactly ready to do again today or ever. After all these years, she is still angry that I left and chased my own dreams, while she gave up on hers for this club. I once would have considered her a friend of sorts, since we grew up together in the club, even though her role was far different than mine. She was property, and I was the princess. We both lived completely different lives. I'd be stupid to think that I could avoid her, while I'm here. We'll have to see each other on a daily basis, but right now I wanted to avoid it at all costs, even if it meant watching a perfect stranger rig up my room in cameras.

At least the view is nice.

Lord have mercy. Stop ogling the bodyguard.

As he reaches up to the corner of the north and east walls, the muscles below his t-shirt and cut ripple just slightly. V isn't exactly what I would call a meathead. His muscles, while smaller than his brothers, are still noticeable under the tattoos that wrap around his biceps. He is lean where the other men are bulky. The kind of guy that I usually fall for. I squint trying to decipher the theme of his ink to profile him a little bit, but he jumps down from the chair he dragged over to the corner, and bends down to pick up a fallen piece of equipment, before I get a really good look at it.

Seriously? Where in the hell is this stuff coming from? Okay, brain. I know you're tired, but this is getting ridiculous.

A smile cracks on my face, as his perfect butt strains against the tight dark wash jeans wrapped around his thin hips. Heated arousal begins to coil in my core, as I continue to watch. Each slight movement from him charges my internal arousal batteries one tick higher, which begins to set me on the dangerous edge of confusion and arousal. I wonder what he is packing in the dick department.

Hey ovaries, get with the program. I know he's good looking and it has been a while, but no. You have someone out there already.

A pained thought enters my mind. There is someone out there who might be wondering where I am or why I have gone quiet. Though I had agreed to cut off contact with the outside world via my government contract, I just couldn't. It's human nature to want to seek out human interaction. After so many nights with Ben and Jerry's and a vibrator, a girl had to do something. I craved affection so badly that I did something really stupid, like set up a dating profile. I tried to make it as generic as possible, and even obscured my face to the best of my ability. It was dormant for months, until a message from another user brought me back to life. That one message turned into multiple messages, which then turned into texts. It was a whirlwind, and I was gladly caught up in it. The man's name is Beauregard. It's old fashioned I know, but in those e-mails and then all the text messages from my hidden pre-paid phone, I found a friend. It was almost like he understood me in a way that no one else had ever been able to before. Even miles away, he could see into my soul and provide me with the relief I had needed for so long. There were no expectations, rules, or FBI agents, when I was talking with him. It was easy, and it was the best damn thing that had ever happened to me.

He was very handsome if the picture he sent me was really him. I'm not naïve enough to believe that I met the perfect guy on the first try, and I also know there is a huge possibility that he might be lying to me. It was an everyday occurrence with Google Images allowing anyone to usurp someone else's identity. Yet, I never got the feeling that what was between us was a lie or a cruel deception by an unhappy person seeking anonymous romantic entanglements, before ghosting away. I have this gut feeling he is telling me the truth, and that the picture really is him.

He is different. I know he is. I wouldn't be this happy if it were all a lie.

After two months of almost constant contact, I felt safe with him. Even safe enough to send him my full picture, and in doing so, our relationship moved from friendly to romantic. It was reckless on my part for exposing myself that way. I knew that, but I didn't care. The thought of meeting him after my contract was over in just a few months, gave me the hope and the drive to finish this job. At the end of this journey, there would be someone that I could call my own and not have to worry about him disappearing or being killed.

My eyes float to the pre-paid phone currently tucked away in the jacket I had worn for days, as we drove across the country. I clung to it like a lifeline the entire trip. Not only for Beauregard, but also for the fact, it was the only form of contact I had with me, other than my purse that I had thankfully left in my un-locked car that day. Without it we would have been dead in that safe house.

As soon as I felt we were safe, I emptied my bank accounts at a local bank branch drive-up window and tossed my card along with my personal cell phone. I knew if I had done it on the trip that it would pinpoint our location, so I pulled the money from an obscure location just within the city limits of the safe house. The men after us could track us easily, if I used my account or card, but cash wouldn't provide a breadcrumb trail for them to follow us with.

The sound of V moving the chair snaps me back into reality. His eyes linger on me for a few seconds, before shifting away again.

"Do you think that someone can get me a change of clothes?" I ask him, while he grabs another camera off the table.

"Shouldn't be a problem," he mutters, while sliding his pad of paper and pen from the earlier meeting, out of his back pocket. "Write down your sizes and what you need. I'll get someone to get them for you."

He hands over the notebook and pen, before getting back to his work. I flip the pages, and I can't help myself but to be nosey, when I see his notes on the meeting today scribbled in his own handwriting across the page.

Would this be how my patients felt if they could see my notes on our sessions?

It's almost like reading an action and adventure novel, as I read back the reality that has become my life. How did I fall so far, when I was only trying to do so well for myself in this world? Maybe my life was meant to be one series of giant screw-ups, like the ones I ran from.

I notice Voodoo grabbing the last camera off the table out of the corner of my eye before I start scribbling down my own essentials. He makes quick work of its installation and returns to the table for his box, before turning on his heels and collecting the list from my hands without so much as a please. His eyes scan the list quickly.

"Just the essentials, I swear." He smiles in return.

"You're all set," he comments, pointing out all the

cameras. "The only room that isn't monitored is the bathroom. For privacy."

"Thank you," I tell him. "At least someone around here isn't a pervert."

He pauses for a minute, and then smiles. "I wouldn't go that far. You just don't know me well enough yet."

I climb from the couch and stalk toward him. His body freezes at my closeness, and I take note of the fact that I can see perspiration dripping from the back of his neck. Not something that I expected of a man who likely kills for a living, just from hanging a few cameras.

Maybe he has an anxiety disorder to go along with his O.C.D.

"Since you're in charge of me, I'll take it easy on you for your first day. I'm going to take a shower and likely turn in for the night. If my clothes show up, just have someone leave them outside my door, and I'll grab them in the morning."

His Adam's apple bobs with a hard gulp. The therapist inside of me wonders whether it was the mention of the shower or the implied nakedness that elicited such a response from him. The need to get him on the couch and pick his mind comes on hard, but I dismiss it. I made a rule a long time ago that if the need to pry open a person's deepest and darkest secrets hit, to back away if I wasn't being paid to do it. Because those are the kind of people whose mind you didn't want to dip inside of.

"Okay," he mumbles. "Goodnight then."

Before I can even respond, he's out of the door. I listen for returning footsteps for a few minutes, before grabbing my jacket and bolting for the bathroom door, seeking privacy.

I shut the door behind me and dig into my pockets for my phone. The screen flicks on, and the low battery notification flashes. I had just re-loaded the minutes the morning before our great escape, but that wasn't the issue. Minutes I had, but the battery dying was going to be a problem without a charger. If I asked for one, my brother or my guardian would be wise on the fact that I had a phone. My brain was too tired to come up with another plan for securing a charger, and I added it to my mental to do list, after I slept.

The battery alarm beeps again, and I quickly unlock the screen, finding Beauregard's name. My fingers fly across the digital keyboard, as I click send. The three days of silence between us was almost too much.

Is it the same for him?

I miss you.

The text goes through, and the phone dies in my hands, just after it sends. My heart sinks, as I realize that may be my last message to him.

I'm truly alone in a prison of my own creation with no escape in sight.

Chapter 8

VOODOO

THE DOOR to her room closes behind me, and I feel like I take in my first real breath, since before I entered.

You were smooth in there, dip shit. Could you have been more of a nervous Nelly? Grow a pair.

She looked so fucking beautiful sprawled out on that couch, and my dick was screaming at me to go say hi. But it was the moment, that her soft hand grazed mine in my sad as shit attempt to be professional, that I knew this was something different. A fucking handshake and I was gone. I was crazy. Absolutely off my rocker crazy, but it was happening. Maybe those fucking romance shows the club girls watch weren't that far off on the love at first sight shit. Well, in this case, there wasn't a big rock and a cash prize waiting at the end. There was something much more than that. The only problem is that she doesn't realize the way she reacted to me is because she knows me. The other me, who was really the real me, without the club bullshit, but that's beside the point.

Fuck, I'm confusing myself.

I caught the shared reaction between us from that touch, as hard as she tried to hide it. She was a shit liar if I could ever call someone that.

Every second that I was in that room, I was in absolute terror of spilling my secret to her. She was so close, yet so far away from me.

Fuck. My. Life. Guarding her wasn't going to be as enjoyable as I thought. Not if I was going to be like this. I'm a raving lunatic when she's around.

As soon as she sauntered over to me with those rounded hips, I knew I had to get out of there. The mention of a shower and the thought of her sleeping naked in that room was my breaking point. It was even worse, when the dark thought crossed my mind of having access to watch her through the cameras I had just rigged up. I heard red alert warnings going off in my head from below the belt. I was running the risk of my other brain taking over, and it wouldn't do me any good right now.

Not happening, buddy boy. That's a prison sentence. You have to wait, until the time is right.

My dick rebutted at my moral high road, but that wasn't a line I was about to cross just yet. Prison colors didn't look good on me, and neither did a dead man's suit. That was the only two possible outcomes of such a stupid fucking idea had I gone through with it in that moment. I just had to play my cards right.

I bolt from the hallway, where Presley likely stands naked, dripping wet from her shower, and charge for my office. Thankfully, I have a nice new selection of porn that I can use to satisfy this itch and pacify it. Just a man and his dick. Masturbating in misery together. *Fucking pathetic.*

My head is so tightly wrapped around Presley's proposed nudity that I didn't even see him standing there just outside our office area. I hit him head on, and bounce back from the contact.

"Where's the fire, V? Damn, that hurt a bit." Raze questions with a curious look.

"Shit, Prez. You've been practicing those ninja skills. Didn't see you there."

Raze's look remains the same, as he assesses the situation.

"V, I live in a house with five kids. Stealth is my middle name," he chuckles. "Did you get her room wired up?"

"Sure did. About to go get started on Ginny's room next."

"Don't bother," he states. "Ratchet took her home with him. Against my wishes, I might add."

"Need me to check the cameras on his house or get Slider over there?"

"I'm already ahead of you. Slider's parked outside right now."

Lockdowns aren't exactly the time to defy our club president's orders, but this is a bit of a different situation. Ratchet loves his sister, that was plain enough to see, and it only makes sense that he wants her in his house the first night back. Was it a smart move? No, but the first night would be their safest here, as long as they weren't followed. The lack of our doors being broken down around us was proof enough for the time being that they weren't.

"She'll be back tomorrow, so you'll have time to do your thing, before she's back."

"Sounds good, Prez. You need anything else, before I get back to work? I want to get the outer cameras ready to go before I install them after dark. If they are watching, I'd rather that they didn't see where I put the cameras."

Raze smiles at my forward thinking, and slaps his large hand roughly against my shoulder.

"If we make it through this alive, I owe you a raise," he remarks.

"Aw, shucks. I'm just doing my job," I mock back. "You know how I love to play with wires and cameras. I'm like a kid at digital Legoland."

Raze just laughs, as he walks away and leaves me to my previous plan. I slide into my office, closing the door behind me and flipping the lock. I think about throwing a sock on the door, but the club girls might get the wrong impression. And so would Presley.

As much as I love pussy, I had to play my cards right with Presley here. No more club girls, and no more one-night stands, until I know where we stand. It was just me and my favorite girl from here on out. Rosy palm and her five sisters.

Tossing the empty box on the table, I stalk over to my personal computer console on my desk that houses my spank bank collection. Business and pleasure don't mix, and that goes for my computers as well. It would be embarrassing as fuck, if I accidentally exposed my pump peep show to an actual website or worse to my brothers. This is one of those things that stays private.

I flick through my collection, and finally decide to try out the parody of the last *Star Wars* movie, *Star Sluts*. It's low quality, but this wasn't going to take long with Presley so fresh on my mind.

I undo the top button of my jeans, as the movie begins to load. My dick is raging against the zipper, and it hurts just from the sensation of the button popping open. I almost want to apologize for putting him through so much temptation. Her beautiful face flashes into my head. Maybe I don't need the porn after all. My fingers start for my zipper just as my *Star Wars* text tone goes off for the first time in days. I now know the season for the silent treatment between us. She was running for her life, and unknowingly, right to me.

My hand flies to my desk drawer, pulling out the old burner phone I had stowed, since her silence began.

The three little words scrolling across my screen makes my stomach seize. She misses *him*. Jealousy punches me in the gut. I'm jealous of myself, and it fucking sucks. This problem was of my own creation. The downside of it is only just now starting to reap what I sowed, except I was its beginning and end. The only person who would be hurt by it would be myself. I guess the old adage of being your own worst enemy was finally making sense.

Presley is texting Beauregard again, and from the confines of the clubhouse. This poses two distinctly different issues. One, she has a phone here and there's no telling if The Zezza's are tracking her with it. The second is that she was thinking about another man, when I was with her.

My sudden need to get my rocks off blinks into oblivion, only to be replaced with the need to tear apart her room and get that phone. The only problem is, if I do that, she'll know my secret, before I even get a chance to explain it to her.

The only thing I can do is play along, even though it is killing me on the inside.

I think for a few minutes before I respond, but the message instantly bounces back. Dammit. It must be dead or she's turned it off. At least that solves one of my problems for the time being. I look down at my dick thinking about starting where we left off, but he's a no go, even with the sounds of a fake Princess Leia sucking off a pretty shitty Chewbacca coming from the computer.

Those three little words and the subsequent emotional avalanche took everything sexy off the menu. I lean down, switching off the video, and re-button my jeans. I guess I'll get started on my intel search, since just about everything I had planned to do tonight has gone to absolute fucking shit.

Pushing off my heels, I head over to my work computers and flick one of them on. Retrieving the pad of paper from my pocket, I notice Presley's list. Half of the shit on it is foreign to me. I snap a picture of it, and text it over to Darcy. She will know exactly what to get. Although, that doesn't solve the real time issue now because Presley is without apparel at the moment. A wicked idea comes to mind, and I smile as I think about it. I unlock my office door, and head to my room on the other side of the clubhouse. The main room is busier than it was earlier. My brothers are home to roost, until the coast is clear. Many of them with their kids and old ladies in tow. Darcy and Dani sit at the bar top, locked into conversation, while the twins and Roxie babble in a playpen between them. Not exactly a sight that I ever thought I would see within the confines of our club. It was a change, but a welcomed one.

With so many people around, I dip unnoticed down the hallway and walk into my room. My dresser to the left of the door was my target. The heavy wooden drawer creaks as I open it, and pull out a few of my club shirts from my prospecting days that I have kept as mementos. They don't exactly fit me now, but they will fit Presley.

"Need anything, sugar?" Misty, one of the newer club girls, asks making sure her ample tits are on display for me. Normally, I wouldn't second-guess her appearance for anything other than what it really was, a satisfying fuck and a happy ending for the both of us. Now, she only annoys me.

"I'm good," I say, trying to dismiss her. Disappointment clearly shows on her face. She starts to leave, just as another idea pops in my head.

"Is there a storeroom for clothes for the new girls? Toiletries? Shit like that?"

"Ruby has a few things set aside. Why?"

Her prying begins to piss me off.

"I'm thinking about cross dressing," I spit back. "Why don't you take your ass over to that little cache of stuff and bring me back a pair of sweats and that girly shower shit you all love so much?"

She starts to question me again.

"This isn't up for debate, Misty. Just get it and bring it back here."

She huffs and spins on the too tall for her heels, stomping down the hall. Her ass shakes with a little more effort as she leaves. Desperate much? I'm almost positive that there are a handful of men sitting right out there in the clubhouse room that would scratch her itch in a heartbeat. Unfortunately for her, this isn't the dick she is hooking up with anymore.

A few minutes later, she comes back and thrusts a bag into my hands without another word. She stomps back down the hall. I force myself not to yell after her to calm her tits, but that might encourage her pursuit of me further. Peeking into the bag, I find a few of the necessities on the list Presley gave me. This would surely get her through the night.

I shove my old shirts into the bag and head back towards her room. Call me a cave man, but I like the idea of her in my shirt. I knock when I reach the door, and she doesn't answer. Do I go in and just leave it by the door? My mind argues with itself like I have someone else living in my head with me. There's no proof that there isn't someone else in this sexy brain of mine, which just makes me laugh at myself.

Snapping myself back to the task at hand, I press my ear to the door and listen for the sound of the running shower, which I hear.

Time to use those ninja skills, V.

Carefully opening the door, I quickly slide in and place the bag onto the floor by the doorframe. I start to praise myself for accomplishing my mission without being detected, until I hear a gasp above me. My eyes trail up from the floor and the bag, and find a towel-wrapped Presley staring down at me like a barrel of a gun. Her long hair is shoved to one of her shoulders, while beads of water slide down her very naked legs.

Abort mission, motherfucker. Abort mission.

"Uh, hi," I squeak, before I scramble out of the doorway and run straight back to my office. My chest heaves as I rush in, slamming the door behind me.

If I had any chance of just leaving Presley alone, it just flew out the fucking window with my man card attached to it.

Chapter 9

PRESLEY

IT'S BEEN ALMOST three days, and my peeping tom bodyguard has been a ghost. No pop-ins to check in on me or any security checks to make sure everything is okay. Even the few times that I visited Ginny in her room on the other side of the clubhouse or ventured out to have dinner with actual people, he was absent. Did my brother pull him from my detail, after what happened? Just when I thought and come to terms with the fact that my person in command changed, I'd find something in my room that could only come from him.

For example, the morning after the incident I grumbled to myself about wishing there had been bacon at breakfast, after coming back from eating. The next morning, I was happily surprised to find a plate of bacon and eggs waiting for me. As I scanned the room, no one else seemed to have it. Just me. Something I know had to be him because he would have heard it on the camera systems. It could have been my brother, but after considering it, I knew it wasn't him. It was V.

Even though he's stayed away, the tingling sensation that cascades down my body tells me he's nearby. It calms me in a way because it's like I'm not alone, even though physically I am.

In my loneliness, I thought about the last time I had seen him over and over again. I have to admit that walking out of the shower and seeing him there, sliding into my room like a burglar was a shock. Maybe more so to him because I didn't find our close encounter that awkward. He was being thoughtful by bringing me clothes and toiletries to tide me over. A surprisingly sweet gesture that I wanted to thank him for had he not decided to Houdini away.

But it added up with the nervousness he seemed to have around me. I had my suspicions about the source of his odd behavior, yet it was unconfirmed, until I could gather more data about him. Some of these questions that I hope can be answered by my recurring visitor.

After getting cleaned up, and ready for the day after another restful night's sleep, I step out of my doorway only to find my brother standing on the other side of it.

"Can we talk?" he asks, gesturing with his hand for us to go back into my room.

"I guess," I reply, stepping back inside with him right behind me.

Mikey closes the door, and the soft click of the hammer striking the plate sounds like a bomb going off in my silent room. The air is so thick with tension that you could have cut it with a dull knife. How did we get to this point in our relationship?

I take my position on the couch, and Mikey shifts to sit on the edge of my bed. His eyes lock onto the HRMC shirt that I have on, and they instantly roll. Was there something wrong with me wearing the club's colors? Every action and reaction he makes, I find myself constantly questioning the motive behind it. Mikey is like watching a bomb with an occasional tick, knowing that at any second that it could blow up in my face.

"Who's Agent Martinez?"

My face falls, and I can feel all the blood rushing out of it.

Shit.

"He's who recruited me. Why?"

"He paid me a visit at home today. Asking questions about you."

My hand rubs across my face in frustration. This is not what we need right now. Martinez being here means only one thing. He knows I'm still alive. As much as I wanted to trust the man who recruited me for this project, there's a part of me that nags that I really can't. The Zezza family had to find out about Ginny's location somehow, and until I could cross him off the list, he wasn't safe.

"What did you tell him?" I inquire, with a hint of nervousness lacing my voice. Did my brother sell me out?

"That I haven't seen you."

"Thank you."

"I don't like that he was at my house, but I think I got him to back off for now. He'll be watching the house and probably Mom's."

"Mikey, I'm sorry for bringing this to you," I apologize sincerely. The last few days of mostly being on my own has left me in quiet reflection. My initial reaction of coming here was propelled by fear, and a deep resounding feeling of regret settled into my bones with the way I treated him. After a few good nights of sleep, the fog of my disdain for the decision to come here was beginning to lift. The club has accepted us with open arms, and I had rejected them all the while clinging to them in help. It was *my* actions that drove the wedge deeper between my brother and me.

Mikey's stern face softens, as his hand raises in front of him in a hushing motion.

"I'm honestly glad you came to me."

"You are?" I shockingly ask. "I thought–," I trail off, as he stops me mid-sentence.

He shoves off the bed and walks toward me, kneeling at my feet.

"I'm not mad that you came here because this bullshit finally brought you home."

"But the club? Ginny? We've put you all in danger because we came home. This is all our fault. The shit hasn't hit the fan as of yet, but we both know it's coming."

Mikey reaches out and grabs my hand, taking it in his. His roughness feels foreign against my smooth skin. It is paradoxical visual of the two different lives that we both have lived. His was rough and tumble, while mine was boring and safe. That is until his world and mine collided head on. Now we find ourselves in the gray middle ground, trying to find our place in it all.

"I know it is. But you are here where I can protect you like I was always meant to do. Whatever happens at the end of this, you will still be here and that's all that matters."

Tears begin to well in my eyes. I thrust forward, removing my hands, and wrapping my arms around his large neck. We hold each other like we did, when I was kid and nightmares sent me screaming in the night. This man. The one right in front of me is the brother that I remember. The man who would never let anything happen to my mom or me.

He pulls his hand away and wipes away my tears.

"I know I can be a son of a bitch. We both know where I get that from," he says with a laugh that I reciprocate.

"Yeah. Just don't turn out like him. You seem to have finally found your happiness," I declare to him, yet another question lingers. "What happened to Maj?"

Mikey grimaces at the mention of his ex-wife's name. He slides from the floor, and shoves his way in next to me on the couch. His large frame makes the frame squeak, under the weight of the both of us.

He begins to tell me about what transpired between them. Each portion of his story starts a fire of rage burning inside of me. She was supposed to love him. That's what nearly all marriage vows say. Knowing that she stood in front of him, shared a home and bed with him, and gave us my niece and nephew all the while working for the enemy, enrages me further. Had the bitch not been dead, I might have killed her myself for putting him and the kids through this.

Woah. I guess there is a piece of my dad still inside of me after all.

"Jesus, Mikey," I exclaim, as he finishes his story. "Why didn't Mom tell me about this?"

His cold, blue eyes shoot a sharp glare in return to my question.

Touched a nerve. Way to ruin it, Presley. This was the best talk we've had in years, and you had to flipping ruin it with bringing up mom.

"She doesn't know, does she?"

"Mom knows what she needs to know."

"And there's dad again," I fire back.

"Ignorance is bliss, LeeLee. Just let her enjoy her years knowing that I'm happy now. She loves Darcy and her kids."

Her kids? Only getting a brief run down from Darcy during odd small talk, as she got me settled in the room, she mentioned her kids. Though I hadn't seen them beside the baby, I wondered if they were my brothers or her first husband's.

"Is Roxie yours?"

"No. Darcy was pregnant when Jagger died. You remember him, don't you?"

My mind flitters back to my early memories of the

club, and the man who sacrificed so much for my family. I can feel a smile forming on my face thinking about how he used to bring me little gifts of candy or a doll, whenever he came over. I often wished that he was my father, when dad was raging off his rocker on drugs.

"You know I do. He was one of the good ones."

My brother nods in agreement. "Speaking of Mom. She doesn't know you are here. Let's leave it that way, until we know for sure how this will all play out."

"For once in my life, I actually agree with you," I laugh, and Mikey smiles back.

"Do you need anything?"

I purse my lips, while I try to think. To be honest, the only thing that I truly need is a charger for my phone, but that's not something I can freely ask for. Finding one somewhere within the club was my only option. I just had to wait, until I could roam freely to search the place.

"No, I'm good, but I do have another question for you. What is V's deal?"

"He do something I need to know about?" Mikey scowls. "If he did, you need to tell me."

"No. It's nothing like that," I stammer. "He just seems so different from the other guys here. I was curious about him."

Mikey smirks back at me, rubbing his hand across his face. Did I miss something about Voodoo? Was this a stupid question to ask my brother or did I cross some unmentioned bro code line?

"V is V. He's a good guy I promise you, or I would have never assigned him to watch you. That being said, if you want someone else, I will arrange it," he offers, looking for some sign of unease about me.

"No, he's fine," I offer. "I can't help, but analyze him. It's what I do. He's a curious case."

Mikey belly laughs like I said something hilarious.

"LeeLee, half the guys in here would be curious cases. We all have to be a little crazy to live this kind of life."

This lifestyle is not for everyone, myself included. It took a special kind of person, usually someone who needed danger and structure in their life, to take up with a motorcycle club, unless you were born into it like my brother and I. We weren't given the chance to live a normal life. I had to make my own version of normal all on my own.

"No shit," I tease back. "Don't forget that I lived this life, too."

"That's something that I will never forget. Had I taken better care of you and Mom everything could have been different," he says with a somber tone dripping with guilt.

"You really think that you could live a civilian life?"

"No," he laughs. "You're probably right. Could you see me in a suit pushing papers all day in some cubicle?"

"Hell no."

We both laugh again because that's the honest truth. My brother's demeanor doesn't exactly make him a great fit for corporate America. He's too independent, and too bull-headed to listen to some pencil pushing manager lording over him. My mind imagines the sight of it, and I can't help, but laugh. Mikey gazes at me in confusion, unknowing of the visions in my head. I start to share the vision, but a soft knock comes from the door. I look up to see V leaning against the doorframe.

"Sorry to interrupt, Prez, but I need to borrow your sister."

Mikey looks between us both and shoves off the couch. He stops short of V and mutters in a low voice, something that I can't hear from where I'm sitting. He slaps V on the shoulder, as he finishes and exits around him.

Voodoo stares at me, staying firmly planted in the doorframe. Keeping his distance, no doubt.

"The prodigal bodyguard returns," I tease him. "Thought you ghosted on me or something."

He runs his hand through his dark hair, while his eyes never leave mine. It's like he's watching me like a predator would watch his prey, whenever we are together. It's unnerving and exciting at the same time.

"I'm sorry for the other night," he mumbles. "It won't happen again."

The ease of our first meeting still lingers in the air of the room. I notice the nervousness of him bubbling just below the surface. He's more in control today, but not by much. This could be my chance to get him to open up a bit more, and try to calm his nerves. I may carry the Sanders name and blood within my veins, but I'm not exactly my father incarnate.

"So, you're saying that you don't want to see me wrapped in a towel again?"

He stiffens with shock registering in his eyes. You can almost see the fictional smoke coming out of his ears, as he tries to come up with something to say that won't get him in trouble.

"I, uh," he stammers, before I put him out of his misery.

"Lighten up, V," I smile, as I rouse from the couch and stalk toward him. He stiffens more, when I stop right next to him, leaving only a few inches between his body and mine. Why is it so much fun to mess with him? I enjoy it way too much for my own good.

The buzz from the first meeting begins to radiate between us again, as we both study each other in silence. He shuffles one foot forward cutting the small distance between us in half. His hot breath sends prickles of goose bumps cascading down my neck and arms.

Is he going to kiss me? Do I want that? Come on, brain. Work for crying out loud.

His lips quiver, and just as he's about to speak, I pull the rug out from under him to break the tension.

"Don't worry," I whisper. "My brother doesn't know a thing about you sneaking into my room, while I was indecent."

He doesn't move. I mean nothing at all. Did I stun him speechless or did his brain freeze up?

"You said that you needed something from me? I hope it's not an encore of the last time you were in my room."

He gulps, shifting back to his normal position, as I just smile wide at him.

Two can play at this game, and teasing him might just be the most amusing thing to do, while I'm here. His curiosities have definitely gotten this pussycat interested in how his mind works.

Chapter 10

VOODOO

HEARING Raze's voice in her room nearly had me calling for a retreat and running away with the circus.

I could totally be a tiger tamer.

Okay. Okay.

Freak show.

When I heard her mention my name, I can't lie and say that I didn't stand outside listening through the door to their conversation, all the while internally begging God to spare me if Ratchet let it slip to Raze. Albeit the brief conversational pieces about me does give me a sliver of hope that I have a chance with her once this was all over. And if we survived, death would definitely hinder my plans a bit, and necrophilia was definitely not in my kinky toy box.

Although I had come here to see her out of investigational necessity, her playful banter was definitely a welcome appearance. This was the Presley that I knew from the months of texting, and to see her come out of her shell was the best fucking thing on the planet.

The only problem is that every time she does it, I act like that fucking Indian guy off of *The Big Bang Theory*. Her beautifully, plump lips move and my voice and nerves just poof into thin air. Fucking bullshit if you ask me.

"Uh, V," she interrupts my mental anguish with a smile. "What exactly do you need from me?"

"Oh," I stammer. "That. I, uh…"

I can't seem to get my thoughts together around her. "I need you to look at some photos. I want to see if you can identify anyone who was involved at the safe house."

She looks to my hands, finding them completely empty, and returns her gaze to me.

"Looks like you forgot something," she laughs.

I look down to my own hands, and just shake my head as I laugh.

"They're on my computer in my office," I say, running my shaking hand through my hair, as a stupid fucking way to break through this wall of nerves. "Field trip?"

She sidesteps around me, stepping into the hall-way, and stops when I don't follow her.

"You coming?" she asks. "I don't exactly know the way to your office."

She's fucking toying with me.

And I like it.

The way she says my office sends all the blood from my braining parachuting straight below my belt. My dick hardens as my mind replays the way those words came rolling off her tongue. Each move-ment of her lips is seductive.

Seriously? That's what turns you on? Come on, dude.

She'll be in my domain. All alone. With me. The things we could do in there.

Get it together, man!

I step out of the doorway, past her and start towards my office. A few of the guys take notice of the fact that she's wearing one of my old prospect t-shirts and whistle, as we walk through the main room. Presley looks back at them, and I catch her confused glare out of the corner of my eye, as I round the corner to the office area.

That's right, assholes. Back off. She's mine.

"What was that about?" she asks me, as we stop before my office door.

"Don't worry about them," I reassure her. "They're all crazy."

She looks back down the hall, before responding back to me.

"I specialize in crazy, V. I'm pretty sure that you know that."

"That kind of crazy out there isn't for you."

I wiggle the keys to my office out of my jeans pocket, unlocking the door. She follows in right behind me, as I flick on the lights to the room. Her wide eyes scan the room, taking in the sights of my fully functional computer man cave equipped with all the latest bells and whistles.

"Wow," she responds. "You weren't kidding when you said that you were the tech guy. I would say that I'm decent with a computer, but this is an entirely different playing field."

Presley saunters up to my main consoles and traces her fingers across the glowing Alienware keyboards. I smile knowing that the one person that I had dreamed about being in my room is now in here. Only she wasn't naked in this reality, but that could be changed in time. I hope at least.

"You better stop that," I chuckle, as she rips her hand away from the keyboard like they burned her. "My computers might start liking you better than me, if you keep caressing them like that."

Presley holds her hand against her chest and just laughs.

"You touch your computers often, V?" she asks.

I stow the idea to tell her that she has no idea and to not use a black light, but that would probably kill the mood. Instead, I settle for something more subtle and subdued.

"I don't touch and tell."

She heartedly laughs at me.

"Good thing my brother wasn't wrong about you. I like a man with a sense of humor."

My dick jerks at her praise of my personality, and I swear to fucking god, I can feel him screaming from inside my pants to seize the opportunity and throw her ass on this desk. But for once, I don't listen to him.

"So where are these pictures you want me to look at?"

I walk over to her, gesturing for her to sit down at the main console she was just fingering. Her body moves in an almost fluidic manner, as she brushes past me and takes the offered seat. The scent of her shampoo wafts into my face, and I fight the urge to take a closer sniff.

Don't be creepy. This is going well for once. Don't fuck it up.

Instead, I lean over her and unlock the console. A collage of photos pops up on the screen. After several days of my self-proclaimed exile from the incident on her first night, I made it my priority to try and track down some of The Zezza men to show her and Ginny. I combed the arrest records of all of their known associates, and I might have hacked into the FBI database as well. That part was actually kind of fun. The ease of which hacking came to me would likely shock most people, but it was an adrenaline rush for me. The chances of getting caught were higher and higher the more I did it. Even with the safety measures I had put in place to mask my I.P. address and location, the chances were extremely high and very real. And if I were to ever get caught, the FBI would find themselves surrounding an abandoned Amish popcorn factory in Indiana. I hope they were hungry.

Jokes aside, it doesn't bode well with me that Raze has had a visitor from the FBI already. Martinez and I would be getting up close and personal as soon as I hacked into their system again. Right after I finish up with Presley.

"What are we looking for here?" Presley asks, she turns her face within inches of mine. Her warmth radiates from her beautiful, creamy skin, begging for me to kiss her rich lips. She pauses, when she realizes how close we are and quickly turns back to face the computer.

So fucking close and yet so far away.

I grab the mouse, bringing up individual mugshots of the men I had managed to track down.

"Tell me if you recognize any of these guys," I instruct her.

I flick through half a dozen of them, before she grabs my hand from the mouse. She pushes herself closer to the screen, getting a better look at the man currently occupying it. Her eyes close and quickly re-open. I notice her body tremors more and more with each passing second, as she stares at his face.

"This one was at the house."

I click on Vincente's file and drag it to the desktop to add to my research file, before clicking to the next one. Thirty minutes pass, and we only add one more to the pile, that one being a strong maybe in her words. At least this was a good start, and I still have Ginny left to repeat the process with. Between the two of them, I would at least have a direction to follow.

I close out the screen, and turn to lean my ass against the computer station desk. Presley shoves back in her chair with her hand covering her mouth in silence. Her beautiful dark brown eyes are filled with terror and fear. Shit, I took her back there.

"You okay?" I ask her, reaching forward to caress her arm. She looks up and a stray tear drips down her cheek. "I'm sorry. I know this is really hard on you, but I really appreciate you helping me get started."

"It's okay," she whimpers. "I guess I can fully understand how some of my clients feel, when faced with the demons of their past now. It's not a great feeling let me tell you."

"I have a couch right over there if you want to talk about it. I can be the head doctor and you can be the patient," I joke, hoping it will bring that heart-stopping smile back to her face. It kills me to see her like this, and I would do anything to fix it. And I mean anything.

"I just want to forget about it," she retorts, as she wipes away another tear from her face.

An idea pops into my head. One that might just do the trick if I execute it to perfection. My mental checklist goes wild, as I decide all the things I will need to make this work. I must be lost in thought longer than I had intended to be, because as soon as I come back to reality, I find Presley staring at me.

"I have an idea. Give me an hour. You in?"

She wipes away tears one last time and her smile returns, lighting up the room like a sunrise. It's a beautiful thing to behold. I'm one lucky man to be witnessing it.

"It'll help me forget?" she skeptically asks.

"It will," I reassure her. "Now you go relax for a bit, and I'll come get you."

She doesn't move immediately from the chair, which makes me laugh. She's so stubborn, and hopefully she'll be mine soon. I clear my throat, nodding toward the door.

"Oh," she exclaims. "You mean wait somewhere other than here."

"Not to rush you out, but the longer you linger, the longer you will have to wait for your mind-numbing surprise. Now, scoot."

She chuckles, as she pushes back from the desk and breaks for the door. I wait for her to round the corner, and I spring into action. If someone had been watching outside, they would have said that my office looked like a tornado trapped in a bottle. Papers, electronic gadgets, and my drones disappear at a record pace, as I put them away for safekeeping. I only wish that I had more time to get this place in better shape, but in honesty, she'd already seen it in its usual messy form anyway.

I shove my futon, which doubled as my bed for so many long nights for the club and the security firm at an angle, facing my open wall that usually held my cork board workflow charts.

"Misty!" I yell from inside my office. "Get in here."

Her high heels clack heavily on the hardwood floors of the office area, as she comes like I beckoned. She breaks through the plane of the doorway, where she stops with her hips popped out with a come and get me smile.

"You rang, babe?" she coos. "You ready to come back to me?"

"No," I cut her off. "I need you to grab me a clean, white sheet, and some of that spray shit that makes fabric smell better."

She arches her eyebrow at me like what I just said had an optional compliance amendment added to it.

"It wasn't a request."

"Fine," she whines, before disappearing again.

A short while later, she returns with everything I asked her to get, and basically throws it all in my face. I almost fire something back at her about her fucking attitude, but I think about how it would feel to be in her shoes. She has been after me for a while now, and I was about to give in to her, when Presley's entrance brought my whole world crashing down around my feet. She was angry and hurt. I would do better to remember that the next time I acted like a pushy asshole.

I make quick work on the finishing touches for my plan, before making one last stop in the kitchen.

With everything set, I go after my girl. Yeah, I said it. In my mind, she's already mine.

Presley rips open her bedroom door, before I can even finish knocking.

"Someone's excited," I tease her, as she steps outside of her door, closing it behind her.

"More like I need to shut off my brain."

"Follow me, my lady. Relaxation awaits."

When we return to my office, she gasps when she steps inside to find what I had done in the hour apart. I had made a makeshift coffee table that currently held a hodgepodge of snacks and sodas, using a few boxes that were filled with various computer and camera parts. The couch is reclined back just slightly with a clean blanket tossed on the back of it, to make it look a bit more home-like and less broke frat boy chic.

On the open wall, I hung a sheet that I had planned a few different uses for, since I hadn't bit the bullet and purchased the projector screen that I had my eye on. The next time, well if there was a next time this happened, I would have one.

I usher her to the couch, and she sits. I plop down next to her. Reaching down between my legs, I pull out two Nintendo Switch controllers.

"Video games?" she questions with a skeptical look.

I kick up my feet on the open end of the makeshift table, and toss one of the controllers into her lap, which makes her jump.

"I promised you mind-numbing fun, and this is it. Well, the start of it. I have a few prime choice movies we can watch, after I get done kicking your ass in Mario Kart."

She shoots me a sly smile and grabs the controller from her lap.

"You're on. Just don't cry when I whip your ass."

We play for hours, before she finally asks to watch a movie. Though she was a bit stubborn about my movie choices, she finally just let me pick, after I assured her that she would love *Super Troopers*. And I was right. Her laugh was intoxicating throughout the entire movie. I couldn't help, but smile. The longer the movie went the closer she scooted towards me. The nerves that had rattled her from the pictures before were completely gone. I smile again, knowing my plan was successful.

A short while later, I take the chance of putting my arm around her in a not so smooth high school first date move. She flinches at first, but settles against it with the popcorn bowl nestled in her lap. Her head begins to dip, as drowsiness sets in. Her head finally eases against my shoulder when sleep overcomes her.

My chin tilts towards her head on my shoulder. I gaze down at her sleeping form, and I can't help myself, when I place a kiss on the top of her head. She groans in her sleep, shifting against me, before re-settling again. I look back down at her sleeping form just as her lips begin to move.

"Beauregard," she mumbles, before drifting off again, while my heart falls to the pit of my stomach. Even with me now, she's still dreaming of him. He was the man who held her heart. Not me. I was crazy to think that I could shove that side of me out of her heart, after just a few days. He had been there for months, where I had only a few days with her.

There was only one thing I had left to do, and it breaks my heart knowing that it was my only option. Beauregard had to break her heart. Without that, I was dead in the water.

Chapter 11

PRESLEY

A COMFORTING BLANKET of warmth stirs me awake. My hand slides from the cocoon of warmth and slips into the chilly desert morning air.

Did I sleep in V's office last night?

My brain is a foggy mess of drowsiness that I can't seem to shake. My brain thumps like a drum line, as the beginnings of a headache start. My bones creak and crack with every labored stretch, until the fog finally lifts.

I'm back in my room. Normally, one would expect to find themselves snuggled into their own bed. But in my situation, I don't exactly remember coming back here.

Did he bring me back? Did I sleepwalk?

The comforter slips from my feet, and the cold chill sends an instant need for the restroom. I try to convince my bladder that I need more sleep, and that if I left the confines of my warm bed, that it might not accept me back again. A ludicrous thought, I know. I mean do blankets have feelings? Not likely, but it doesn't mean that I want to leave their heat for the chilly outside air.

I slip another foot out of the covers, which only makes the need to pee intensify.

"Goddammit," I grumble, throwing off the blankets, putting both of my feet down on the cold floor. I pad to the bathroom in a huff and take care of business. My body shivers, as I head back to bed. For a split second, I consider just getting up for the day, but decide against it. A day in bed sounds much better, than facing the world.

The comforter thankfully allows me back into the bed. Welcoming me with semi-warm arms. I flip over the pillow to the cool side, snuggling into it. The quietness of the room begins to lull me back to sleep, until my brain has other ideas. The scene from last night floods my sleepy mind.

The care and thoughtfulness of V's gesture makes me smile into my pillow. He knew exactly the kind of distraction that I needed, after facing one of the men that sent my life spiraling back out of control again. His dark eyes and cold, emotionless face haunted my dreams, during the sad attempt of the nap I had tried to take before V's planned evening. Had it not been for his distraction, I doubt I would have slept so well last night.

My consciousness re-focuses to V. His bright eyes were beacons of laughs and smiles, throughout the entire night. After so many days of nervousness and avoidance, I think he was finally ready to show me the man behind the mask. He was goofy, as he explained the game to me, and his personality really came out to play. While I had pegged him as an anxiety-riddled man, my diagnosis may not exactly be accurate. Anxiety may not have been his folly at all. His issue with the situation was definitely centered around me. From the moment I walked into this club, I felt like there was something different about him. He was overly cautious, yet caring when he needed me to identify my attacker. He was also oddly protective of me. Try as he might, I noticed the way he sneered at the men looking in my direction. He was like a male trying to mark his territory. Thankfully, he didn't try to piss on my leg.

It was perplexing to me to think about the day and night change in him. But somehow, some way, last night changed it all for me. The games were meant to be the distraction, but in reality, it was his company that distracted me more. My core was a heated mess of need and desire, the minute he closed the door to his office, leaving us alone like two teenagers trying to fool around without being caught. He was an attractive man, and any woman would turn a head to look at him.

But the feelings developing inside of me can't be real in such a short time. It was confusing, especially with a piece of my heart firmly in Beauregard's hands. If the feelings I have for him are even real. When I leaned into V's arm, I felt pangs of guilt inside of me because of Beauregard. Was he out with other women in our silence? Was I even the only woman he was talking to? These were all questions that I couldn't answer without him. Ones that would likely go unanswered, until I found a phone charger. Something that I had already shoved into the not going to happen inbox of my mind. Which is where I should be storing V, but for some reason, I was wavering on it.

There was something about him that I wasn't seeing on the surface. I shouldn't even be considering seeing where it goes with him, yet I can't shake the thought from my mind. My heart was leading me to Beauregard, but my mind was pushing me towards V, despite the fact that it would never last. If the dangers lurking around me finally settled, my plan wasn't to stick around. My life would never be back in this club, and getting involved with V, would only complicate that plan even more. The other side of that coin wasn't a pretty picture either. I would be the one to lose.

I try to shove the ridiculous notion of a relationship with V out of my mind. The silence of the room is near deafening and is soon broken by the sound of my stomach betraying my plans of lying in bed all day.

Traitor.

I shove the blankets back off of me, stalking to the chest of drawers, where the clothes V had gotten for me lay folded inside. The old wooden drawer squeaks as I open it. I reach inside, grabbing another simple t-shirt with the club's logo on it and grab a pair of black leggings.

I dress quickly in the cold, and sweep my long dark hair into a messy bun on top of my head. You could say that was a perk of being in my brother's clubhouse because I really didn't need to care about how I looked. I wasn't here to impress anyone. Well, not everyone. V might me the only exception to that rule.

Stop it, Presley. Why are you doing this to yourself? It's only going to end badly. Cling to Beauregard. With him, there's a future.

My stomach vibrates and grumbles, snapping me back from mentally berating myself. I walk to my door, throwing it open, and step into the hallway. With each step closer to the main room, the smell of breakfast wafts into my nostrils, causing my stomach to growl in protest again.

The room is busy with tables of people chattering about, all the while shoving food into their mouths. Everyone seems really happy here the longer that I watch them. I have to admit to myself that Mikey really did have a positive effect on the club. It was almost like the family I had once envisioned this place could be as jaded child. It could all be just a mirage though. Like the calm before the raging storm that Ginny and I had brought upon them. Guilt hits again knowing that the delicate balance of this club may be tipped back into the darkness because of us. It is a thought that doesn't settle well in my heart and soul. I make a silent promise to myself that I will run, before I ever let that happen to my brother's hard work.

"Presley! Over here," Ginny's voice calls out to me. I spot her over at a smaller table, off to the side with her brother flanking her. I smile back at her, as I walk towards them.

"Morning," she beams at me. "Sleep well?"

"I did," I respond, sounding almost too formal with her. It's hard to remember that we are no longer just a doctor and patient. "And you?"

"Like a baby, except when this big lug was snoring," she says with a giggle and elbows Ratchet's rib cage.

"I don't snore," he snarls. "That's you."

Ginny scowls at his rudeness, and elbows him again.

"Don't mind him. He's an asshole in the morning."

He scoffs at her accurate observation of his mood, and shovels a spoonful of eggs into his mouth.

"I'll go grab some food, and then I'll be back."

Ginny smiles at me and just laughs, pointing behind me.

"I think your food is already on the way."

I peer over my shoulder, and find V balancing two plates through the tables, heading right for us. He strides up next to us, depositing a plate in front of me.

"First it was video games, then a movie, and now breakfast. Is there anything that you don't do, V?" I smile, as he slides onto the stool next to me with his own plate, loaded with what has to be about a pound of bacon and one lonely scoop of eggs, that are barely holding onto the plate.

"I guess you'll just have to wait and see," he teases back, while he stuffs a few pieces of bacon in his mouth. His sense of humor and smile are just as intoxicating as his touch. I could seriously just stare at him for hours, and never grow tired of it.

What the hell? Where did that come from?

I just shake my head at his absurdity and the random thought I just had, focusing on my own plate of delicious smelling food. I smirk when I see that my own plate has a mountain-sized pile of bacon, but instead of eggs, there are two pancakes covered in butter and syrup.

I ferociously tear into the pancakes and moan when I pop a butter-soaked piece in my mouth. V stiffens next to me, and I can feel his stare, as I take another bite.

"Where were the pancakes?" Ginny asks her brother. "I didn't see those up there."

Ratchet huffs and just stares a hole through Voodoo, who only smiles in return.

"Must have run out," V says with a mouth full of bacon.

"Suck up," Ratchet mutters, under his breath.

V exchanges another look with Ratchet, before making his plate and fork his priority.

"There she is. Hello, Presley," I hear from behind me, which makes me spin on my chair turning to find the person responsible. The Viking looking man, who tried to deny my entry into the club on our first day, is shuffling his way towards us. He stops just to my left, and steps way too close into my comfort zone.

"You ready to trade V in for a younger, more experienced keeper, yet?" he quips. V goes rigid when he notices how close he is to me. "Name's Slider."

"And I'm not interested. Why don't you slide on out of here and away from me?"

"Oh, come on, doll face. You'd have more fun with me than him. I wouldn't put a bunch of computers up on a pedestal if I had you around."

"Back off, fucker," V growls behind me. Slider jerks in response to V and jolts around me to get to him.

"Not in this lifetime, Slider," Ratchet warns. "Why don't you get out to the garage and get started on waxing bikes? Mine seems to be a little dusty. You've been slacking off."

Ratchet's low-voice insult doesn't go unnoticed to Slider. It doesn't take a doctorate degree to see that there's bad blood between these two men. Not to mention the fact that V is seething himself.

Slider's glare bores into V then Ratchet, before retreating back. I don't remember prospects being this high-spirited back when I was a kid. My father would have never stood for such insubordination. Had Slider said something like that to his face, he would have never been seen again. Respect is a major principle of a motorcycle club, and I fear that it was one hard lesson that would be taken out of Slider's hide, if he didn't learn it fast enough.

I watch as V's heated stare doesn't leave the back of Slider's head, until he disappears out of the room. The rest of breakfast is done in an awkward mix of silence and brooding alpha male.

"Voodoo wants me to look at pictures today," Ginny interjects to break up the silence. "Would you, uh, come with me?"

She looks at me with somber eyes. Seeing the faces of those men affected me deeply, so I knew it was going to be even harder on her. It was also only a natural reaction on her part to want me there to comfort her, as a therapist and mostly as a friend.

"Of course, I will."

Ginny's sad façade cracks just slightly, as she finishes the last bite of her breakfast. "You ready?" she asks Voodoo.

"Whenever you are, Little G."

"That's not her name, ass hat," Ratchet fires back at the nickname Voodoo called her.

"I like it," Ginny adds.

Ratchet rolls his eyes, but doesn't say anything else. He loves his sister enough to stow whatever distaste he has, in another one of his brothers, branding his sister with her own nickname.

Voodoo shoves off the stool obviously wanting us all to do the same. Ginny wipes her face off with a napkin, before popping up from the table herself. I do the same, and the three of us walk to V's office. I was a little surprised that Ratchet didn't follow, but maybe he has something else to do.

It takes about two hours for Ginny to make it through all the photos. Knowing how important it was, she took her time. I was proud of her for only squeezing my hand twice, as she forced her mind back to the darkness of her past.

In addition to the two men I had picked out, Ginny added six more to the pile than she had seen prior to the safe house, Gio being one of them. Her body trembled at the sight of him, and even as I pleaded with her to step away, she didn't. Ginny wanted to end this part of her life, and she was putting herself through mental hell to do it. She still has a long way to go, but this also showed me how much she's grown as a person.

After we finish, Voodoo texts someone on his phone, and Ratchet soon arrives to collect Ginny. She needs time to process all of this, and I make sure to tell her that I will stop by to check on her later, which earns me a semi-fake smile.

I linger in the office, as V collects random wires, circuits, and some different pieces of a computer that I couldn't even begin to tell you the proper name for.

"Spring cleaning?"

V pauses with a slew of cords of various sizes in his hands.

"You could say that. There's an electronics recycling drop off this weekend, and I want to free up some space."

He shuffles over to the box on his desk, where he begins to pile the junk, and shoves in the fistful in his hand. While his back is turned, I notice the familiar end of what looks to be a bundle of phone chargers hanging over the side.

Shit. He might have the kind of cord I need for my phone.

Guilt pangs me, as I consider stealing it from him. I force myself to think about the situation in a different way. He said it himself that this was trash. Taking it would just be my own way of recycling.

"Be right back," he tells me, as he heads out the door. "Need another box for the old DVD burners."

I pause, waiting to make sure he isn't coming back before I dart for the box. A few different sizes of phone chargers lay right on top, and I grab them, coiling them as tightly as I can and stuffing them into my box. I know he might notice, so I shift around a few more of the wires to make it less obvious.

He steps back in just as I return to my place. My heart stops as he peers into the box, but he goes back to loading up the next box without a word.

"Almost done." He tells me, as he shoves a large metal box on the top of a very full box. "Let me get these out to the garage with the other recycling shit, and we can play some more Mario Kart."

As much as I want to say yes, I can't. Mario Kart isn't what I had in mind, knowing the pilfered cords in my pocket might just bring Beauregard back to me.

"I actually think I may head back to my room and lie down. I've been battling a headache since I woke up, and I think helping Ginny only made it worse. Rain check?" I lie. His smile falls.

"Sure. You know where to find me." The disappointment is clear as day in his voice.

Now who's the asshole.

I spin on my heels, and trudge out of the room with guilt weighing heavily on me. I stole from him to facilitate my need to speak to Beauregard, despite the growing feelings I'm starting to have for V. A man who is real and right in front of me.

So, this is what it feels like to be a complete, train wreck.

Not a fan. Definitely not a fucking fan.

Chapter 12

VOODOO

I'M a miserable sack of shit.

For the past week, I've watched the beautiful life shining out of Presley drain, and it's my own fucking fault.

She wanted so badly to contact Beauregard. I had given her the perfect opportunity to make that decision, when I purposely left the box with every single kind of charger I could find for her to choose from. It was a psychological game, and one she didn't even know she was playing. That box was a test.

If she took the charger, she lost.

If she asked for the charger, she lost.

If she didn't take it, I won.

Except instead of being shocked by an electric jolt for making the wrong decision, I was the person who was being punished. That shock hit me like a bolt of lightning.

It hurt more than I thought it would, when I peeked into that box, with her standing so innocently there in front of me, and found them tucked away. The pain only increased, when she blew me off to go back to her room and wait for her phone to charge.

You could say that I was just guessing at what she was doing, but I knew for a fact that's what she did from the cameras. She paced the floor, constantly going back and forth to the bathroom.

I watched her excitement of connecting with him again, and as soon as the tone went off on my burner phone, I hit rock bottom.

Why couldn't I be enough for her? I had tried my damnedest to go out of my way to make her happy. Breakfast, the movie, video game night, and giving her more breathing room than I should have, with the level of danger we were waiting on to show up at our doorstep at any minute.

But it ate away at me.

It ate away at me because I never responded back to her. Message after message from all hours of the night went unanswered. With each passing day of continued silence, a darker shadow settled over her. She was disappearing in front of me, and it was all because of me. She just didn't know it. Listening to her cry last night almost broke me. The phone was cradled in my hand with an "I miss you too" typed onto the screen, ready to send. But I couldn't do it.

I was a chicken shit because I was still clinging onto hope that she would pick me over him. The playful banter that we had prior was gone. Her one-word answers were proof of that.

I had to fix this because my plan of having Beauregard ghost on her wasn't working. As I listened to my brother's discussion in Church, I made another promise to myself to handle this situation, as soon as Church was over. It was time to nut up or shut up.

Ratchet stands, and directs our attention to a news report pulled up on the big screen behind Raze, that I had installed just this morning.

"Local police are reporting the recovery of the body of a local woman tonight," the news anchor begins. "Sabrina Townsend was found early this morning by San Bernardino police alongside I-10 near the Ontario exit. Townsend was reported missing just three days ago, when an eyewitness saw three masked men at a convenience store throw her into a black van. She is the third woman in the last week that has been kidnapped and dumped."

The news reporter continues on with a map of where the bodies of the victims were taken and found, over the course of the last week. Each dot was inching closer and closer to us. The Zezza's knew the girls were in California. That much was true, but whether or not they knew they were with us, was still a dangerous unknown.

Each of my brothers looks around the room. We are all thinking the same thing. The devil that's coming for Ginny and Presley is closing in on them and us.

Ratchet pauses the video and sets down the wireless remote on the table.

"You all know what this means," he declares. "The Zezza's are moving in."

Ratchet pauses for a brief moment, before continuing, "All of the women who have been kidnapped are similar ages, builds, and have physical characteristics to either Presley or Ginny."

I can literally feel my blood boiling, as it courses through my veins. The threat to Presley is circling like a fucking vulture, and I have been more distracted by a fucking fake identity crisis, instead of doing my damn job. Fucking stupid. I have never let a woman get into my head like this before, and it could cost Presley her life, if I don't get my shit straightened out.

"We need to double security," Hero adds in. "I've called in a few of the guys from the Oakland Chapter and Orange County. Thor will be taking the lead on getting those guys up to speed."

Thor nods. After the last scuffle a few months back, I'm surprised to see him so eager to return, after his injuries. But knowing he is willing to join in with us again makes me proud to call him my brother. Accepting his transfer was one of the best decisions we had made. He came to us looking for a better position, and we gave it to him. He has the kind of muscle that would make most thugs piss their pants in fear. He was our personal badass Fabio.

"Like I mentioned before, if you need to move your women and children out, this would be the time to do it," Raze reminds us. Darcy had initially drug her feet on leaving, when Raze had insisted she take the kids and visit her parents for a while, but she finally gave in to his wishes. Hero had followed suit, and sent a very pregnant Dani and the twins, along with Darcy. Together and away from us, they would be safe, until this played out.

"I'll get Maria and the kids out first thing in the morning. They're overdue for a vacation," Hot Shot adds in.

"Mikayla won't leave, even if I tied her to the back of Maria's car. She'd just gnaw her way through the ropes," Thor chuckles about the woman who latched onto him, after the death of her brother. "She'll stay no matter what I tell her."

"Worst case scenario, we hole her up with Presley and Ginny," I comment. Not exactly the best plan, but it might be the only hand we have to play.

Raze peers down the table and catches my attention.

"Show us what you have, V."

I get up from my chair, as Ratchet tosses the projector remote into my hand. I wanted to make a remark about the use of the new tech in the Church room, but this wasn't the time or place to do it. I will just have to wait, until all this shit is over.

"Ginny and Presley have identified the eight men seen here on the screen as Zezza members or associates."

I click to the first full picture and rattle off the dossier of information I was able to gather off of them, via the FBI's database.

It isn't until I get to the last one that I pause.

"This is Gio Zezza. Oldest son of Don Rigo Zezza."

Ratchet scowls, as he peers up at the man who is responsible for getting Ginny into this mess and for the necessity of faking her death. His stare makes it clear as fucking day that, if we get a shot off on this guy, he wants him to himself. And I can't blame him.

I would want the kill shot on the man who had hurt my sister. Although, my sister Remy would probably have already killed them, before I got there. She was the one who was all bitch and bite, where I was the calculating dark horse who planned, before he struck.

"I wasn't able to track down any safe houses for The Zezza family in the area through their various shell companies, but I'm still looking."

The amount of money going through that crime family would make Bill Gates look like a lucky lottery winner. They had hundreds of millions of dollars spread across various real and fake enterprises all over the world. They had their hands in import, export, and even the skin trade, as far as I could tell. These were the kind of bastards you didn't want on your bad side, but here we were in the exact spot we didn't want to be.

"Any idea on the weapons cache?" Thor asks.

"The sky is the limit with them." Flipping through a few slides, I land on the screen I'm looking for. It has the listings off all the so-called olive oil importation logs from their cargo ship that comes in and out of Long Beach on a monthly basis.

"Their last shipment came in about two weeks ago. Manifest said it was olive oil, but we all know what the contents of those containers really are."

"Drugs, guns, or pussy. Maybe all three." Hero interjects into the conversation.

"Winner, winner, chicken dinner there, VP."

"They're armed to the teeth and moving closer to us by the day. It's a safe bet that their toys are far better than ours. Possibly even Soviet military grade."

"Which is why I pulled a few strings and have some new gear headed our way. It should be here in a couple of days," Raze happily informs us. "Let's just hope it's not too late."

I add in a few more bits of information, into my part of the meeting about things I had found out from Ginny directly. Gio had a penchant for high-end escorts, and I had taken the liberty of hacking into the surveillance cameras, near the more popular clubs that were rigged with facial recognition software. If he showed up, my cameras would alert me. I had also greased Red's palms a bit to filter in any chatter from the streets straight to us. He was a slimy bastard, but he proved useful from time to time with shit like this.

"Good work, V," Tyson offers up to the entire room.

We discuss alternative action plans for various scenarios for nearly three hours, before we finally decide to call it a day. The more practice we have the better off we'll be in the long run.

Raze concludes our meeting with a bang of his gavel. Each of my brothers all begin to file out, except for Ratchet and myself.

"The girls doing okay?" my club president inquires, once the last man leaves the room.

"Ginny's good. I've been keeping her busy and away from the news. The less she knows about those murders the better."

"I agree, but I'm concerned about Presley. She seems off. Shed some light on that, V."

"I'm honestly not sure what's up, Prez. She was fine a few days ago, but has retreated a bit," I lie.

You fucking know what is going on, dip shit. Why don't you go ahead and fess up now? Maybe he'll wait to kill you, until after The Zezza's try to make us extinct.

This situation with Presley is one that might just fucking get me killed. Ratchet shoots daggers at me with his eyes. Thankfully hiding them from Raze.

"I'll talk to her, and figure out what's going on."

"Good. If you need me to get involved, just tell me," Raze heartedly concurs.

Our president shoves out of his chair and smacks Ratchet on the shoulder, as he stalks out the door. I can't help but notice the slump of his shoulders, as he disappears from sight. He's miserable without Darcy and the kids, and it's clearly showing. Even more of a reason to just get this over with.

Ratchet jerks my arm, as I try to leave myself.

"What did you do?" he snarls.

"I fucked up, man. She's pining over the fucking fake me."

I fill him in about my original plan to just ghost. He growls when I mention the fact that she has a phone, but I remind him that I can't exactly storm into her room and demand it without outing myself in the process. It's a hot damn mess, and I'm smack dab in the middle of the firestorm.

"Fix it," he growls, as he stomps past me.

I would if I fucking knew how. Believe me, I would.

I leave church and head back down to my office to think about what I can do. Just as I get to the edge of my door, I spy movement in Raze's office, through a crack in the door. I peek in and see Presley rummaging through his desk.

"What the fuck are you doing in here?" I yell.

She freezes and drops the papers in her hand. They float to the floor in a pile at her feet.

"I know," she angrily reveals. "I know fucking everything."

Chapter 13

PRESLEY

VOODOO'S VOICE cuts through the air and stops me dead in my tracks. I don't want to look up at him, but it's not like I can disappear like an apparition. I can feel the color drain from my face as soon as I peer up at him. The papers that were on the top of my brother's desk slip from my hands. No one was supposed to see me in here, looking for keys to one of the club's daily drivers that set dormant outside in the outbuildings. I waited until they were all in church to take the risk of doing this, and what did that get me? I'm caught, and my hand is in the fucking cookie jar.

I sputter out the only thing I can think of in response of being caught in the act.

Way to be nonchalant, Presley. You could have played this off as just looking for a pen or something like that. But no, you just show your hand, before the other cards have even been turned over.

"Know what exactly?" he questions, slipping into the room and shutting the door behind him, effectively cornering me with no way out.

"I know about what has been going on here," I sputter with the vibrations of fear dripping with every word that comes out of my mouth.

V cocks an eyebrow, but I see right through him. He's just as scared as I am. *Does he know? What has he not told me?* I know that being in a motorcycle club that everything is done behind closed doors and without a woman in earshot, but that shit ends now. Not after what I just saw.

"Go on," he urges me. "What exactly do you know?"

He inches closer to me, treating me more like an injured predator about to strike, than a woman who is petrified. V circles me slowly, making sure that he is between me and the door when he stops.

He does know. Why else would he want to prevent me from walking right out of this door and screaming at the top of my lungs? I was supposed to just keep on living ignorant to the things directly affecting me, because that's the way the club wanted it to be. Had they even told Ginny?

"I know about the women."

He stills, and I notice a small sigh escaping his lips, like this wasn't what he expected me to say. Why does he seem so relieved? People are dead, and he's relieved. He's insane. No person in their right mind can find comfort in the death of innocent people. Maybe my original diagnosis was right after all. There should be textbooks about men in clubs like this. Abnormal psychology professors could probably teach an entire class about the psyche of a male biker.

"You know already," I hiss, with rage beginning to course throughout my entire body. I have been very angry in my life before, but that was nowhere close to how I felt right now. I'm pissed because I let my guard down, enough to think that this was an even playing field. That the club was my partner in this, instead of my controllers. How stupid I have been.

"I do."

The rage inside of me takes over my mouth before I can stop it.

"You hid this from me. Are you fucking kidding me right now, V? I thought you and I were a team on this, but you kept me in the dark. I had to find out about it on the news."

"Team?" he fires back, anger clear as day on his face. "You came to us for help. That's exactly what we are trying to do. Nowhere in that agreement was the bullet point for sharing all the information. You left it up to us to take care of this issue. There were no terms."

Seeing the news report, about the women who had been murdered, devastated me. Their deaths are on my hands, and I hadn't even wielded the instrument of their death. Though the news anchor didn't come out and say that it was the work of a crime family, it doesn't take a rocket scientist to see the patterns. No motives. No armed robbery. Just a snatch and grab, and then a body dump. A person with an interest in criminal investigations or a healthy obsession with crime shows would be able to see what wasn't being said. It also didn't help that every victim had looked eerily similar to Ginny or me. No, this wasn't some random crime spree. It was a manhunt, and innocent women were paying the price for our actions.

That was going to come to an end.

"You shouldn't have even been able to see the news. I blocked the fucking channels from your room, and Ginny's."

"You did what!" I yell at him. "How dare you try to play God and keep me in the dark. I would expect that from my brother, but not you."

V flinches, and I can tell my words cut him to the

quick, like I had intended for them too, but it doesn't stop his approach. V's hard footfalls are almost deafening the closer he gets. Each step sounds like a cannon fire, booming off the walls of the Mikey's office.

"Keep your voice down. Do you really want your brother rushing in here and finding you ransacking his office?"

I didn't give a shit about what my brother or anyone else heard. They knew about the murders, and are all just as guilty as V. Hell, I'm sure that their little church cult meeting was all about this new insight. I would bet my life they discussed it like the planning of the next patch party, taking no consideration to the fact that the two people at the center of this, should have been told first. Ginny and I were the afterthought to their madness.

"Fuck them. Fuck my brother. And fuck you!"

He growls at me, and the sound coming from him sends a chill down my spine. It was primal and fucking terrifying. The V I knew wasn't home right now. A dark shadow stood in his place, lacking everything that made him Voodoo. He was gritting his teeth hard, and the cool darkness of his eyes were swirling like tornados. This was a side of him that I had never seen before, and I honestly hoped to never see it again.

"You will never say anything like that again in this place," he orders. "This club is protecting your ass, and you will respect that."

"Not anymore, I'm leaving."

"I don't think so, Presley. Just how exactly do you think you're going to pull that off? Call an Uber? Ride share? Those things require money. You'd get made by The Zezza's the moment you stepped into a bus depot. You know about the women, so why do you not think that they have every place of mass transit monitored? Still want to leave now?" he asks with a cocky fucking smirk on his face.

"Yes, I'm taking one of the club's vehicles."

"And you'll lead them right back to us and to Ginny when you're caught. How could you not see that?"

Shit. I hadn't considered that.

"Are you going to try to stop me, if I still want to leave?"

"Yes," he hisses. "You're not going to slink out of here without so much as a fucking word. You want to leave, then you march that ass of yours out there and explain to Ginny and the club why we wasted our time to protect you before you go off on this suicidal mission of yours."

His words sting like a shot to the heart. V's angry, and he's not sugarcoating the truth that I know is right. It is a suicide mission, but I can't keep hiding here, while others are being hurt. That's not a guilt that I can live with for the rest of my life. I'd rather die than to do that. There's no deeper wound than knowing someone else is dead because of you.

"I can't do this anymore. It's not fair that I'm alive, and they're dead," I plea to him. "People are dead because of me."

V steps forward with his frame nearly touching mine. His blue eyes bore into me, and I can't look away.

"Do you think I don't feel for the women who have died? Because I do. That's all I have thought about since the news story broke. I want those motherfuckers taken care of just as badly as you do, but if we rush into this, the next person who dies will be a member of this club. Or worse, one of their family members. I've kept you in the dark because I wanted to protect you. Just like every other man in this club. We're putting everything on the line for you and Ginny."

He pivots and raises a hand, pointing to the closed door.

"Every man sitting out there has a family, that by agreeing to protect you, has put them into jeopardy. Do you know why?"

"No," I sheepishly whisper.

"Because they know that we'd do the same for them if the roles were reversed. Sacrifice is a part of who we are. We accept the risks, knowing that we may not make it through the next day. That's why you can't leave because if you do, you are throwing that faith and love back into every man's face. We both know what waits for you on the other side without us. Can you live with the fact that your death would not only affect your brother, but the entirety of this club, especially me?"

I remain silent, as I take in everything he just said. Guilt and rage still flows inside of me, but my brain begins to rebel against my plan to go to the FBI in exchange of Ginny, if I made it that far. I couldn't dismiss that part of the argument.

Was I making the wrong decision after all?

V's hand falls back down to his side, as his attention shifts back to me.

"I don't want anyone else to die for me. Leaving keeps all of you safe, especially Ginny."

V steps one foot forward, pressing his chest to my front. I can feel his arms lifting upwards. His large hands move to cradle my face, and I'm frozen in place.

"People die every single day, Presley. It's a fact of life."

"But I can control who dies for me if I leave. Just let me go, V. Let me spare you all."

"If you leave, I'll just follow you."

Wait. What is he saying?

"Why would you do that? What would be the point of it? If you're right about my leaving, I would just be leading you into the slaughter."

Why would it matter so much to him, if I left? I'm just one woman. Dispensable by the rules, that corner stoned hundreds of motorcycle clubs. Is there something I'm not considering? Oh shit.

"I think you know why."

Before I can reply, his lips press into mine. Shock of the unexpected kiss flares to life, but soon fades away into arousal. His lips are soft against mine, but this isn't a normal kiss. The sensation was that of desperation and need. My arms slide from my sides and wrap around his neck, inviting him in closer, before my fingers slip into the dark strands of his hair. The roughness of his tongue licks across my swollen lips, as he pushes inside. My tongue caresses his in turn, as the kiss deepens. They dance together like two ballet dancers, during the final piece. It's methodically beautiful in its rhythm, and best kiss of my life.

V severs the connection abruptly. My heart slams against my sternum from excitement and surprise.

His blue eyes are wild, searching for a sign that I want this to continue further. He tests the waters, as he rubs one of his thumbs over my bottom lip, and it's still damp from the kiss we just shared.

Is this what I want? What about Beauregard? Am I willing to risk the relationship I have with him for Voodoo?

It's in that moment that I finally let go of everything holding me back. My life could end tomorrow just as he plainly pointed out. This could be my last kiss. My last chance at feeling something other than fear and hopelessness that I know is coming my way. This may not be the perfect situation or the right man standing in front of me, but he's here, unlike Beauregard.

I want this though I may regret it later, but right now, I want him to kiss me like that again.

"More," I whisper to him. He smiles back.

"With pleasure."

His lips connect with mine again, and I am lost.

Chapter 14

VOODOO

I DON'T KNOW what came over me to kiss her. One minute I was so fucking pissed at her for trying to leave and throwing blame at the club. And the next, my lips were on hers. My selfish need to taste her took over, as my last-ditch effort to keep her where she would be safe, and more importantly with me.

It was a dick move, but it was working. There was no doubt in my mind that momentary pause when I pulled away from her luscious, swollen lips that she thought about him. Knowing now that she'd seen the news reports, I told myself that her aloofness the last few days was a mixture of guilt for their deaths and for the feelings she was developing toward me.

What she didn't know was that my feelings were more than just new lust bearing fruit. I had loved her for months from afar. She was the siren calling me home for the first time, and I couldn't resist it anymore. Her brother might fucking kill me, but seeing her so soft from my kiss and begging for more in his very office, trumps all reservations that I once had about this.

Her call was my doom, and I accepted my fate with open arms.

Our tongues tangled together in a passionate dance of wills for several minutes, before she pulled away, gasping for air. The break was momentary, before we were smashed together again.

She whines, when I pull my mouth away from hers again, but moans as my tongue licks down her neck and across her collarbone. Goosebumps flourish down her skin in a dotted disarray of desire.

Her body wants this just as badly as mine does, but it doesn't stop me from asking. I'm a gentleman after all.

"Are you okay with this?" I ask against her neck.

"Did I say stop?" she moans, pulling my face back up to hers and shoving her lips against mine.

My hand leaves her neck, sliding down to her pulp breasts, taking a nipple between two of my fingers. She moans in my ear as I tweak it, before releasing it again and cupping her entire perfectly sized breast in my hand. Her pelvis begins to grind against mine, and my cock strains against the fly of my jeans. Just like before the zipper is problematic, but my cock doesn't care knowing that it will soon be nestled so tightly inside of her that pain will mean nothing.

My fingers slide from her breast and travel down her stomach, passing her navel. She jerks as I slide a finger against the thin fabric covering her pussy. I gently maneuver her back to Raze's desk, which squeaks, as we run into it. Her eyes go wide, as her mind realizes where we are.

I try to distract her by returning my lips to her neck, but it doesn't work.

"We shouldn't be doing this here," she protests, with a breathy voice heavy with need.

"You sure about that?" I retort, as my hand slips inside the band of her yoga pants.

My fingers brush just outside of her wet lips, before sliding inside. My index finger finds the pulsating nub, glistening with wet arousal.

"You're wet already," I tease. Her hooded eyes look up at me and roll back, as my finger begins to move.

"Oh god," she sighs, shifting her legs farther open for me.

She wants this release so badly that she has

forgotten the fact that I'm finger fucking her against her brother's desk.

I flex my finger like I'm beckoning someone forward, and her moans grow louder. Each move I make, excites her more to the point that her wetness begins to soak her leggings that are so tightly wrapped around her hips.

"Do you know how fucking sexy you look right now?" I whisper to her, before bringing her into a deep kiss. "So exposed just for me. Any second now your brother could walk in here and see you like this, and that excites you. Doesn't it, Presley?"

"Uh-huh," she whimpers.

"Your pussy is greedy just like you."

My finger slides away from her clitoris and into her entrance. Her thighs tighten around my hand, locking it into place, as I add a second finger, plunging it into her core.

"Faster," she pleas. "I'm so close."

I comply, adding a second finger into her slick entrance, and I feel the shudder of her orgasm hitting the brink of release. Her thighs clamp like a vise around my hand, as she rides the wave of her orgasm. Her beautiful, soft body jerks for several minutes, until her eyes finally open and look up at me, completely dazed.

"Did we?" she asks, as reality sets in.

"We did."

My hand slips from her pants, and I bring it up between us, glistening with her juices over my fingers. Her eyes widen, as I lick her taste off of each one with a moan of my own.

"The next time I taste you will be with my tongue," I promise her.

She starts to protest, but heavy footsteps start down the hall. The party is now over, before I could even get my cock out. Fucking figures.

Presley jolts from against Raze's desk. Her hands tug at her pants, and she tries to straighten herself up, after a good fucking orgasm. Thankfully as the footsteps grow closer, they pause and head into the office to the south of Raze's.

"It's just Hero."

"Thank god," she exclaims. "But what about you?"

"Don't worry about me, Presley. This," I motion with the same finger that just I just fucked her with between us, "is just beginning. I'll be by later to finish what we started."

She shallows hard with excitement.

"And don't worry, the cameras will be off."

She smiles, as she pulls me into another kiss, before breaking the contact and slipping out of the door. I give her a few minutes head start, before sneaking out of the office, but apparently my ninja skills aren't exactly on par because I walk into Ratchet.

Fuck we almost got caught.

"Hey Ratchy," I smile, trying to play off what just happened. He scowls. Yup, he knows. Just great.

"Do you think that was wise?" he inquires with a cocked brow.

"Probably not, but it happened."

"He's going to fucking kill you," he mutters, as he passes by me and heads out the door to the garage area of the property.

I just smile, as he passes and mentally tell my cock that his time is coming. What just happened was out of desperate need, and the next time Presley came for me, it would be because that need outweighed the need to forget. I slide into my office, and try to drown out the sound of my cock screaming at me to go find her. I make sure to grab the footage from the hallway earlier and load it onto a flash drive, before deleting it. My work takes up what I think is hours, but the clock moves at a glacial pace. Only ninety minutes has passed. I groan. Each tick and tock seems to take an hour instead of seconds, as my need to feel her body again grows more intense.

"Fuck it!" I exclaim, giving up waiting any longer.

My fingers fly, as I code a few programs to run to scan for more information about the dead girls in the area to run, while I reach for the orgasmic stars with Presley. I slide over to the computer monitor that is connected to the camera in Presley's room, and find footage from a few days ago, as she napped uneasily. I start to record it and write out a few lines to play, while I was in her room. If Raze accessed the feed to check on her, all he would see would be her sleeping in her bed alone. Even though sleeping wasn't exactly a part of the plan, until afterwards. And she would definitely not be sleeping alone.

Raze was going to find out one way or another, but seeing me and his sister dancing the horizontal mambo was not the way to break it to him. But until I knew where this was going, my plan was to keep it on the down low. The less he knew the better, until we were both ready for everyone to know. We would just leave out the part about hooking up in his office. That was a definite need to only tell a portion of the story.

I notice Presley pacing in her room with her hands wrapped around her body, while the distraction loop records. She looks beautiful, even in deep thought. Her lean legs fall into her beautifully round hips with each step. She's a breathtaking sight to behold, and someday soon, she will be all mine.

I watch until she moves off-camera, before setting up the video loop. I double check my work, and even view the feed on my own phone before I walk away from it. Mistakes are easily made in coding. All it takes is one period to be off and it would be a disaster, like in *Office Space*. The next thing you know there will be copiers being beaten to death, buildings being set on fire, and my happy ass with Presley drinking piña coladas on the beach. Now that I think about it, that would be pretty fucking sweet.

I force myself to stow that plan in the file for a plan z, should I ever need one. Climbing off my office chair, I make a quick stop over to my desk to grab the flash drive containing Presley and I's jail break from Raze's office, into the pile of other flash drives set to be destroyed. My heels turn on a dime, as I spin around ready to see her again, when my burner phone pings.

Fuck my life. After what just happened, she's texting him again. Does she already regret what happened between us so soon?

Pacing the floor, I debate with myself whether or not I'm going to look at it. If I read that message, it has the potential to negate everything that happened earlier. Her words to him could break me, and I honestly don't know if I can recover from that. On the other hand, it could be the opposite of my worst fears. Maybe she was telling him goodbye. My mind wavers and refuses to make a decision.

Where's a good therapist when you need one? Oh wait. She's the root of the current problem at hand. Just my luck.

Before I can change my mind again, I retrieve the phone from the desk drawer, unlock it, and click on her nickname on the screen.

> I miss you a little less today. Hope you are okay.

After days of her pleading messages for contact from him, today's message seems almost mild. It's neutral in the realm of what she could have said to him. I'd be stupid to think that after what happened between us, that she would drop him like a bad habit. Moving on takes time, and I wasn't being considerate of that fact. Her feelings for the man standing before her now were just blossoming, but Beauregard had been in her life much longer. Their bond was stronger, and it would take more time to break and bend to let her move on with the real me.

My overzealousness of wanting to keep pushing forward would have been a mistake, and had she not texted him, I would have never seen it, until it was too late. I consider replying back, but that would only drive the need for contact between them.

No. It was best to let it lie, until it was the right

moment. We needed more time to find our footing and make a real connection. One that wasn't driven by sex.

With the change in plans for tonight, I decide on a much different course of action. She would probably be confused at first, but after the fact, she and I would both be happier for it. I flit across my office, grabbing a few things, before heading out to the kitchen for the rest of supplies. The main room is mostly full, but my brothers are engrossed watching the LA Rams kicking the Arizona Cardinals ass on one of the big flat screens, mounted on the wall.

I quietly slip from the kitchen, unnoticed by them and head down the hallway to Presley's room. She cracks open the door, and her brown eyes grow wide, when she sees what's in my hands. I push through the door, closing and locking it behind me, after I put down what I am carrying.

"I thought–," she stammers, clearly confused as I suspected she would be.

"I know. Earlier was amazing," I truthfully admit, "but it was in the heat of the moment. I want to explore these feelings I have for you and not rush this."

She smirks like I'm telling the world's biggest lie to get into her pants.

"So, what do you have in mind?"

"Well, you've heard the phrase Netflix and Chill, right?"

"Yeah, but I thought you were wanting to go slow."

I smile, as I grab the popcorn bowl from its perch and pop a few kernels in my mouth.

"That's right. This isn't Netflix and Chill. What we have here is Hulu and Hug."

She shakes her head and just laughs.

"Maybe if you're lucky, you might just get a kiss," she teases back. "What are we watching first?"

Chapter 15

PRESLEY

THE SPOT next to me is cool for the first time in nearly a week since V's proclamation of slowing things down. It was something that I would have never expected to come out a man, associated with my brother's club. Their usual modus operandi was to fuck first and ask questions later. The brain below the belt often was the prevailing thinking in their man to dick relationship. But he was different, and I couldn't thank him enough for it. The brooding alpha male ego was hard to deal with, and finding someone who was still all male, yet so down to earth was refreshing.

Night after night, we spent time together in the confines of my room out of my brother's watchful eye, getting to know each other mentally. Though he made sure that he kissed me silly, until I feel asleep in his arms, after watching one of the many movies in his collection. *Super Troopers* was a little crazy for my tastes, but he had slowly introduced me to the new Marvel comic book movies one by one. In sequential order of course. It was a little odd to find out how much I was starting to like them. The characters reminded me so much of some of the men in this clubhouse, and of V. I think I could have knocked him over with a feather, when I told him that I hadn't really seen many movies. How could I when the government controllers dictated so much of my life? Leaving my house outside of work was too much of a risk, and I found myself drowning in books rather than movies to pass the time.

The attraction I felt for V was growing every day we spent time together. And again, his drive to make time for me was just as unexpected, as the way I felt about him. He made me feel important as odd as it sounds. I was always an afterthought with my dad, with my brother, and with the few guys I had dated in my life. Maybe it was the kind of guy I was seeing or the situation of my childhood, but until V, I was never someone's number one priority. Even though, some of it was the fact he was in charge of me. It just didn't feel like I was a job for him.

It was exciting. For the second time in my life, a man had swept me off my feet in tremendous fashion. The only difference between this time and the first was that he was right in front of me, living and breathing.

Beauregard's hold on my heart seemed to be slipping away. The initial driving need to talk to him was fading, but I still found myself texting him from time to time. Maybe it was out of habit or maybe it was for closure. The answer was lost to me despite the fact I knew that many days without contact could only mean one thing. He'd moved on in my absence, which both relieved and frightened me all at the same time. My mind was a category five hurricane of confusing emotions. It raged out of control, and the only time it seemed to still was when V was around, even though he was the exact opposite of Beauregard. He was dangerous and walked on a thin line on the right side of the law. Yet as I learned more about him, my stance of no bikers and definitely no members of this club were slipping.

The nights that V spent with me here in my room was a constant barrage of new information about him. He talked about the loss of his parents to a drunk driver, while he was studying computer technology at Tulane with so much heartfelt emotion. It was like I was living with him right there in the moment. I could feel his pain, fear, and most of all the love he had for them, and his sister, Remy.

Growing up in New Orleans had been rough on his family, but together they had made it through. He was first and foremost a family man, and even years later, V still looked after his little sister and nephew Beaux from a distance. His eyes swelled with pride, as he told me stories about them, and shared a few photos. His nephew was a spitting image of him with a mess of black hair and striking blue eyes. Even at the age of five, Beaux was already too smart for his own good, something that made V laugh. His sister was in a heap of trouble should he end up having a tenth of his uncle's spirit inside of him.

The smile he wore was genuine when he spoke of them, and it warmed my heart like a hearth on a cold day.

V's presence was comforting to me. He listened, as I talked about my family life growing up. He listened to me like I do to a patient. Never casting judgment, and I even caught him a few times growling, as I talked about my father's reign of terror. He had thankfully been gone when V joined the club. I doubt my father would have even allowed him to join because he wouldn't have seen the usefulness of having someone that was good with computers on the roster.

Am I crazy for even considering moving forward with V? This wasn't the life that I had wanted, but now I had caught myself on more than one occasion thinking about what life would be like here with Voodoo. A thought that baffles me because I didn't even know this man's real name. In any other courtship, that would have been the first thing exchanged in polite conversation. Just another reason why this entire thing was such an enigma for me. I wanted him, but to possess him would mean giving up every plan that I had made, since I was a little girl. Was I willing to do that?

After sliding from my bed alone, I make quick work of showering and getting ready for the day. Just as I'm about to leave my room, I spy a surprise waiting for me on the edge of the bed. V had been back in here. Why else would I find a little brown teddy bear with a leather vest wrapped around its body? I snatch up the small token of his affection in my arms, and cling to it, detecting just a hint of the woodsy scent of his cologne lingering on its plush fur. Smiling, I tuck it between the pillow at the head of the bed, and head out the door in search of food.

The smells of sizzling bacon and waffles float down the hallway, making my stomach growl. Most mornings, V leaves my breakfast in my room, but today, it was nowhere to be found. He had warned me that there would be days where he would have to be away to work on the case. His absence hurt, but I had to understand. He was trying to protect Ginny and I along with his brothers. I couldn't fault him for doing his job, even if I missed him.

I peer around the room and find that nearly all of the brothers are missing in action. The tables are empty, except for a few of the club girls seated off to the far side of the room, and Ginny sitting alone. She twiddles her fork in a circle as I approach, and she smiles when she notices me heading her way.

"What's good around here?" I ask, trying to open up a dialogue with her. Ginny's eyes seem distant today. A sign that she was battling her anxiety that I had learned to recognize in the years I have worked with her.

"The bacon is a little burnt, but the waffles are pretty good. Get the blueberry syrup," she advises me, with a monotone voice.

She's definitely about to have an episode. I just have to hope that I'm in time to help her through it before she hits the bottom. Ginny's mental situation is volatile when she's like this. One small misstep, and it would blow up in all of our faces.

I step away to grab breakfast, and keep my eyes trained on her the entire time I shovel a few waffles on my plate with three nearly black pieces of bacon. I'm not sure which of the club girls cooked, but they really need lessons because I'm almost positive a necromancer couldn't resurrect this slice of pig. It was about as dead as it could get.

I re-join Ginny at the table, while she remains silent. Her emotionless expression indicates that her mind is a sea of turmoil. I shovel my food in quickly, as I realize this needs to be handled now rather than later.

"Ginny?"

"Yes?" she answers flatly.

"Why don't we go over to my brother's office and talk? You look a little lost today."

"Okay," she replies, as if she was a robot answering to his designer. Her mind has taken her personality away from her, and she's slipped into the darkest realm of her psyche.

I pop up from the chair, reaching out for her. She takes me by the hand and doesn't let go, as I lead her down the hallway towards the office. I peer into the room, and find as I has suspected that my brother is absent. While I probably should have asked for permission to use it, Ginny is more a dire need. I'll just ask for forgiveness later.

I gesture for her to sit in a wooden chair at the front of his desk, and I take his overly large executive chair that overwhelms me. Ginny nervously fidgets in front of me, breaking my heart.

"Let's talk about how you are feeling right now. Any feelings at all?"

"I'm scared," she admits.

"Fear is a very real thing, Ginny. We've talked about that in so many of our sessions in the past. But the real question is what has triggered your fear impulse this time? I want you to close your eyes and really focus on it. Take the darkness and mold it into words."

Ginny complies, closing her eyes and steadying her breathing like I had taught her to do. She remains like that for several minutes, before peering back at me.

"It's like the fear is taking over my brain. Every noise scares me to death. One of the bikes backfired this morning, and I dove under my bed. I didn't move for a few hours, until Ratchet found me there."

"And what about your brother? What do you feel when you think about him?"

"I feel shame and betrayal. Looking back now, I should have listened to him. He was trying to protect me, and I was hurt when he sent me away."

I let her reflect further with a silent pause. For nearly three years, I had been waiting for Ginny to reach this point. She had placed the blame wherever she could for her situation, but deep down, the root of the cause was the one she was finally revealing to me now. I had to let her keep going without interjecting, as long as I could. The more fear and anxiety she released from her mind, the better she would feel later.

"My brother was always the stronger of the two of us. When mama and daddy died, he watched over me. When that man tried…" she mutters, stumbling to find the words. I remind her to take a deep breath and continue when she is able. "When that man tried to molest me, he fixed that problem, too."

My heart aches for her, as the demons who inhibit her mind are being set free.

"Jude was my everything. My rock, and I threw him away as soon as he started making decisions that I didn't like. I thought I knew better, and I know now that I was rebelling against him trying to control me."

And there it was. Ginny breaks down in sobs, as her head falls into her hands. I move from the chair and kneel down beside her, taking her in my arms, as she cries away the pain. She sobs uncontrollably, until there's nothing left inside to cry about. She pulls away from me, and wipes the tears from her face.

"I ruined your shirt," she remarks, looking down at the stream of wet tears that stain the fabric.

"It can be washed," I declare to her. "How do you feel?"

"I feel free. For the first time in my life, I feel free."

She smiles the first genuine smile that I have ever seen, since I met her. Her aura even seems lighter.

"I think you know it's time to talk to your brother. Tell him everything that you just told me. I think you'll find after you do that your mind will be clearer."

Ginny nods as I stand up. We walk to the door together, and she slips outside of it ahead of me to find her brother. My eyes fall to V's closed office. I take a few short steps over to the door, pressing my ear against it. There's nothing, but silence inside. My heart aches just a little bit knowing that he's still not here.

I return to my room, as an eerie sense of dread wafts over me, when I notice the door to my room is cracked open and Voodoo sits inside with a dark scowl across his face.

Something has clearly happened, and it's not good news.

Chapter 16

VOODOO

WATCHING her sleep is only second best to feeling her soft body against mine. Her hooded eyes, the way her mouth turns to a smile when I pull her closer, or how her hand reaches out for me, when I'm not lying next to her. The way her dark hair cascades around her shoulders and frames her face makes her look like a haloed angel. It's pure magic the way we can talk all night, until we pass out from exhaustion. Every word that leaves her lips is precious, and something that I will never forget, as long as I live. Call me sappy or a pussy, but it's in these kinds of moments that I realize how much I love with her. We are completely alone, and she is completely mine.

The memories we have made over the last several weeks mean more to me than anything in the world. Well, maybe one of my computers. Okay, both of them, but if I put my bike or drone, Rhonda, in the mix, I might be pushing it. That's a lie too. She is like finding the rarest of all comic books in pristine condition. She's so beautiful, and I yearn to touch her.

Presley is the single most important thing in my life, and each day I spend with her, the guilt of hiding our previous relationship haunts me. The messages between her and Beauregard have dwindled each day. I can feel her reaching out to me, rather than him, like she did in the early days after her arrival to the club. But she was still seeking his correspondence during the times I had to be away for club business or work. I had hoped that she would have been done with that relationship in her life by now, yet I also understand her dependence on him. He was her rock, during the pit of loneliness. Until he pushes her away or she knows the whole truth, she will still have a piece of him inside her.

I know that I have to tell her soon, and when I do, I'm risking that this will all end.

But she deserves to know.

She *needs* to know.

And when she does, it may all be over.

Even if things do end, the memories of what we had together will have to suffice because after her, no one else will ever compare. The man I am will disappear with her. She will take my sunshine and replace those skies with rain. She is my life and quite possibly, my demise.

Jesus, I was starting to sound like an episode of Sesame Street. Where was the Cookie Monster, when I needed him?

I didn't want to leave her side this morning, but a text from her brother asking me to join him in his office couldn't be ignored. The only problem I had was how in the fuck was I going to keep a straight face knowing what we had done on his desk. The answer? I have no fucking idea.

I grab my jeans and shirt from the floor, and slip them on. My phone buzzes, as I pick it up again with another message from Raze.

"I'm coming, boss. Get your panties out of a fucking bunch and give me a second," I mutter to the empty room.

My cut lies on the back of the couch, and as I throw the worn leather over my broad shoulders, Presley shuffles in the bed. She eases, stretching out her body across the newly vacate space and re-settles. I peer back at her sleeping form, before walking out of the door.

One day, I won't have to leave you. Unless you leave me first.

The sun peaks through the windows of the hall-way, as I creep quietly with my Ninja mode activated. I start playing the sound effects of *The Pink Panther* movie in my head, as I slink from the hallway into the main room. "Dun-nah," I sing to myself, when I make it across the main room and into the office hallway undetected. Another successful escape achieved.

The light from Raze's office beams from under his cracked door. It's unusual for him to be in so early. Most of the time, it was like pulling teeth to get him away from Darcy and the kids. But with them out of town, I'm sure he couldn't sleep. Happiness was a good look on him, so we didn't mind him being a little late. A happy Prez equals a happy club. Well, most of the time.

I peak inside and find my president with eyes glued on his open laptop. Without turning his attention away, he calls out to me.

"Stop fucking sneaking around, and get your ass in here," he orders.

"Shit, Prez. Grouchy this morning I see," I remark, as I slip through the door. He gestures to the chair in front of me, and I park my ass. This time remembering to not put my feet up on the desk, like I do with Hero. I can joke with him. Raze is an entirely different story. Getting on his bad side wouldn't exactly help my pursuit of Presley.

He shuts his laptop with a hard clamp. How the

plastic case didn't break, I have no idea. You'd be shocked to know how many laptops I've replaced for the man stewing in front of me. Poor damn laptops didn't even see it coming.

"Care to tell explain to me what I have been seeing on the cameras?"

Shit. Shit fucking shit. Sweet zombie Jesus take me to hell now.

"Uh, I can explain."

His face grows sterner by the second, as I feel my life slipping away from me. I was sure that the death date test I had taken online a few weeks back, had clearly said that I would die of an ass kicking in 2050. Apparently, what you read on the Internet isn't always true. This isn't how I saw myself dying. There were far more balloons and streamers in my version of it. Plus a few sexy zombies, but that's another story for a different day.

"Please do. I'd love to know exactly why I just watched my sister sleep in the same pajamas for the last seven days."

Be cool, V. You can explain this. No verbal diarrhea. Stick to the facts, well the sugarcoated facts.

"There's a loop on her feed that runs every night," I admit.

"For what purpose?"

"Her privacy," I half-lie. "She wasn't too keen on the two of us watching her sleep."

"Did she ask you to do this?"

"No. I did it on my own. Keeping her happy seemed like the better course of action, considering the circumstances."

He considers my answer carefully. The pause in the conversation sends my heart pounding like a bass drum against my chest wall. I bet if he listened hard enough, he could probably hear it from the other side of his desk.

"Do you have the original feed still active?" he inquires, raising his eyebrow slightly.

"I do. The alerts are all still in place for movement and sound," I declare, hoping that he isn't seeing through the thin line of my bullshit.

"I don't like it," he gruffly mutters. "But I get her point. Just make sure those damn alerts still work."

"I check them every day."

"Good," Raze says, with just a hint of relief in his voice. Did he have suspicions about Presley and I or was this more out of a concern that we had been compromised?

The chances of the latter happening were about the same as Ratchet driving the Sunday school bus, slim to fucking never. Our mainframe and networks were kept in several off-site locations. I had set-up back up servers to piggyback off each other should one fail. Even the back-ups had back-ups, and I had hard drives full of information stashed all over the city in safety deposit boxes.

I had wired our systems to be harder to hack than Fort Knox. The only way someone was going to get our information was by fire-bombing the clubhouse, but even then, my back-ups would be safe. I was a technological doomsday prepper and proud as shit of it.

"I need you to go see Red today." Raze states.

That sleazy motherfucker was not the biggest fan of our club, after the last time we came for information about Rex. He had other ideas at first about the inside track of breaking apart Rex's skin trade ring. Mikayla being in our possession now was proof enough that Rex had lost.

But Red was a different story. He was a sly businessman who dealt secrets and bounties like that jolly giant selling paper towels. The underbelly came to him for answers, but also for a price. If Raze was sending me to Red, either he had called us with a tip in the middle of the night, or Raze needed me to press him for more information.

"Sure thing, Prez. What about Presley?"

"I've got her covered," he growls. I want to press him further, but that would only piss him off more, and possibly make him suspicious of my relationship with her.

"Red going to be home this early? He usually keeps the same hours as Dracula," I laugh. Raze's face remains stoic. Yeah, definitely too early for jokes. I would have made a comment about him needing to get laid, but his woman was gone, and I liked my balls where they currently hung.

"He'll be there. Take Slider with you."

"You got it," I agree and start for the door.

"Another thing," he calls out after me. "Is there a reason my sister is wearing your old prospect shirts?"

I come to a screeching halt, pausing just long enough to take a deep breath, before turning back around.

"She needed clothes in a hurry. Figured they'd fit her."

"I see."

"Anything else?"

"Nope."

I nod then exit his office with my life. Does he have a suspicion about us, or did I manage to play it off? We need to be more careful, until I'm ready to tell him. Maybe I should wear a disguise, when I sneak into her room, or I could throw him off giving Presley one of Slider's shirts as well. As soon as the thought of Presley wearing one of his shirts blossoms, I growl inside. Nope. Not happening. My shirts only. No man will put his scent on her body, but me.

The dread of leaving Presley here alone hits hard. She's been here for weeks, under my care. Now, I had to leave her alone because defying the orders of my president wasn't something that I could do without outing myself. Raze will keep her safe. I have no doubt he will, but when it comes to Presley, the only person I trusted completely was myself.

Knowing that I could be gone for an extended length of time, I unlock my office door, and snatch the surprise I had planned to give her tonight off my desk. It's cheesy as fuck, that I will admit freely, but she'll love it.

I make quick work slipping back into her room and tucking it away on the now empty bed. The spray of the shower is inviting. My cock stiffens at the dangerous thought that crosses my mind about joining her. I was testing the thin resolve of keeping my promise every single night, but until I knew where she stood with me, slow and steady was the torturous race.

I leave quietly and head out the backdoor toward the garages. Slider is already waiting, a sleepy and pissed off look plastered on his face.

Just great. I dealt with Mr. Moody, now I get King Asshole all in one morning. I must be the luckiest guy on the planet. These guys really need to figure out how to wake up on the right side of the bed like me. The early bird gets the tequila worm and all that jazz.

"Morning, sunshine," I call out to him.

"Fuck you and your sunshine," he fires back.

"Fuck you too, princess."

He growls and grumbles like a fucking toddler. I've said it once, and I'll say it again. His attitude adjustment will be happening soon enough. I might just request to be the first in line to do it.

Slider slides over his bike. The engine rumbles to life, just as I reach mine. The light reflects off the finish of my 2012 Softail Convertible, and I smile. Black Betty is a sexy fucking piece of machinery. She's got an all-black metallic body with chrome details, and an engine that purrs like a kitten. She's sleek and fast, just the way I like her.

The leather seat is cool when I climb over her stocky body. She purrs, as I flip the ignition switch and pop the kickstand. Slider pulls out of his parking spot, as my fingers wrap around the accelerator. The air is cool, when we hit the outside of the garage and ride towards our destination.

Red's shit hole bar is dark when we arrive. The

nightlife has long since called it a night, which bodes well for us, and our task at hand. Slider and I park next to the backdoor entrance right beside Red's beater of a pick-up truck. I laugh, when I see the array of his sexual innuendo bumper stickers all over the tailgate and back window. Red might have a dirty mind, but the chances of him getting laid are just about as high as Ratchet and that bus. He is a grease stain on the community. A piece of shit who exploited his female employees that came in search of quick cash. That much was apparent, after Dani and Ricca's experience here. It was shitty we still had to use him as a middleman, but necessary evils still had to live, until their usefulness was spent.

Slider and I both climb from our bikes, heading towards the door. Slider shoves the door open, before stepping inside ahead of me. Motherfucker still thinks he's here to run the show, instead of being the back up. The need to beat some sense into him was strong with my inner asshole force. Where was a lightsaber, when I needed one?

Red's office sits just inside the backdoor, and when we enter, he's sitting at his desk.

"Hell of an entrance there, Slider," he remarks with a toothy grin. Has the guy ever tried to audition for American Horror Story? He'd make a great creepy clown.

"Shit happens," Slider says, as he pops a squat in the chair in front of Red's desk.

"Voodoo."

"Morning, Red. Heard you have some information for us," I start, getting down to business.

"A couple of fellas popped by last night asking around about two women on the run."

"You get a name?" I ask.

"No names, but I'm pretty sure these are the kinda men you don't want to cross. Nice suits, expensive watches, and a high-end car," Red explains, grabbing a toothpick off of his desktop and starts cleaning his teeth with it.

"You get the plates?'

Red slides a piece of paper over to me across his desk, after he ditches the toothpick into the trashcan next to him. He's a disgusting little shit. I glance down at the paper, before sliding the number into my pocket.

"You get anything else from them?"

"Yeah, I did, and you're not gonna like it. The man happened to mention that one of the women he was seeking had a million-dollar bounty out on her. The younger one I believe, a two hundred thousand dollar one on the other."

"Shit," I exclaim, looking over to Slider.

"You can say that again. Every underground

bounty hunter and assassin for hire is going to be looking for them."

I thank Red, before charging from his office and back out to our bikes. This situation just went from bad to fucking doomsday, and we're not prepared for the hailstorm about to come raining down on us. I pace around my bike, trying to make sense of it. Ginny's bounty makes sense because she could turn the tide of the court case against The Zezza's. But Presley's is an enigma. She was a witness to their snatch and grab, but why would they want her? Her involvement is microscopic compared to Ginny's. Unless... fuck. They must know she was treating her. That has to be the reason. They're afraid Ginny confided her secrets to Presley, and she could be the second star witness in the case if they got to Ginny and took her out. While Ginny was the ultimate prize, Presley was almost just as important.

Slider climbs on his bike and looks to me.

"You better call him," he advises.

I slip my cell phone from my pocket and dial Raze. He answers on the first ring.

"Houston, we have a major fucking problem."

I fill Raze in, as I mount my bike. The stakes have grown even higher, and the target on the girl's backs has grown exponentially with the bounty.

Chapter 17

VOODOO

VOODOO'S GAZE locks onto mine as soon as I enter the room.

"What's wrong?" I inquire. His face falls instantly.

"I'm that easy to read, huh? I should probably practice more or get lessons from your brother," he deflects.

I walk over to him, settling in beside him on the bed. He leans over and plants a chaste kiss on my lips. When we pull apart, the turmoil swirling inside his blue eyes is clear. The look so clearly not hidden from his face is one that I have seen many times on my old patients. It's one of guilt and fear. Those two emotions wrapped into one is the recipe for a disaster. Those emotions are also like the Molotov cocktails of serious conversation starters. It's combining the ominous "We need to talk" sentiment and adding in an extramarital affair or declaration for wanting a divorce.

"What is it?" I ask him. His hand gently engulfs mine on my thigh, giving it a squeeze.

My mind instantly starts to run the worst-case scenarios of how this conversation is going to go.

Have The Zezza's found us? Have they struck again killing another innocent victim? Is Ginny not safe? Are we being asked to leave?

The possibilities could be all or none of the thoughts flickering in my head like a streetlight about to blow.

"I went to see one of our informants today."

"Oh, that's why you left without saying goodbye."

The ache of his leaving without kissing me this morning hurts just a little less, knowing that it wasn't intentional, but the relief will be short-lived judging by the look on his face. His brow is creased, and his jaw is set as hard as stone. He's putting on a brave face for me, and that terrifies me even more.

"Yeah," he mutters. "Not exactly how I had planned the morning to start off."

"So, what did your informant have to say? Are you even supposed to be telling me or are you breaking your club code by doing this?" I offer, trying to bring him back to the topic he started.

"Raze knows so it's fine, but I want to warn you," he says, squeezing my hand again. "This is going to change everything."

My heart falls. We *are* getting kicked out. My brother is going to serve me up to the wolves circling outside to protect himself and his club.

"Just tell me," I plea.

"There's a bounty on Ginny's head. A big one."

I gasp. My hand grabs at my chest, as my heart thuds. I know what a bounty means, and the kind of people that it brings. Lowlifes for hire looking for a quick cash grab.

"How much?"

He hisses and turns his head away before he mutters a dollar amount that sends my head spiraling. Really? A million dollars for one girl. That's unimaginable. Crime families usually come with deep pockets, but this was pushing it. Back when my father was alive, the club used to contract out some of the wet work for men just like The Zezza's. Twenty thousand is the largest number that I heard whispered around the club, when no one thought to censor themselves around me. This is fifty times that.

"Does she know?"

"Ratchet is on his way to tell her now."

"Her anxiety is going to be off the charts. I need to go to her."

I start to get off the bed, but his hand reaches up and grabs me.

"There's more."

Oh no, this can't be happening. Please don't let this be real.

"How much?"

"Two hundred thousand."

Those three little words send me spiraling to the floor. Silent tears fall down my face like a babbling brook about to flash flood. This can't be real.

Why would they want me? What use could I be for their court case?

Until we came here, I only knew bits and pieces. Not enough to be anything more than circumstantial evidence.

My chest constricts in what feels like a panic attack. The room begins to spin, as my lungs scream for air. The sensation of vomiting punches me in the gut before Voodoo's hands cup my face. His distorted voice calls out to me, trying to center me again.

"Breathe, baby. Come on, breathe for me."

He starts mimicking breaths in and out like one would do with a woman in labor. I begin to mimic his movements back, and after several minutes, the room stops spinning and air begins to fill my lungs again.

"That's it. Breathe, beautiful."

I sit in silence with him kneeling beside me, cradling my shaking body.

"I'm going to die, aren't I?"

His fingers pull my chin away from his chest and up to his face.

"You'll never die, as long as I breathe, Presley. That's one promise that I will keep, until my last breath."

His lips descended on mine in a fevered rush. My chaotic filled mind hushes, and I lean into his deep kiss. My arms instinctively wrap around his neck, as I pull myself into his lap. His rock-hard erection is clear as day through his jeans and my leggings. My pussy feels so fucking good, as I gyrate against it.

"Presley," he mutters against my mouth. "We shouldn't."

I pull my mouth from his and smile up at him, as my fingers begin to pull my shirt over my head.

"You're upset," he protests, while his eyes move to my bra-clad chest. Thank God, I picked out a cute bra today. This was definitely not what I had expected to happen when I found him in my room, but I'll take it. "We don't have to rush into this, baby. You're not in the right headspace right now."

I smile up at his sincere gesture, but the only thing I want right now is him. The hesitations I had about him have faded away and along with them, Beauregard. I need V more than ever right now.

"The only head I'm concerned about is the one positioned perfectly between my legs right now," I purr back at him. Voodoo's face freezes, as he fights to try to find the right words to say. For the first time since I've known him, I've stunned him speechless. No jokes. No puns. Just stunned silence.

"Pussy got your tongue?" I tease him further.

"You keep talking like that, Presley, and I will be breaking that promise I made to you."

"Break it."

His hands fall to my waist, as he shifts underneath me. The bulge in his pants hits just the right spot and sends my head back in a moan. His large hand grabs the back of my neck and brings his mouth crashing back to mine. Our mouths are all need. After he's finished with my lips, he shifts down to my neck. Each kiss and lick are like mini-lightning bolts to my core. He descends further down, before his mouth grazes my nipple through the lace of the bra. His hands join his mouth on my breasts. His teeth lightly bite against the sensitive pebbled nub before he reaches behind me and slowly unclasps my bra.

"You like it when I bite you, don't you?"

I bite my lip and shake my head in return. The smile on his face as I invite him to put his teeth on me further is deliciously predatory.

"Show me where you might want me to bite you."

My eyes cascade down my body, and I stare at the space between my thighs. He cocks an eyebrow, and in one swift move, he shoves his hands under my ass and lifts me like I'm a feather. His mouth connects with mine again, as he turns us around and places me on my back on the bed.

His hungry eyes rake over my half naked body that is fully exposed in front of him. The warm heat inside of me turns to a raging inferno of needy greed. I feel small as he stands over me.

"Please touch me," I beg him to take action.

"I've been waiting for this moment for far too long to rush this, Presley."

His large hands fall to the waist of my leggings. He inches them down first over my right hip then the left. The sensation of his hands on my legs feels so fucking good, as the leggings fall away from my body. The jumbled-up ball of black fabric flies through the air, as he throws them behind him.

"So fucking beautiful," he mutters, as he kneels between my legs. I jerk when I feel his rough tongue against my inner thigh. His long fingers brush against the material of my underwear, and I wiggle my pussy closer to him.

"I knew you had a greedy pussy, baby."

"Please, V."

"In good time. Quit rushing me, woman."

My head falls back again, as his tongue moves higher up my inner thigh. His hot breath tingles against the sensitive mound of flesh between my legs. His face is so close that it's taking all I have not to squirm closer and bring his mouth against me. The kisses continue to the top of my thigh, before he pulls away, making me groan in disapproval. The licks resume on the other thigh.

He's fucking teasing me.

"Missed a spot," I gasp out.

His fingers graze against my panties in retaliation. The sensation of the fabric being pushed aside is nearly too much to bear. He smiles, as the sound of my panties ripping fills the room. They end up in the pile with my leggings. Before I can moan, his mouth is on me. V's tongue caresses between my lips, and instantly finds my clit. He circles it a few times, before making good on my request. The pain from his teeth lasts only seconds. An intense burst of plea-sure shoves the painful sensation aside and takes over. He alternates between precision strokes and gentle bites, building an even more intense fire to the point that I'm about to explode into a billion fiery shards.

He laughs against my flesh when I squirm closer and force him harder against my pussy. My orgasm is pulsating at the edge of explosion. He pulls away, just as I'm about to have what feels like the biggest orgasm of my life.

V smiles from between my legs, knowing that he's torturing me.

"The only way you are coming today, baby, is around my dick."

I watch from the bed, as his shirt pulls away from his torso in one quick movement. I lick my lips at the sight of his defined abs, perfectly contouring his chest alongside his tattoos. This man is fucking beautiful, and he knows it. He meets my gaze and smiles.

His hands start for his fly, but I lean forward and grab them.

"I want to undress you."

"Your wish is my command."

He bends down to kiss me, while my hands fall against his hard chest. I let my fingers explore his hardness, before sliding down to the waistband of his dark jeans, popping the button free. He straightens his body up, watching me with hooded eyes, as my fingers gently work his fly against the clearly defined bulge in front of me. The zipper reaches the end, and my mouth drops open in surprise, when I realize that he doesn't have underwear on.

I beam up at him, as his hands come to his hips and slide his jeans from his thighs. His length springs from his pelvis, as they fall away. His cock is so much larger than I had imagined. There are women in this world that would be intimidated by the sight in front of me right now, but all I can think about is what his large, wide cock is going to feel like inside of me.

My fingers grasp the wide base, as I bring my tongue to it. V groans when I run my tongue up and down his length.

"Fuck," he hisses when I pop the head into my mouth. My fingers move from his length to his hips, pulling him farther into my mouth. Deep throating him would be impossible, but I take him into my mouth as far as I possibly can go without being uncomfortable. Using my tongue, I swirl around the sensitive dip on the underside of his head. I pause then do it again.

"Presley," he growls above. "I need to be inside of you."

I release his cock from my mouth.

"I thought you'd never ask, slowpoke," I tease him.

"Baby, there will be nothing slow about the poke

you're about to get. The moment that I'm inside of you all of my control will be gone."

Holy fucking shit.

"Condom?" he asks, with a worried look on his face.

"I'm on the shot. We're good," I reassure him.

"Thank fucking god."

Voodoo's hands reach for me, pulling me off the bed. He turns us both in his large arms, kissing me the entire motion.

"I want you on top," he orders me, as he falls backwards on the bed.

I climb up on the bed, straddling my legs against his muscular hips and positioning his length at my entrance. A deep breath exits my lips, as I lower myself on him. The pressure is so intense. I feel like the farther I lower myself that my body will split into, even with how dripping wet I am. His hands fall to the underside of my thighs. Each inch is a sultry mixture of pain and pleasure before he's fully seated inside of me.

V gives me time to adjust to his length before he uses my hips to pull out then thrust inside of me.

"You okay?" he asks.

"Fine," I tell him. "So fucking fine."

He smiles, before he thrusts again. This time the pain is almost completely gone, and pleasure soon takes over. The orgasm that was on the cusp of blossoming flares intensely comes to life again, and I know that it won't take long for him to bring me over the edge. My clit grinds against him, as I take over the rhythm from him.

"That's it, baby," he urges me. "Give that orgasm to me."

My ass slaps against his pelvis, as I quicken the pace.

"Ride me, Presley. Make me come."

His words bring my release throttling over the edge. My entire body feels like it's on fire, as the intense waves of pleasure rocket throughout me. The prickling heat feels like a thousand tiny electric shocks. I grind against him, lengthening my orgasm as his hits.

"Fuck," he cries out.

He thrusts inside of me riding out his own orgasm, until I fall on top of him in a tangled mess of limbs. V sweeps my hair to the side, and pulls me in for a long kiss.

We lie there for nearly an hour in each other's arms before he shifts underneath me. He slides me off to his side and climbs from the bed. I smile, as I watch his perfect ass sway, as he stalks to the bathroom. The toilet flushes, and he reappears from the bathroom and slides back into bed with me. Exhaustion begins to set in, as he pulls me tighter against him, and nuzzles his face into my neck, before soft snores vibrate from his throat.

Just as my eyes begin to close, I whisper something that I never expected to say to him.

"I love you."

Chapter 18

VOODOO

DAYS PASS, after the revelation of the bounty that now haunts us all. It lingers on, like a storm capable of dropping an F5 tornado on us at any time. The tension and mood around the club darkens as every day passes. Many of my brothers already operate with paper-thin hair triggers on a good day, but this was nothing like I had ever experienced before. This wasn't even comparable on the fucked-up Richter scale to Maj's Mexican holiday last year. It would be the storm of the century, and no weather report would be able to tell when, where, and how bad the devastation was going to be. The only thing we could do was plan, prepare, and pray that we were going to be able to do our jobs to the best of our ability at a moment's notice.

I spent my days with my brothers in Church or

chained to my computers trying to pinpoint the location of The Zezza's stronghold. My pursuits were coming up empty, but I wasn't going to give up. Not when it was Presley's life on the line. If I had to outsource it to those little fuckers on the other side of the pond, I'd do it no matter the cost. I'm willing to do anything to keep her safe, including breaking every single cyber law in the country. Time was my enemy, and every second that ticked away with no information was putting her closer to danger. It wouldn't take long for the bounty hunters to come knocking on our door. We were the largest club network in the entire state, and what better place to look than within our clubhouses.

My days were spent with my brothers, but the night belonged to her. Though the guilt of our first time together being under duress still bothers me, she's keeping my head above water. Her presence centers me better than any hit of weed. Her heavenly scent better than any drugs I've tried in my more reckless youth. After another unsuccessful night of backdoor hacking, I give up and sought comfort and solace with Presley. Her body entwined with mine was just what the hot head doc ordered.

"Good morning," she whispers to me from my chest, where her head sits nuzzled against me.

"Morning, beautiful," I respond back, placing a soft kiss to the top of her head.

Her arms slink around my stomach, and her fingers begin to dance along my side. I pretend to jump like she's tickling me, which sends her into a quiet giggle.

"That's one of my favorite sounds."

She repeats the motion again, and I pull her face up to mine, giving her a proper good morning kiss. My cock stirs awake and practically yells at me to get him in on the action too. She notices and smiles back up at me with a come and get me grin.

Her hand slides down to my morning wood and grasps the base of it, twisting upward. Pre-cum glistens at the tip, and she uses it to lube her hand. I prop myself up against the pillows to watch the show my girl is giving me. If every morning started off like this, I would die a very happy man.

"Fuck, baby," I growl, as she increases her motion. She kisses down my lower belly, shifting her position as she goes, but never releasing my aching cock from her hand. Presley looks up at me. "I want to taste you." I have no words. I'm stunned fucking silent, but she already knew I wasn't going to stop her anyway. She lowers her mouth to the tip, and pops my cock in her mouth. Her tongue traces every vein, as she explores. Her tongue twists in a figure eight around the tip.

My orgasm is going to hit hard, and she knows it.

"You're going to kill me with that mouth of yours," I groan. Her laugh vibrates around my cock, and it sends my head into a tailspin. She sucks and glides her mouth over my length, until I'm about to explode in her mouth.

"I'm going to come," I warn her, but she doesn't move away.

My balls tighten with my release impending, just as my phone rings.

"Fuck!" I exclaim, reaching over on the nightstand to grab it. Raze's name and face is flashing on the screen. Boner… meet boner killer.

"It's your brother." Presley looks up at me, but doesn't even move.

"Hello," I hiss into the phone, as Presley licks another figure eight around my tip. I cover my phone with my hand and moan.

"Church in five."

"Okay," I grunt, as I bite on my knuckle to fight off trying to moan, with what Presley's mouth keeps doing my cock.

"You alright, V?" he inquires. Fuck me sideways, he knows my voice is off. Presley chooses that exact moment to graze her teeth around me, and sends my orgasm spiraling over the edge. My come shoots in her mouth, and she takes every drop.

"Yup, fine. I'll see you in a few," I bark out, before hanging up and tossing my phone to the floor.

Presley smiles at me from between my legs, and all I can do is shake my head at her.

"Jesus, you are going to kill me. You fucking got me off, while I was on the phone with your brother, woman. That's not exactly something I can explain away."

She crawls back up to my side and snuggles in.

"I was thinking about that. I think we should tell him."

Oh shit. Red alert. Death imminent.

"Can we talk about that later?" I offer up as a distraction. She side eyes me knowing exactly what I'm trying to do. I really need to work on my deflect and redirect skills.

"Either you tell him," she says rolling over into her pillow putting that perfect ass of hers on full display for me. "Or I will."

I groan. Maybe I should check on that life insurance policy of mine and make sure it's up to date.

"We'll talk about it later," I repeat, before slipping from the bed and smacking her ass as I stand. She jumps at the sting then laughs.

I take a look down at my phone and see the time.

Fuck. I'm late for church already. No time for a shit and shower. That would have to come later. I grab my jeans from the floor, stuffing my half-hard cock inside, and zip them up. I would usually be good for a while after that kind of orgasm and the two from last night, but with her, I can't get enough. I grab one of the shirts I stashed in her room for emergencies, such as this and my cut, throwing them both over my head.

I plant a quick kiss on her cheek before I turn for the door.

"I'm not kidding, V. He needs to know," she calls out from our bed.

"And I need to live."

I close the door behind me, and start making my bucket list of what I want to do before he finds out.

Church is surprisingly uneventful, except with the news that Don Zezza, Gio's dad, has died. While any other time that news would mean nothing, this time it did. Italian families are notoriously close knit. When a patriarch dies, they flock together. With Don's death, we would have a momentary break in in our high alert status. With time being of the essence, it could be the break I needed to find my way in. Raze dismisses church shortly thereafter, and my brothers disburse from the room.

I bolt for my office knowing that I was going to

have to deal with Presley's ultimatum, sooner rather than later with a very uncomfortable conversation with Raze. Just as I make it to the door, I spy Ratchet coming down the hallway. `

"Dude. Office. Now," I spew out in a quick, nearly unintelligible word vomit. Ratchet cocks an eyebrow at me, before I grab ahold of him. I pull Ratchet in my computer room, and quickly look around the hall, before quietly closing the door. Ratchet's cold stare of concern is locked and loaded on my panicked face.

"Jesus, V. You look like someone is hunting down your ass for sport. What the fuck is going on?"

Ratchet arches his brow, probing me for answers.

"Because I'm being hunted, fucker."

"You didn't?" he gasps. "Please tell me you didn't tell him yet because I want to watch him kick your ass."

"No, but she wants to tell him."

A smile cracks on Ratchet's face followed by a chuckle rumbling from his chest, as the dam of laughter breaks free. He grasps his stomach as he laughs at my pain.

"Shut up, asshole," I bark at him. "This shit isn't fucking funny."

"But it is," he forces, while still gasping for air. "He's going to kill you."

"No shit, Sherlock. Tell me something I don't know."

I push off my heels, and pace the floor in front of him like a father expecting his first child. He's right, and I know it. Sleeping with Presley was the point of no return, and I hurtled past that barrier with recklessness abandonment. Maybe Ratchet was right about the box of screws being loose in my head. I have to be one thousand French fries short of a happy meal to do what I just did.

"What the fuck do I do, Ratch? I've run this scenario in my head about a million fucking times, and every single one of the ends with me pushing up daisies in Darcy's flower bed."

"You're on your own with this one, V. I tried to tell you to just leave it be. She didn't even know who you were."

I sigh and stop my pacing to face him again.

"That's the problem, Ratch. When it comes to Presley, I have no restraint. I didn't have any restraint when I started the charade online watching her for you. I sure as fuck didn't have any restraint when I fingered her on Raze's fucking desk. And don't get me started about what happened in her room last night," I trail on, pacing again.

Ratchet's hands begin to jerk quickly, as I continue to pace, naming off all of the places that

Presley and I had christened, while I was supposed to be guarding her. His movements become quicker, and that's when I notice the stoic look on his face. My body freezes in place when I hear heavy breathing coming from behind me.

"He's behind me. Isn't he?" I whisper to Ratchet.

"Yup."

"And he heard everything. Didn't he?" I whisper back.

"Yup."

"Fuck." I exclaim, before turning around and meeting the eyes of my very pissed off club president.

Sweet fucking zombie Jesus, I am a dead man.

"Office. Now," he growls.

"Nice knowing you," Ratchet taunts. "Can I have your bike when you die?"

"Fuck off," I mutter under my breath, while shooting him the one finger salute. I'm not even dead yet, and Ratchet's after my shit. Fucking typical. I consider bolting out the back door when I reach the hallway, but Raze would find me. And what would happen then would be so much fucking worse.

If I really wanted Presley in my life, I had to do this. For us. The only problem now is that she might be in a relationship with a ghost because of what Raze just heard in my office. Good thing I took notes, when Presley made me watch that stupid Patrick Swayze movie with Demi Moore. I might need those romantic otherworldly skills soon enough. I just wish I had learned to throw clay first.

I take a deep breath in and walk into my doom. Raze is pacing the floor and sharply turns when I shut the door behind me.

"Is it true?" he screams, charging towards me. Raze stops just inches from my face. "Are you fucking my sister under my fucking roof?"

"Yes," I freely admit.

His growl comes right before his haymaker comes at my face. It's like watching Neo dodge bullets in *The Matrix*, except it was a fist coming straight for me. I had that split second to decide whether to dodge it or throw one of my own, but I waste it thinking about the fucking *Matrix*. His fist connects with my right eye and nose, sending me stumbling backwards into the door with a thud. I can feel the thick stream of blood beginning to flood from my probable broken nose.

"I deserve that," I tell him, using the back of my hand to wipe the blood.

Raze's chests heaves, as blind rage courses through him. All of this is my fault, the blame landing completely on my shoulders.

"How long has this been going on?"

"A few months."

He looks at me processing my admission, likely doing the math in his head. It wasn't adding up, and the part I really didn't want to tell him was about to be put out on the table. I say an internal apology to my right side and possibly my balls, for what is about to come my way.

"Explain."

One-word questions disguised as demands. Danger Will Robertson. Danger.

I take a deep breath, and tell him about the whole online relationship. Raze listens intently pacing around and growling, as I talk my life right into a six-foot grave. He growls and balls his fist, as I spill my secret. I finish my admission, and he stands there in a silent rage, likely imagining all the ways he can kill me.

"And Ratchet knew?" he finally asks.

"Yes, I did what I had to do in order to help Ricca adopt Asher, but I didn't expect to fall for her."

Silence again.

Just keep talking asshole. You've got a broken nose, and a black eye. Wonder what else will be broken when this is all over.

"I'm in love with her, Raze."

"You should have fucking told me, Voodoo. From the very beginning. The moment you realized she was my sister, you should have come to me. But you didn't. Now you're standing here in my office telling me that you love her. Does she even fucking know that it was you on the other end of that conversation?"

"No. I have wanted to tell her so many fucking times. It's eating away at me. But with all this shit going on, I just couldn't do that to her."

Raze charges again. His hot breath and glare burning me without even touching me.

"You're gonna tell her, and after you do, I'll let her decide what to do with you."

"I'm not dead?" I stupidly ask.

"The jury is still out. You fix this, V."

"Believe me, I will," I promise him. "But, I need a favor first."

I tell Raze my plan to expose the truth, and while he doesn't like it, he reluctantly agrees that Presley deserves privacy when I deliver this blow. He throws in his own requirements to my plan, and I stalk back to my office in desperate need of a raw steak or a frozen bag of peas.

I survived this time, but that was going to come into serious question, after I started the spiral of no return. I sigh, look to the drawer in front of me, and slide it open.

Beauregard's silence was about to break and with it, my heart.

Chapter 19

PRESLEY

BLISSFULLY HAPPY.

Those are the only two words that can describe the feeling soaring through my heart and soul right now. A feeling in these circumstances that shouldn't even be in my vocabulary. I was being hunted, and I was smiling.

Was I finally losing the grip on reality? Maybe I was, but I would do it all over again for him. Voodoo came into my life unexpectedly. His nervousness around me in the beginning was shocking in comparison to the man who I was sharing my bed and body with now. The pre-conceived ideas that I had about the men who serve my father's former club had been on point, except for him. Voodoo was the odd ball. His kind, gentle nature, as I was struggling to come to grips with the bounty placed on my head, was more than I could explain with words. His kiss was meant to be a distraction, but it was so much more.

With his lips upon mine in that moment, he took away all the pain in my life, and with our bodies, we created something new. It's a connection I can no longer deny. The last few days have been amazing, and even as I caught myself thinking about Beauregard in fleeting moments, the love I had felt for him was melting away. He would always be a part of my life, even if I didn't get closure from our sudden break.

Voodoo had replaced him in my heart nearly entirely, and it was a switch that I welcomed with open arms.

But V's reluctance to tell my brother was fast becoming a sticking point for me. In normal cases of a brother's friend and his kid sister hooking up, the emotions would run on high. Mikey would be like that, but turned up to eleven. Voodoo was his non-blooded brother, and our relationship without first seeking permission or at least telling him about it, would be seen as a low blow. Possibly even a betrayal. Something that I know scares V. My brother held power over him. He could make his life miserable or rip away his cut, effectively taking a piece of his soul with it. I wanted to give him more time to tell Mikey, but suspicions were starting to run high around the clubhouse. The club girls watched us like a hawk, and whispered about us sitting together every morning. As careful as he was, I had no doubt that one of them had seen him slipping away from my room, after so many nights together. It only takes sex before dawn escapes, to put two and two together, and these girls were experts at floating from bed to bed.

I had a selfish reason for wanting our relationship out in the open. Waking up alone was beginning to get old. I wanted to wake up next to him, and cling to him like a normal couple. I wanted to be able to hold his hand and kiss him without having to slink away to his office or my room. With my life in jeopardy, I wanted those moments of normalcy because it could all change in the blink of an eye. Death was a possibility, and with the grim reaper's scythe so close to my neck, I need to feel normal. Just for a little while

I made a plan once V bolted for his church meeting to tell my brother. I had hope that the news coming from me would be a softer blow, than it would be coming from V. With a wave of his hand, he could cast V out. My protection would go with him if I chose to follow him. The decision between my brother, my safety, danger, and V wasn't going to be an easy one to make. But I knew in my heart, which way the decision would swing. I just had to accept it.

I make short work of my shower and getting dressed. I admittedly spent far too much time rehearsing my grand speech about having the right to love who I choose, and my brother's opinion being only that just an opinion. I had to cling to my strength if I was going to make it through this.

I take one last glance in the mirror, before heading out the door to my brother's office. My eyes scan the main room quickly as I stalk through it, finding that most of the guys are out and about. Church must be over, and knowing my brother, he would be holed up in his office, just where I want him.

Just as Mikey's door comes into sight, I watch from afar as Voodoo beelines for his office with blood all over his shirt, face, and hands.

"That motherfucker," I growl, under my breath.

I don't even knock when I reach my brother's door. I shove it open, and then slam it behind me.

"Please do come on in," he sarcastically fires at me, from behind his desk.

"Are you *fucking* kidding me right now, Mikey? I just saw V. Did *you* do that to him?" I point out the door towards V's office.

"Sure did," he says with a smile on his face. "No one touches my sister without permission."

He's fucking gloating over the fact that he's assaulted one of his own men. And for what? Because he dares have a relationship with me. It's like fucking high school all over again. A man gets close to me, and my brother runs him off. Unfortunately for him, I worked around that little issue, and he is about to get a huge surprise. No one tells me what to do. Not anymore. I have lived that life for far too long, and look where that got me. That ends today.

Rage fuels my every move. Before I can stop myself, I charge towards him. He slides his chair back, glaring up at me, but standing his ground. Mikey sits like a coiled viper. Cautiously monitoring the situation without inserting himself. He's waiting for me to make my move. My hand goes rogue, slapping him hard across the face. Mikey remains steadfastly still, as I recoil my hand from the pain of hitting him.

"That wasn't a bright move, LeeLee. Are you okay?"

"My hand is fine, asshole," I hiss. I cradle my hand against my chest, trying not to think about how badly it hurts and praying it's not broken. My fingers extend when I try to move them. Not broken, thank God. "I want to make something crystal clear for you, Michael. I'm an adult. I do what I want, and I fuck who I want. You have no say in that."

"The fuck I don't. He's one of my men," Mikey says, on the verge of yelling. His finger points to the door mimicking my own gesture. "He is supposed to be protecting you. Not fucking you." He hisses as he stands, planting both of his hands on the table. I can't help, but notice the specks of a bruise forming on his hand from hitting Voodoo. The sight of it enrages me.

"Not your decision. You had no right to do that," I yell back at him. His eyes narrow as angrily.

"I have every right to be pissed off, LeeLee. It is my decision when your life is on the line. What if he was with you and didn't see The Zezza's rolling up? What if they came into this clubhouse and killed us all? Do you see what I'm trying to tell you?"

The hypothetical scenario he presents does make sense, but he's thinking so analytically. My brother has always been hardwired to look at all the angles of a situation, except for the emotional part of it. Right now, I can almost bet that he's sitting there trying to decide what else he can throw at me. But the bottom line is that this isn't a fling like he thinks. Though there is the complication with Beauregard, I've fallen for V despite my best attempts not to do that very thing.

"I do see, but you aren't seeing the whole picture."

"I see it perfectly fine. You're my sister," he says with a bite to his voice. He pushes off the desk, rounding it and comes to a stop before me. "My only sister, and I will break off every man's hand in this club, if they touch you, if I feel so inclined. This is my club, and these are my rules. No one trumps me here."

"And I'm a human being. You can't keep running away every man that comes around. My life could end at any moment, and you're systemically trying to deny what could be my last chance at happiness."

"Not with him," he demands. "Over my dead fucking body will I allow it. I'll kick him out, before I let that happen." Mikey doesn't budge. His stern stance is proof alone of that. While his intentions are noble, he has to let me go. I want my own life, and I'll have it without his permission.

"I'll just go with him, Mikey. I love him."

My brother stills in front of me. As a man who has loved, lost, and found love again, he has to understand what that means for me.

"I love him," I repeat. "And despite what you think about us, I will not let you shove us apart. You don't know him like I do."

"If you only knew," he mutters.

"Knew what?" I inquire.

"Nothing," he interjects.

His arms reach out, pulling me tightly against him. Standing in his embrace makes me feel so small. His large build hulks over me.

"I want you to be happy," he whispers against the top of my head, before pulling away. "But this is not the life I wanted for you. I joined this club and took over when Dad died to protect you and Mom. Everything that I do is for your protection."

"I know," I admit to him. "But you can't keep me in a gilded cage, Mikey. I need room to breathe, and a chance to live my own life, if we make it through this. Please just give me the space to see where this ends up."

My brother's stern face slips just ever so slightly into a crack of a smile. It doesn't last long, but it was there. He does understand.

"I don't like it, but if it's what you want, I won't stop you. But if that asshole ever hurts you, I will kill him," he states making sure to exaggerate the last part to drive home his point. "And don't fucking suck face in front of me. That's all I ask."

"I promise to keep it at a minimum."

He hugs me again, before I leave his office. I pause at V's door, but decide against knocking. He just went toe to toe with my brother over me. He would need time to process it all. While other women would fear that he would have a change of heart about our relationship, I knew better. No man would take a hit from a guy like Mikey, if he planned on ditching the girl afterwards. It was better this way to give him space. When he was ready to talk to me about it, he would come to me.

I practically skip back to my room. V and I didn't have to hide anymore, and the thought of being so open about our relationship is positively electric. No more closed doors, secret rendezvous, or hiding. We were free to be ourselves, something that I would be taking full advantage of once V came back. All I had to do was wait.

I try to pass the time watching one of the movies V had packed into the top drawer of my dresser, but without him here doing his running commentary or directly quoting the movie he had clearly seen a hundred times, it wasn't the same. My next pursuit is reading one of the books that Ratchet had brought Ginny fails as well. I nearly give up when a sound echoing from the bathroom freezes me in my place.

It can't be. No. There's no way. I'm hearing things. It's just the boredom messing with my head.

The sound rings again, and then I know I'm not crazy. I uneasily slide from the couch, padding to the bathroom, and pulling open the vanity drawer containing my burner phone. As I reach down to grab it, the screen lights up as another message pops up on the screen. Beauregard. After all this time, he reaches out, when I have just fought my brother over V.

Was this a sign from above that I was on the right path with V or the exact opposite? The fates were playing a cruel trick on my heart. I mull over the decision in front of me. Do I delete the texts without even reading them and turn off the phone, shutting Beauregard out of my life? Or do I read them, opening myself up to threaten the relationship I have with V?

Where is a damn therapist to talk this over with? My mind swirls with indecision. Would this be betraying V if I looked at the messages? What about responding to them? The love I had for Beauregard was essentially gone, but the part of him left inside of me needed that closure between us. I may regret what I'm about to do, but I can't ignore it. My finger touches on his name, and the messages pop up.

Hi.

I'm sorry for not responding.

We need to talk.

I start to type out a message, but another one comes in.

> I want to be honest with you. I've met someone, but I still think about you.

I can't stop myself from replying. Beauregard had moved on just like I had. Maybe replying back wouldn't be as bad as it was making me feel.

> I have too.

> Are you happy?

His response is quick.

> I am, but there's a part of me that still wants to meet you. Would you be open to that? I know you're out east, but I would be willingly to meet you halfway.

I pause. Am I crazy for even considering this? My heart pounds in my chest. I'm already in danger. Leaving the clubhouse will be impossible.

What would Voodoo think if I did this? Would I tell him? I know it would hurt him, but I would try my damnedest to explain my reasoning to him. Closure would be a good thing for all of us going forward. V holds my entire heart, but my mind would be finally clear of Beauregard. This would be good for us in the long run or at least that's what I tell myself. If I had any chance of making a clean break, I have to take this no matter the risks. I gulp as I type out my reply.

> I'm actually in California.

> What do you have in mind?

We text back and forth a few more times. Making the plans to meet each other the next day in Los Angeles. How I'll get there is an entirely other problem in it's self, but I'll figure it out. Meeting Beauregard closes that chapter in my life. I'd be free and clear to pursue V with a good conscience. I have to do this.

For me.

For V.

For the relationship I want with him.

I only have one choice. V can't know, and the only way to do this. So I tuck my tail between my legs, and walk back to my brother's office, blatantly lying to him about a need to get away.

"It's not a good idea," Mikey fires back immediately.

"I know, but I need this. Please. I'll take extra protection with me."

"V is enough."

"Not him," I blurt out.

My brother cocks an eyebrow at me. His deep scowl cutting into his face. With a brief shake of his head, I watch his shoulders slump.

"Fine. You have an hour. That's all I'm willing to go you."

"Thank you," I beam back at him.

"Don't thank me yet. There's going to be rules."

He lists them off one by one, but no matter how many obstacles he puts in my path, I agree to them all.

"If anything happens to you," he growls.

"I'll be fine," I reassure my brother. "I'll follow your rules."

"I'll tell the guys," he grumbles. "I'm trusting you, LeeLee."

"I know."

I left his office with permission and a sense of dread.

Why does meeting Beauregard seem like it's going to destroy my world?

Chapter 20

VOODOO

THE LAST HOUR has been agony. The wavering of my decision to finally tell Presley that Beauregard Martin, tech guru is really me, has been the hardest decision of my life. I know that Presley feels something for me that is more than just the amazing sex. What we share is less primal and more deeply connected. Raze finding out not only about this precursor, but our current relationship as well was just not in the plan. She needs to know that much I knew, but his ultimatum blew my timeline to shit.

Which is why I find myself waiting in the cocktail bar of Le Petite Belle in the heart of Beverly Hills, dressed and cleaned up like a respectable individual for the first time in years. Suits and ties weren't exactly my go-to wardrobe, but I had to play the part.

Getting Ratchet to agree to be her chauffeur for at least the first part of the night was the hardest part of it all. He had been on my ass for weeks to tell her who Beau really was, and he was right. The time is now or never. She would either forgive me or forget me, but it was a risk I had to take with so many threats lurking around us. Like her brother. My life was dangerous, and hers was currently thrust into the middle of the murky waters of living on the edge of right and wrong.

After living in so many years of terror with her father, how could I even ask her to stay here with me? This club is what her nightmares were made of, and I selfishly wanted her to stay if she would have me. There are things I would do in this world that would make a normal man shutter in fear, and I would do them over and over again just for her. Presley was the princess in the castle, and I desperately wanted to be the one to rescue her from the dragon. But depending on how tonight goes, I might just find myself pushing up daisies and out of lives in this game. The decision was all hers on where we go from here, and that terrifies me.

The bartender in his tiny, little bow tie and French cut suit slides over to me with a bottle of champagne and a fluted glass in his hand.

"May I offer you a sample of our finest French

wine, monsieur?" he asks, in a voice with a heavy-laden fake French accent.

I stare at him, and he stands there looking like an idiot with that glass and bottle of champagne, waiting for my answer.

"No thanks, Garçon," I respond back, in my own version of a fake accent. "I don't drink that frou-frou bullshit, but I'll take a beer, if you have one."

The bartender starts to open his mouth, when I notice the door opening out of the corner of my eye. My phone chimes, as a text from Ratchet flashes across the screen alerting me to Presley's arrival.

The moment I lay my eyes on her, all of the air is sucked out of my lungs. She's so beautiful. While it should hurt that she's all dolled up for another man, I can't be hurt since that other man is me. Her long, dark hair is twisted and braided like a crown at the top of her head. The simple black dress that drapes her body hugs every curve and highlights her figure perfectly. The urge to want to switch places with that dress hits hard. But it's the heels on her tiny feet that add the knockout punch to the gut with her beauty tonight. The black straps of the shoes wrap up her calves and adds a few inches to her height. I don't know what it is about heels on Presley, but my cock goes ridged in my pants to the point it could prob-ably cut through a steel beam.

Her dark eyes glance around the room, as I quickly turn my back to her. If she makes me now, I will never get a chance to explain, and every single chance I would have to make this right, would leave with her right out of that door.

The too sweet voice of the hostess I met earlier fills the air of the room, as she greets Presley. I turn around and watch her lead Presley to the private dining area that I booked, and as soon as she's out of sight, Ratchet slips into the door and beelines towards me.

"Sir," the bartender interrupts, before he gets to me. "You need to have a tie and jacket to be served in this restaurant."

I laugh, as Ratchet just glares at the guy.

"I'm not staying," he barks back. The bartender begins to protest again, but I wave him off with a quick gesture. Ratchet takes a few more steps, and sidles up next to me on the bar stool.

"You ready for this, V?" he asks. "There's still a chance to turn back now."

"No, it's time. She needs to know, even if it means I risk what she and I have now."

Ratchet lifts his hand and grips my shoulder tightly.

"You may be a son of a bitch, but I'm proud of you, V."

"Aww Ratchy, is this your version of a father-son talk? You getting practice in for Asher?" I tease back. "What's next? Are you going to give me the talk and threaten to kick my ass if I hurt her?"

Ratchet laughs loud enough that a few of the patrons sitting farther down the bar turn and glare at him. He just smiles at his disturbance of the peace.

"Nah," he quips. "I'm sure Raze has done enough of that shit for the entire world."

"You aren't kidding," I coolly respond, thinking back to my run in with the club president. Raze's ultimatum may have been the tipping point of telling Presley, but like I said before, it's the right thing to do.

I notice the hostess leaving the area where Presley is waiting to meet Beau, and she turns towards me. Ratchet notices her coming close and abruptly stands.

"Good luck, brother," he offers, before retreating back outside to the waiting car. When I decided to do this, I made Ratchet promise that he would wait in case she bolted. I didn't want to take the chance that Presley would be exposed if she ran. If her safety was compromised because of me, I would never forgive myself.

"Sir," the hostess calls, "Your party is waiting."

I inhale a deep breath, and slide from the barstool.

With each step closer to the room, my heart thuds more intensely.

You can do this. She's the best fucking thing in your life that isn't circuits and motherboards. It's time to man up, and see what you're made of.

My feet fall in line, one behind the other, as they lead me to my fate. It's like I'm a condemned man walking to the gallows, knowing that I'll hang or be pardoned.

My hand tremors slightly, as I reach for the curtain separating the two lives that I have lived for the past few months with her. They say that the truth sets you free, but why do I feel like it's damning me?

I take one last deep breath and slide inside.

Presley's head is down, and her hands are wrapped tightly around the fabric napkin she grasps. Her gaze rises to meet mine, and she freezes, speechless.

Her eyes flash from nervousness to rage in a split second, and I briefly wonder if she might be related to Ratchet with how fast the switch flipped in just a second flat.

"You son of a bitch. It's been you the entire time," she seethes, standing up.

Fuck. Where's the fucking abort mission button when you need it?

"I can explain, Presley," I beg, rushing toward her,

in an attempt to block her escape. She shoves me, but I stand my ground. Every part of me is screaming to grab ahold of her, bringing her in tightly, until she screams out her pain and anger, but I can't do that. Presley isn't some spoiled little girl who wants to put on a show or be pacified like a child. She's an educated woman who is angry as fuck at me for my deception. If I have a chance in hell of repairing this, I have to let her talk, and I have to hope she listens to reason.

"You want to explain why you've been lying to me? How long have you been catfishing for the fucking club?"

I raise my hands up in surrender, as she tries to push me aside.

"Please, Presley. Just sit down, and I will explain everything. This isn't what you think it is."

She shoves me again.

"Hear me out, and afterwards if you still want to leave, you can. I won't stop you," I offer to her. She glares at me, and I can't help but notice that her hand is clenched at her side. I stand my ground, and she slowly eases back into her chair. Her beautiful face is plastered with judgment, as I sit down across from her, making sure to keep my distance. I have no doubt that she knows how to throw a punch with her parentage, and I want to get through this without being branded with another black eye. The one her brother gave me was finally starting to fade away. I didn't need another one so soon.

"You have five minutes."

I sigh at her angered indifference, and open up to her like a patient on her therapy couch.

"It looks bad. I'm fully aware of that fact, but I wasn't catfishing you," I start. My hand slides from the table, and into my pocket, as I retrieve my wallet. Fingering my ID, I slide it over to her. I watch intently as her eyes fall to the thin piece of plastic containing my most personal information, including my real name.

"Beauregard Martin is my real name. I'm a tech guru, and I work for your brother's security company as a technical specialist. That is a private sector job."

She scoffs audibly at my explanation. *Jesus, I'm going nowhere fast.*

"The man you met online is me. The only thing fake about what transpired between us was the photo I used on the profile. When Ratchet came for Ricca, he asked me to look into you and make sure that Ricca was not only safe, but that you wouldn't hinder her chances for getting Asher. I never thought that what started off as protecting my family and my brother would turn into this," I tell her, motioning between us with my hand.

"I was just a job to you," she retorts. "A job that you just so happened to start falling for the target. How do you expect me to believe a word that you are saying? You're a part of a club that buys and sells deceit like a fucking candy store. You forget that I lived that life, and I ran from it."

I try to reach out for her, but she quickly tucks her hands under the table, effectively shutting me out again. I grab my ID and slip it back into my wallet, as this train continues to derail in front of me.

"The club isn't like that anymore. Can't you see that? You came to us for protection, and your brother and my club has put everything on the line to protect you," I fire back. Her insistence that the HRMC is the bad guy in this situation starts to grate on my nerves. This is my fuck up, and she isn't allowing me to take full ownership of that.

"Presley, I know you're angry with me. I own that lock, stock, and fucking exploding barrel, but the club isn't the enemy in this. I am."

She scoffs again. Jesus, she's just as stubborn as her older brother. I guess the apple really doesn't fall far from the pig-headedness tree.

"Angry? You think I'm angry? Try pissed. Disgusted. You've lied to me. Deceived me into thinking that you felt something for me, and for what? To spy on me for your club?"

I try to reach for her again, and yet again, there is nothing from her. This ship is sinking faster than the Titanic, and the only lifeboat left is reserved for her.

"I fucking love you. Don't you realize that," I loudly proclaim. "I have guarded you, protected you, and while doing so, I have fallen in love with you, despite the fact that this entire fucking thing has been eating away at me. I wanted to tell you from the moment you walked into my clubhouse, but when the target was painted on your back, I had to put my club above my personal agenda."

Presley stands and takes two steps towards me, stopping just in front of me. I rise to meet her, and am met with her hand slapping me across the face.

"That is the problem with men like you. Everything else is more important than the truth. You lied to me, and what's worse is that I let you in. I let you break down those barriers I spent so many years building, after my father's club tore them down. I gave you a piece of me that I can never get back, and I'm sick just thinking about how stupidly I played into your plan."

Presley glares at me one last time, before heading toward the curtain. She stops just short of exiting the room, like she is fighting an internal battle.

"Give me a chance to make this right."

"You are all out of chances, and I'm all out of fucks to give" she yells at me, and stomps out of the room.

"Fuck!" I scream, and lay a punch to the doorframe that once held Presley. "Fucking idiot."

I center myself, and start out after her, before the hostess and the manager I assume storm into the room. Both of them yell at me, and threaten to call the cops before I grab my wallet, throwing a couple hundred dollars back into their faces to shut them up. I shove them both out of the way, and chase after Presley.

As soon as I break the threshold, I know something is wrong. Presley is nowhere to be found, and Ratchet is lying on the ground with blood seeping from his shoulder and leg.

The sound of screeching tires a block north tells me that this has gone from bad to the worst fucking night of my entire life. I do the only thing I can. I slide my phone from my pocket and call Raze. If he was thinking about killing me for sneaking around with Presley, then he is definitely going to kill me now for losing her.

Chapter 21

PRESLEY

HE *BETRAYED* ME. He *lied* to me. And I fell in love with a man who entered my life twice, and destroyed it. Beauregard was real. That much had been answered, but finding closure with him was more damning, than I could have ever imagined. I couldn't stand to be in his presence anymore. I needed to think, and I couldn't do that with him there watching me like a wounded deer. An audience to my self-destruction was the last thing I needed right now. Not even Ben and Jerry's or a fifth of whiskey could make this situation better in a calm manner. The happiness I felt coming here was now a figment of my imagination, on my road to instability and insanity.

He did this to us.

Voodoo had played me for a fool, and I fell for it. I

was ashamed of myself for not seeing this for what it really was. Our relationship was a convenience where the victim fell for the manipulator, like a witless child seeking a Popsicle from a stranger.

I came here seeking closure, and the only things I was leaving with were a web of lies and illusions. Everything good in my life just collided and imploded right in front of me. There was no coming back from this at all.

The cool night air rushes into my lungs, as I bolt from the restaurant. Ratchet leans against the car parked just outside. His eyes are wide when he sees me. Did he know what V did? Or should I say Beauregard? Just thinking about his admittance too duping me kills another piece of me inside. My heart shatters knowing the two men that held my heart were responsible for breaking it.

Ratchet shoves away from the car, and then everything becomes a blur. A shot rings out from behind me, and I watch as Ratchet clutches his shoulder, falling to the ground. It's like slow motion when I turn around. My hair flying up in the air, like a cloud wrapping around me as I spin. Three large men, one with a smoking gun drawn, stand right me behind.

I try to scream, and I try to run, but they're on me, before I can. I feel their large hands enclosing around my body, pulling me away from Ratchet and completely away from safety.

"Ratchet," I finally screech. He tries to stand, but the man with the gun shoves himself between us, firing again. This time the man hits Ratchet in the leg. He stumbles back, and collapses onto the sidewalk by the car in a heap.

"No!" I scream out, before a large hand clamps over my mouth, drowning out the sound of my pleas for help.

Tears streak down my face like molten lava. The man with the gun turns and faces me. His dark eyes are cold pools of evil. He shoves his gun into the waistband of his slacks, and stalks towards me.

"Good evening, Dr. Matthews. It's nice to finally meet you."

His mouth curves into a horrifying smile, as I feel a pinch, and I know something has been jabbed into my neck. A warm sensation drips into my veins at the injection site. I can feel my stability slipping away from me, as my legs begin to weaken underneath me. Inch by inch, my muscles seize, losing control to the unidentified drug coursing through my body. I try to speak, but my muffled voice sounds like I have my head underwater. The man in front of me sways, as my vision blurs in front of me.

"Put her in the car," I hear a voice demand, as a

cold blackness pulls me under, closing me off from the world.

———

Hello? My voice calls out to the empty vastness inside my head. *Can anyone here me?* I try to reach out, finding something to pull me back from the dark oblivion of my mind, but I realize that there's nothing to move. I'm trapped inside of my own head, as the world continues to tick along outside of my body.

I panic when dark thoughts begin to cross my mind.

Is this purgatory? Am I dead? Why can't I wake up?

My internal pleas only illicit silence in return.

Just wake up. Please wake up. I scream, but there's no one to hear it in my personal prison. I try to will my eyes to open or my limbs to move. There's no response. *I* was the voice in my own head, and it wasn't because of a split personality. The drugs had done this, and all I could do was wait for them to release me.

Hours pass. Well, what seemed like hours, when you're left with nothing to do, but think, stew, and worry inside your own head. I had read case studies, before about coma patients who had been in a similar situation as this. They were awake, but their body wasn't. Where one could say they had an out of body experience, mine was purely an in-body experience.

Muffled voices speak, breaking the silence. Their words are unintelligible, but I can hear them. I'm not dead. Well, for now. There was no telling what I would see or find when I fully woke-up.

The ripple of my body stirring rushes through me. The sensation of being moved stirs me more than the voices. I can feel myself on the brink of consciousness. Fiber by fiber, my muscles begin to stir and stretch, as the drug begins to wear off. A few more minutes pass, before my eyes flutter open.

Distorted blobs of color fill my sight, and my head aches like I have a major hangover. I try to focus on my surroundings, but it's too soon. My eyes need to adjust. The voices continue to talk, not noticing that I'm stirring. I try my eyes one more time, before shutting them again. The drugs haven't fully released me, and if I fought, they'd notice I was awake.

"She's been out for two days, man. How much Ketamine did you give her?" a thick accent mutters near me. His voice is low and unfamiliar.

"I didn't exactly check the dose, Ricliss. We were exposed. I just shot her up," a different voice replies. This one person is local without a trace of foreignness to his voice.

"The boss will kill us, if she dies," the first voice declares.

I test moving my lips next. The small movement is met with the resistance. My tongue explores the barrier preventing them from parting, and the bitter taste of glue hits my taste buds. Tape. There's tape on my mouth. My throat feels like sandpaper, as I try to swallow the taste of the adhesive.

"Did she just move?" the local man asks. I still. His footfalls come closer, and I can feel his gaze peering down at me, without even having to look at him through tiny slits. I count the seconds, before he finally moves away. Forty-five seconds pass, before he shuffles away from me again.

I wait unmoving, until I hear two sets of footsteps leave the room. A heavy lock clicks, as the door shuts, and my eyes fly open to assess the situation alone. The room is dark with very little light peeking in from the single barred window. Bars only mean one thing. That this isn't exactly the first-time the people keeping me has done this. Reinforcements such as those aren't just a fly by night addition, when the mood to hold someone prisoner strikes your fancy. This is a professional set-up, and not a good sign for my chances for escape. There's no denying that I need to get out of wherever I am, but the chances were becoming slim to none, the more I take in my surroundings. A silent prayer slips from my lips, as I sigh in relief to find myself still fully clothed in what I wore, when they grabbed me. At least, I hadn't been touched in my drugged state, and that was a miracle in itself.

My hands are bound behind me. My fingers stretch out and feel a rough, thick cord tied around them. I try to move my feet, but the tug on the cord around my hands pulls with the motion. They've bound my legs and feet together. My muscles scream with each movement I make from stiffness. If the men were telling the truth, I'd been out for two days. Far outside the normal forty-eight-hour recovery rate. My chances of being found were growing slimmer by the minute.

Had Ratchet lived or did he die? What if they went back for Voodoo? Thinking of him jolts my heart. I couldn't think of his betrayal right now. My sole mental pursuits had to clearly focus on how to get out of here. My judgment of his actions had to wait, until I escaped. That's if I survived long enough to do that in the first place.

The springs of a thin mattress creak under my weight. The squeaking gets even worse when I shift my body to see more. I shuffle my feet trying to reach the edge of the bed when the door slams open. The man who shot Ratchet stands in front of me, smiling down at me. His suit is now gone, and he has changed into a pair of worn jeans and a black shirt. I freeze in terror not knowing what to do.

"Sleeping Beauty is finally awake," he declares. His accent is thicker, than the man earlier. This man's tones are gravelly dulcet tones. Fog still clouds my mind, but I force myself to focus on his face. His olive skin is almost perfect, and contrasts with his deep, dark eyes that resemble black holes of pain and despair centered on his face. A swatch of stubble dots his thin, angular chin. His hair is slicked back tightly against his scalp.

My worst nightmare has finally come true, and I'm helpless to stop it. The Zezza's have me.

The man approaches me, leans down by my body, and rips away the tape from my mouth in one brisk movement. The stinging pain informs me that the adhesive pulled away my skin and small hairs with it, and it brings hot tears welling in my eyes.

He eyes the tape, before wadding it up and tossing it in his pocket like a seasoned professional. My DNA would have been on that tape along with his fingerprints. His mind was already erasing the ties between us and tying up loose ends. I knew in that moment that I wouldn't make it out of here alive unless someone came for me soon.

"I've been waiting for you to wake up. Dr. Matthews, or should I call you Dr. Sanders?"

My face gives me away, and his demented smile broadens. His hot breath blows down on my face causing me to shiver. I peer up into his dead eyes, and it's like looking into the face of the devil.

"Let me introduce myself, my name is Gio Zezza, but I think you probably know that already."

"Why am I here?" my voice cracks. My throat burns with each word I force out. My throat screams for water that I know is probably not coming. Why would you give a condemned prisoner a drink, when their life was nearly at an end? The answer is you wouldn't.

"Don't play coy, Doctor. You know why you're here."

I lay silently, while my mind tries to plan its next move. His hand lazily grazes my dirty hair with his hand. He starts to speak again, before an older man walks into the door. He's in black suit, and the air shifts around him. He was someone important to the crime family, and to Gio as well. The new man speaks in a foreign language to Gio, as they both stand over me. Gio speaks back to the man in a clipped pace. I try to listen to pick up what I can, but I don't understand a single world. The older man looks back down to me, before turning on his heels, leaving the room.

Gio re-focuses his attention back to me. He roughly grabs my shoulders, pulling me from my forced fetal position and shifting me upright. My knees and calves scream in pain with the uncomfortable position. He releases me, before turning his back on me.

"You and I are going to have a little talk. Let's get you a little more comfortable, shall we?"

He calls out to the hallway, and two huge giant-like men walk through the door. The only way I can describe them is if the Incredible Hulk was Italian instead of green. These were the muscle to Gio's crazy. In another life, these two monster sized men would probably be on one of those fake wrestling shows in spandex. If they could have only gone down that career path.

"Tie her to the chair," he orders them. A chair appears, and in a blur, my hands are released and then retied to a stiff back wooden chair. I stifle a sigh of relief, as my legs and arms stretch for the first time in a few days.

Gio moves in front of me, as his men finish securing me to the chair.

"She's all yours, boss," the man with a foreign

accent utters, as he and his partner leave the room again.

Gio's thin lips purse, as he takes me in. I notice the glint of metal seated at his left hip. He smirks when he realizes what has my attention. The long fingers of his hand slip to the gun, and he un-holsters it. He spins the gun in his hand, before turning the muzzle towards me. I flinch, and he looks on in joy. He knows I'm afraid, and he's toying with me. Gio is a Grade A sociopath, and I would have known that without even having to be his captive. His mind was a dark place of death, destruction, and disease. No amount of medication or counseling could ever alter the way it ticks.

"Where's the girl?" he orders, inching the gun closer to me.

Could it be? Does he not know Ginny's real name? I stow a sigh of relief because Gio would be able to sense my ease. I had to play my cards the right way for as long as I can. My brother would come for me, and I had to try to keep the game going, as long as I could.

"Go to hell," I spit back.

"Tsk, tsk, tsk, Dr. Sanders. That's not how you speak to someone who has a gun on you. Didn't you cover that at Stanford?" he sneers.

Fuck. Not only does he know my real name, but

also where I went to college. That can only mean one thing. He knows about my brother, and his club.

Oh god. No, this can't be real. No. No. No. I've put them all in danger.

The rescue plan I was clinging to was just pulled out from under me like a rug, if my brother was even still alive. Gio and his family could have already attacked the clubhouse for all I knew, and this was a sick fucking way to use them against me. I would not break.

"Someone just figured it all out," he smiles, pushing the gun in his hand into my forehead and giving me a shove backwards. "I know all about you. The club your brother runs. The men in it, and even their families. You really should be more careful, Presley. Did you really go out for a nice dinner knowing we're looking for you? Someone with your education should be much smarter than that."

Gio paces around me, tapping the gun against my head with each rotation.

"The minute you walked into the restaurant I had you."

"The waiter," I croak.

"See you are smart," he laughs, tapping the muzzle of the gun against my head several times in a row. "There's that education coming out."

My head drops in shame at how stupid I was to

believe that I could have met Beauregard slash V, and not have been made. My mistakes have put the crosshairs on every single person involved with the club. And for what? Love that may have never been real.

"Now it's sinking in," he utters with a pause. "I'm going to ask you one more time. Where's the girl?"

I remain silent. My death would not be for nothing, if I stood my ground, and protected Ginny with my last breath. In death, I would be able to save her, even if I couldn't save myself.

"Kill me because I will never tell you where she is," I hiss.

Gio kneels in front of me. The gun is between us, terrorizing me with every movement.

"All in good time, Doctor. All in good time."

Chapter 22

VOODOO

THIS WAS NOT SUPPOSED to happen. She was just supposed to be pissed at me, not get fucking kidnapped, while leaving my brother sporting two new bullet holes. I fall to my knees beside Ratchet, as my phone calls Raze. He rips me a new asshole when he picks up. I try to give him as much information as I can with Ratchet also adding in what information he could. I rip my tie off my neck with my free hand, and tie a tourniquet above the bullet hole in his thigh, to slow the bleeding. I'd seen it in movies, and that was just about the extent of my medical training. His shoulder was seeping blood, but at a much lower rate than his leg. The greatest chance of one of the bullets puncturing something important was in his leg, and that's where I put my focus. His care was now in my control with the Calvary back at the clubhouse preparing to strike back and get Presley. Ratchet pulls himself off the ground, and leans his upper body against the car.

I try to check his shoulder wound more closely, but a female bystander comes running up to us. The older woman's eyes are wide with panic. Not what we need right now. A witness who wants to stick her nose in our business and inserting herself into a situation that doesn't concern her.

"Oh my god. I heard gunshots when I was taking groceries out of my car. Are you okay? I'll call an ambulance," she rattles, fumbling around with her phone. Her hands shake, and I reach over to her, steading her.

"I'm a doctor, ma'am," I lie. "The ambulance is on its way." I had to get her away from us so we could slip away. Raze had already called Doc by now, and he would be waiting to patch Ratchet up if he could. Hospitals were our last resort, especially with the particulars of this case. If he were to hobble up to the emergency room, questions would be asked that we couldn't answer and the police would be called. I just had to hope that the Doc could handle this.

"Ma'am," I calmly say, raising my hand to silence her. "Thank you for wanting to help, but I have this situation under control."

"Did you see who shot him?" she asks not wanting to let this go.

"I did. Like I said, I have the situation under control." Take the hint lady. Just leave.

She gives me a look, and I nicely dismiss her again. My patience was running thin, and I was about to snap at her to drive the point home. The woman tries to continue to insert herself into this situation, but she finally takes the hint. I have no doubt that as soon as she rounds that corner, her phone will be dialing the police. She disappears from sight, and I spring to action, knowing that we don't have much time before the cops show up.

"Let's get you up, big guy," I mutter to him, slipping an arm under his un-injured shoulder, and helping him to his feet. His jaw clenches from the pain as he groans. I carry most of his weight, as we limp around to the other side of the car. I pop open the door, and help him slide in.

"Fuck," Ratchet growls, as he uses his injured leg to slide into the low car seat. "Should have driven the truck."

"You didn't exactly know you were going to be shot."

He throws me a serious side eye, as I close the door and run around the front of the car. I climb into the driver's seat, and get the fuck out of dodge before the cops show up. Ratchet's head dips back against the seat rest, and my eyes snap to him.

"Stay awake, fucker," I order him. "Do not go to sleep."

"Ain't tired, shithead," he grumbles.

I throw a look over my shoulder at the oncoming traffic, before peeling out of the parking spot into traffic. A few cars honk their horns at me, but I don't care. Ratchet's bleeding all over the interior of the car is more important, than their road rage sensibilities. Some people just don't know what a real emergency looks like.

I hit the gas, jerking the car forward, and begin to change lanes like a mad man. The exit for the freeway north comes up far more quickly than I anticipated two lanes over, and I perform the standard merge with cutting off people not caring if it pisses them off. Some blue pick-up brakes in front of me, and I jerk the wheel narrowly missing his tailgate.

Ratchet glares at me.

"Fucker, this is Ricca's car."

"Do you think she'll care if it's a little dinged up versus you bleeding out? Pretty sure she'd side with me," I fire back at him, cutting off another line of cars and bolting onto the freeway.

"I'm not dying."

"How do you know?" I declare, looking at blood covering his entire right leg.

"I just know. Besides, you're the fucking doctor," he teases back.

"Shut up, asshole. It's all I could think of to get the bitch out of the picture."

He manages a laugh, but it quickly turns into a grunt of pain, as I hit a pothole. He shoots another look my way about the car, and I just smile back.

I make good time, and pull into the parking lot of the clubhouse with a cloud of dust behind me. I drift to stop by the backdoor. I'm out of the car in a flash, ripping open Ratchet's door, when the heavy hand of one of my brothers comes behind me.

"I got him," Thor insists, shoving me out of the way and thrusting his hands inside of the car. In a nearly flawless move, Ratchet is out and on his way into the clubhouse with Thor's help and me hot on their heels. Doc waits on the other side of the door.

"I'll take it from here," he urges, pointing Thor and Ratchet toward the living quarters of the club-house, where he has likely set-up up his gear. Ginny comes running from the direction of her room, and screams when she sees him.

"Jude!" her small voice wails. "Oh my god."

"I'm alright, Ginny. Just a little banged up," he says, trying to ease her fear.

"You've been shot. You aren't alright at all."

Ginny clings to his side, and I watch as they disappear. His ass better live through this. I already owed him enough as it is.

I exhale the first real breath I had taken since I walked into that restaurant, and turn to find a fuming Raze standing behind me.

"Prez, I–," I stammer out, before he cuts me off.

"Save it, until after we get Presley back. Church. Now."

I follow behind him, my head hung low from shame. This could have all been fucking avoided if I hadn't insisted on such a dramatic meeting place to tell Presley. She could have been here and safe, instead of with them. The thought of what she could be going through kills me inside. I know what men like that do to women who don't cooperate. If she left with her life still intact, it would be a miracle. I just had to hope that the same fighting spirit to survive that ran in her brother's veins was in hers too. Her death would mark the end of mine. I couldn't live with that kind of guilt.

The meeting room is full to the brim of my brothers. Each pair of eyes is on me as I enter. They know. They all know why this happened. It's my fault. The blame for this rests solely on my shoulders.

Raze stands in front of my brothers and addresses us all, but his eyes never leave mine.

"Most of you know what's going on, but I want to go over what we know. Presley was taken from outside a restaurant downtown. Ratchet was shot in the process of the snatch and grab. While I don't have confirmation it was The Zezza's, we all know that the possibility of this being someone else is slim to fucking none."

The crowd murmurs, throwing more glares at me. I stand strong. I have to be strong for her, even if it means that I'm fucking crumbling inside like an old broken building collapsing under the weight of its own bad decisions.

"Effective immediately, I want all the club girls out. Take them anywhere, but here. That includes Mikayla," Raze adds shifting his stare over to Thor, as he enters the room.

"Already ahead of you, Prez," he agrees.

"The calls have been made. Oakland, Long Beach, and Orange County are already on the road."

The reinforcements coming are only a drop in the bucket to the numbers The Zezza's have in their disposal. For the first time in our history, we were staring down the barrel of our enemies, out-gunned and out-manned. This fight would be an uphill battle, and every death would stain my soul with a dark smudge. The guilt of knowing that begins to eat away at me one big bite at a time.

"What do we do in the meantime, Prez?" Tyson asks.

"We try to find out where they are holding her, and then we wait. They made Ratchet as a threat, and his cut will lead them right here. They'll make contact."

I led them to us like a butcher to the lamb for slaughter.

And wait, we did. Two days pass without a word from them. While my brothers scoured the news, and our network of sources, I chained myself to my desk. Not eating. Not sleeping. Just working to find her. I had to find her. Nearly fifty hours straight of nothing but my computers, that were failing me for the first time. The glare from the lights on the screens begins to kill my eyes. I try to wipe away the pain and drown it with another Five Hour Energy shot, but it's no use. My eyes blur, and I know that I'm pushing my body to the limit. I resolve to step away for just an hour, while my programs continue scanning for news through the dark web. It's only a temporary break, and not me giving up, I convince myself. I wouldn't do that, until my heart ceases to beat in my chest. My last breath would be lost still trying to find her if it came down to it.

I find my feet leading me to the room, where Ratchet lay recovering. The door is cracked, and I peer inside to see Ginny by his bedside. Her hand is tightly wrapped in his, as she sleeps with her head on his bed. I start to walk away, but Ratchet's eyes lock onto mine. Caught. He nods his head, calling me inside.

My steps are quiet as I enter the room, and I park my ass in the chair on the other side of his bed that Ginny's not occupying.

"How are you feeling?" I ask. Ratchet looks to his bandaged-up shoulder and leg, then back up to me.

"Like I was shot twice, genius," he snidely comments. "I'm okay. Doc says I'll be good in a few weeks. He was a shit shot. Missed every single artery."

I exhale a sigh of relief. Ratchet and I both knew he was lucky. Men like that are trained like professional hitmen. He should have been dead, but the commotion and exposure must have affected the shot. Under normal circumstances, I would be burying Ratchet, instead of talking to him right.

"Any news about Presley?' he asks with a low voice. He looks at Ginny, watching if she stirs at the mention of Presley, but she snores quietly at his side.

"None. No chatter," I sigh.

My heart thuds like lead, as my mind thinks over

what they could be doing to her right now. She could even be dead, and everything we are doing to get her back would be for nothing. My body trembles, as the picture of her lying beaten, abused, and dead flashes in my mind. Her dead eyes looking right through me while her cold, blue lips whisper to me.

This is your fault. You did this to me.

"We'll get her back," he reassures me.

"I wish I had your hope, Ratchet. Two days is a long time for them to not contact us," I admit, under duress the thought that I had tried to shove out of mind after the first day.

He shifts in the bed, taking care to not disturb Ginny, and allowing a groan of discomfort slip through.

"Do you know how I know we'll get her back?"

"I'd sure love to know where you get your crystal ball answers."

"Because of her," he nods his head back towards Ginny. I cock an eyebrow, confused.

"If it were Ginny, I would be doing the exact same thing you are doing right now. Even if you don't want to admit it, we're realists, you and me. We see things for what they are."

He's not wrong. I didn't fill myself with false hopes like others might to get them through this. On paper, we were looking for a body not a person, but my heart told me otherwise. She was still out there. I know I would have felt her life being taken away, as crazy as it sounds. She was still out there waiting for us to find her. I know that now.

"Presley is a pawn in their game. The Zezza's want Ginny. They'll use her to get to Ginny, and when they do, we'll be ready."

Ready to fight. Ready to die. All for Presley and Ginny. It was like being on the final level of a game, waiting for the big boss to strike. It was coming, and I would *be* ready.

Chapter 23

PRESLEY

GIO'S INTERROGATION lasts for a few hours. He yells, screams, and threatens everyone I love, dangling them in front of me. But I don't give in. My resolve to protect Ginny to the end stays strong. Even as his fist connects with my face then my stomach, I keep my resolve. Not getting what he wants, Gio leaves my room, leaving me in a painful silence of the tears that I hid from him. Tears would have meant he won, and I wouldn't give him the satisfaction. Not one wet drop of emotional exhaustion and fear would fall for him.

I will not give in. There's too much at stake if I do.

My mind shuts off the horrors happening on the outside, and I focus on happier times.

I think of Ginny first. She is the spark that keeps me going. My life would be lost for hers. That much I knew. Despite how hard my brother would fight for me, I was willing to lose it for her. Ginny has so much life left to live, and she deserves to have a chance at it. Her childhood may have put her into this precarious and life-threatening series of events, but I could change that. Her life was so much more important than mine. I imagine her future. Her being so happy and peaceful. She will find love, and start a family. I cling to those imaginative dreams, until they too fade away.

Voodoo soon follows. No matter how hard I want to push him away, his face slips back into my mind. His smile beaming down on me in a loving embrace settles my nerves, as I focus on his face, and not Gio's. I should be furious at him, but as I feel my life slipping away by the minute, I find that I can't. Like Ginny, he is a beacon of hope in such a hopeless situation. I know he's out there looking for me with everything that he has. Just like my brother and the club. Yet Voodoo's devotion to saving me would be much stronger than a familial bond. His drive was powered by love, and that trumps all. I just hope that if I somehow survive this that I get the chance to tell him that I forgive him.

The foreign man who tied me up returns a short time later with a glass of water and a plate of food that resembles dog food. He shoves it on the floor in front of me, and shuts the door behind him. I peer down at the meal in front of me, and though my stomach retches at the thought of consuming, I can't ignore the hunger pains. The only problem is that I'm still tied to this fucking chair.

Ideas float in my mind like clouds in the sky, but there's only one solution to this problem. Planting my feet firmly to the ground, I lift the chair and lean forward, letting my weight take me off balance. My body hits the cement floor with a thud, and pain floods my left side. It wasn't the best idea, but it was all I had. I scoot to the best of my ability, until the glass of water and plate are directly in front of my face. I nudge the glass until it topples over, spilling the content in front of me. My tongue slips from my mouth as I lick the water like dog from the dirty floor. The wetness coats my throat, relieving the pain from days of thirst. I lick as much as I can, before turning to the food. The smell is enough to take away any chances of eating it. The glistening slime atop the brown lump of mush disgusts me. Even the thought of it makes my stomach turn the longer I look at it. The growls radiating from my stomach scream to eat it and take away the hunger pains, but I can't. It will only come back up. It's better to starve, than to taste the foulness presented in front of me.

I slide and scoot myself away from it, until the

legs of the chair hit the edge of the bed. I lay like that for hours, slipping in and out of sleep, until the door clangs open with a bang against the wall.

"Well now," Gio's voice calls out. "Someone was thirsty."

His brown loafers step around the plate and toppled glass, stopping in front of me. I crane my neck up to look at him, as he smiles down at me.

"You weren't hungry, Presley?" he teases, before turning to the plate and then back to me. "And Alpo spent such a long time preparing that cuisine for you. You're disrespecting my hospitality."

Dog food. The fucker was trying to serve me dog food. I'm so glad that I didn't eat it now.

"What do you want, Gio? I'm not going to tell you anything. I thought you'd have realized that by now. Starve me, beat me, or do what you want. It won't change anything."

His hands grip the back of the chair and toss me upright like I was a weightless being. He was strong, but I had already figured that out by the velocity of the jabs he delivered to my stomach. He took no pity on me as woman. Gio is a heartless, soul-sucking monster, and is currently shoving his nose right in my face.

"Such strength you have, my dear. It's almost endearing. But the clear fact remains that you're nothing to me. I have all the information I could ever want sitting back in my office. Bios on your family, your friends, your nieces and nephews who you think are safely tucked away in Arizona. We know everything about you."

"If you have everything you need on me, then why are you torturing me?"

"For pleasure, of course," he declares, smiling like one of V's movie villains. He means what he says. If I had balls, he'd be holding them right now. But why if he has that information has he not charged the compound and taken what he wants? The realization hits me. He doesn't know that Ginny is there. The only thing he knows is that I was there. That's the piece he doesn't have one hundred percent certainty on. He's trying to appeal to my feminine weakness to try to get me to slip up. That will not be happening.

Gio rotates quickly, heading back to the door. He abruptly stops.

"On second thought. You might rather enjoy what I'm about to do. Ricliss!" he calls out. "Bring her along."

The hulking form of one of the guards bursts though the door. He pulls a small silver knife from his pocket, popping it right in front of my face. I flinch in terror. I can defend myself against mental attacks, but physical ones are a different story.

Ricliss grins, as he uses the blade to cut the ropes binding feet, leaving the binds wrapped around my hands. Using the rope as a leash, he jerks me upright, and my legs falter underneath me. They tingle and burn, as feeling and blood return to my lower limbs. Ricliss doesn't wait for me to get my bearings. His strength is over-powering. He practically drags me from the room and into the hallway, like a dog who refuses to walk.

Plain gray colored walls line the corridor. I try to memorize each twist and turn that we take, but I lose count. We pass a series of doors just like the one I came out of. Gio and his family have built a fortress with enough cells to hold more than twenty people just in this hallway alone. These were sick men who killed for pleasure and territories. Why it surprises me to find this kind of place in their possession is lost on me. Sick men often have twisted realities. These men were no different. Ricliss and Gio chatter like two teens at the mall as they walk. The language is still foreign to me. I should have paid more attention, during my language studies in school.

Ricliss shoves me forward into an open doorway. I crash to the floor in a heap. My eyes peer up from the ground to find dozens of men staring back, including the old man who was in my cell the day I woke up. His face is unchanging, as Ricliss picks me up again, jerking me into a chair. He pulls a small roll of duct tape from his pocket. The knife he used to cut me free returns, he uses it to unbind my hands. I rub my wrists, trying to get the blood back into them, but he uses the duct tape to bind them to chair.

"Stay there, and shut up," Gio whispers into my ear. "If you don't, I'll gut you."

His threat hits home, and I comply.

"Gentlemen, shall we?" the older man asks at the head of the table. Gio moves beside him, and presses a button on the table. The sound of a dial tone fills the room with the dialing of a phone number after it. It rings and rings, until a voice finally answers.

"Hello," the voice on the other side of the line answers.

It's Michael. This is what my purpose was for them.

"Good afternoon, Michael," Gio nearly sings. "You're a hard man to find my friend."

"I take it this is Gio Zezza," Mikey calmly growls.

The men in the room look around, grinning at each other like they've won an award. Gio leans down closer to the speaker.

"So, you know who I am, and I presume then that you know what I want. Yes?"

"Yes," he hisses. "You want the girl."

"That's right. I seem to have something in my possession that you might also want."

"Is she alive?" Mikey inquires. He's playing this smart. This isn't his first rodeo dealing with murderers and thieves. Proof of life is the first thing you need to establish, when dealing with kidnapping. That much I had learned from watching my father. The dead are of no value. The living were worth a hundred times that.

"I want to make you a deal," Gio offers. "The girl for your sister."

No, Mikey. Don't do it. Please, I'm not worth Ginny's life.

I squirm and my chair squeaks, as I do. Gio's eyes flash up to me. His finger cuts across his throat, as a warning to shut up.

"You'll have to be more specific. We have a lot of girls around here. You in the market for pussy?" Mikey deflects. Good. Keep him talking. V is no doubt on the other side of the call trying to trace it. My heart skips a beat, when I think of his face listening to this all go down. Is he thinking about me?

"Don't be daft, Mr. Sanders. You know damn well what girl I'm talking about. Your sister's traveling companion. She's told us oh so much about her."

Lie. My brother has to know that.

"I want proof of life, before we discuss the particulars."

Gio looks to me.

Shit. What do I say?

"She's right here, Michael. Why don't you say hello?"

"Presley?" his voice shakes. "Are you okay?"

I remain silent, until Gio nods.

"Mikey," I cry out.

I can hear his sigh over the phone in relief. He thought the worse, and I just put his fears to rest.

"Don't do this, Mikey," I beg him. Gio's face flashes with rage. He nearly runs from the end of the table toward me. His hand flies backwards in the air and comes down in a fist across my face, as he throws a haymaker. I feel bones crack under the force of it. Blood cascades from his fist onto the floor next to me. My mouth fills with the disgusting metallic taste. I spit it out onto his pristine floor, and return to look up at Gio.

You will not break me.

"Shut up," he yells. "You know the consequences."

"Don't touch her." I hear V's voice break through from the other side of the call. "Don't you fucking touch her."

"Shut up," my brother hisses to him. Hearing his voice sets my spirit on fire.

"Don't trade her for me," I yell again, bracing for

the hit that comes with my insubordination of Gio's only command. His strike this time is harder, knocking the air right out of my lungs.

"Stop!" Mikey yells. "We'll agree to the trade."

"Coming to your senses. That's much better. I'll send you a location."

"No. You'll come to me, and I want to see my sister, before the trade. Up close."

"And why do you think that I would agree to that?" Gio huffs, returning to the head of the table with my blood dripping from his knuckles. "Do you think that I'm stupid enough to come on your turf?"

"Our turf or no deal.

He's leveling the playing field. Home turf advantage will put them in a well-protected and secluded area. He can control it, even if he can't control the rest of the situation. My brother knows that I'm ready to die, but he won't give up on the chance to save me. His stubborn pride will fight, until the last drop of his blood spills to the ground. Yet he's still angling for something as the conversation continues. What is he hiding?

"I have a stipulation if I agree to this. My men can search your grounds. No guns. No cops. The clubhouse will be empty and the girl outside. Do you agree to these terms?" Silence fills the room for what seems like an eternity.

"Do you agree?" Gio asks again.

"I agree. Tomorrow at noon." Mikey concedes, before the line goes dead.

The room of men all erupt in a joyful glee. Each of them has smiles plastered on their faces a mile long. Celebrating their victory of wills over my brother. Gio stalks back toward me, and grabs my face with his hand. The pain shoots from my open wounds on my face, as he brings me to look him in the eye.

"Tomorrow, we get the girl, then kill your brother's club in front of you. You will watch, until every one of them is dead, then it will be your turn."

Chapter 24

VOODOO

I DIDN'T SLEEP last night.

Not one fucking wink.

Counting sheep didn't even help.

Believe me I tried, but knowing that today was the end of all this shit for Presley and for Ginny put my mind in a nightmare tailspin. The possibilities of how this would end were endless. She could live, or Ginny could die. Maybe vice versa, we could all die. There was no way this ended without bloodshed. Anyone who believed or hoped for that was lying to themselves. Someone would pay for this with their life. That was the only certain in a sea of uncertainties.

As soon as my eyes closed, I saw their bodies riddled with cuts, bruises, and bullet wounds bleeding out in front of me. Presley's skin once so beautiful had traded its luster for a dull, lifeless yellow and blue of dead, rotting flesh. Her milky eyes staring up at me for help. No. Sleep wasn't for me. I refuse to allow my last memory of her to be that of a nightmare.

Instead, I spent most of the night pacing the floor, trying to find an alternative out of this mess that I had caused. Presley didn't deserve to be put into this predicament in the first place. She should be safe by my side. Hearing Gio beating her over the phone broke me. The visions of him laying his hands on her beautiful flesh would haunt me for the rest of my life, however long that might be.

Raze had a plan, and it was a good one. One of the best ones we'd ever had in fact. It was smart. Unexpected. One that Gio wouldn't be able to anticipate, but it had its flaws. Raze was relying on Gio's blind need for Ginny to cloud his mind enough to not see it coming. It was a risk.

A risk that I wasn't willing to take with Presley's life. I thought about the different angles we could take. Was there some avenue I wasn't considering? The hours of pacing cleared my mind, and I formed a plan of my own. It's not necessarily better than Raze's plan, but it would tip this fight into our favor at a price. A price that I was willing to pay as long as my girl, my brothers, and Ginny walked away from this.

The clubhouse was eerily silent, as I leave Presley's room and stalk to my office. A man wouldn't often admit to needing their woman in front of their brothers, but I did. Raze didn't want me to be in her room, but I needed her scent around me. She almost felt close again lying in the bed that I shared with her for so many nights. I remember the way she smiled at me when I kissed her goodbye in the morning. The way she sounded just before the brink of an orgasm. The sweet taste of her lips that I hope to one-day kiss again. Those are the happy thoughts I cling to now.

The closer I get to my office I think about how things will be, when we get her back. Will she still be pissed at what I did? Will she even consider forgiving me? I could live with her hating me for the rest of our lives as long as she was free. My life would be pointless without her in the world, and that's why I have to do this. Her life for mine was a trade I was willing to make, and make it I would.

I close the door to my office once I step inside. My computers are still working trying to find another solution, but the time for that option is now gone. I failed at the one job I was good at for the first time. I didn't pretend that I was God's gift to the computer world, but at the end of the day this was a low blow.

The thought of trying one more time pushes forward in my mind, but it's futile. The devil was coming to our doorstep in just a few hours. Time was the most precious thing I still had left, and I wouldn't waste it on trying to do the impossible. I was bested, and I had to own that, even if my pride refused to do so.

I pull my phone from my pocket, and dial the number I had sworn to never use, even if I needed Batman to kill the Joker. That's how far I was willing to go down the rabbit hole to ensure this ends in our favor. The call goes through, and an answering service picks up on the second ring. I ask the operator to direct my call to the man I seek. She relents after I give her a few pieces of information that I knew would fast track me right to him. The right words for the worst situation.

"Hello?" his gruff voice answers.

"I want to make a deal," I say into the receiver.

Our conversation lasts nearly an hour. My contact was reluctant at first to agree to my plan, but after I sweeten the deal, he agrees. The key is knowing the right words to say and how to play the cards you have in order to win the hand. He took what I had to offer, and ran with it. Now it was in his hands to follow through with it. I had made my bed, and I would lie in it, when the time comes. I slide to the floor when I hang up, as I realize what I just did. My trust in my brothers was unwavering, but I needed this to be an absolute. Like Presley, the apologies would have to wait, until after the fact.

I tinker around in my office, making additional preparations for the deal I just made. My wheelie chair is in constant motion for nearly two hours, before a knock comes at my door.

"Prez is looking for you, V," Hero says through the door.

"Be out in a few, VP," I answer him, as I click on last button and send a backup to our server offsite for safekeeping. The mouse flies over the screen, as I pull up a program that I designed for such an occasion. The red wedding box of doom pops up on the screen. I hesitate when I see it.

"It's for the best," I mutter to myself, before clicking it. Lines of code scroll down rapidly. One line after another, before the monitors systematically go black. Every trace of our past history is gone. Hidden away from prying hands for safekeeping. If I die, Raze would be sent the location to the secure server with instructions on how to retrieve the information. A system that had been set-up from the very beginning of my time here. Life always seemed to find a way to pull the rug out from underneath a person in their prime, so I made plans long before this day had ever come.

I take one last look around my office, before shutting the door on it for likely the last time.

Be good girls to the next person who fondles your keys.

The meeting and main rooms are packed to the brim of my brothers from my club and others in the area, when I finally step into it. When Raze's call for help went out, they answered in full force. Our numbers swelled nearly reaching sixty men ready to fight in less than a few hours.

I notice Raze exiting Church with the presidents and vice-presidents of the other chapters present here today. His face is stern, yet oddly calm. He too had obviously prepared himself for the worst. He looks to me and nods.

Though this was my fault, he wouldn't hold it against me, until the dust settled. He would be angry, of that I have no doubt, but he would be proud of me for protecting my family.

Ratchet limps into the room from his sickbed, and hobbles to one of the couches not fully occupied. He spies me, and motions me over to him.

"You should have gone with the girls, cripple dick," I tease.

"Like hell. Not with Ginny here. Besides, I can't let you guys have all the fun."

"She ready?" I ask. His face falls from mentioning

her. Like Raze and I, he has a personal reasoning for worrying about this meet.

"As much as she can be."

He pauses, looking back down the hallway where she sits waiting. Is she doing the same thing that Presley is right now? Praying for a miracle? As to where Ginny is well protected, Presley's fate would be much different, if it was as bad there as it sounded on the phone. My fists clench at my sides when I think about her cries of pain. If I got the chance to put Gio down, I wanted the kill shot. He would die at my hand for the shit he did to her.

"You ready?" Ratchet says, breaking the silence of my mental escape into dark thoughts.

"Yup," I reply. "Just like old times. Say, do you remember the first time you and I went on a run?"

He laughs, shaking his head at the memory. Raze had given me to Ratchet for my virgin club business trip, after one of the club girls who used to darken our doors came back nearly beaten to death. Her lowlife boyfriend had taken his fists to her because his dinner wasn't warm enough, while he was tweaked out of his mind. Gigi had been one of the club's favorite girls, and Raze wanted the problem to end for her.

"You mean you nearly shooting your fucking foot off, when he charged at you?"

"I told you. There was cat dander in my eyes from that fucking four-legged terror she had. It slipped," I defend myself.

"Years later and you still won't accept the fact that you nearly pussied out."

"Did not."

"Did so."

We both laugh. Not a forced laugh, but a good old belly laugh. The few guys standing around us, look at us like we were clinically insane for laughing when doom was headed our way, but I needed this. Just a chance to remember the good times, before they went to shit.

"I need to thank you, Ratch."

"For what? Getting shot?" he questions. "Because I sure as fuck didn't want to do that."

"No, not that. I mean for helping me find my way here. I doubt that I could have done that without you and Jagger here to help me. I wasn't exactly the kind of guy you wanted for the club, but you still voted for me."

"Where is this all coming from, V?" Ratchet asks, with a hint of skepticism dripping off his gravelly voice.

"Can't a man tell another man he appreciates him?"

He cocks an eyebrow at me. "What have you done, V?"

Even now, Ratchet can see through my bullshit barrier to know that something is up. It was beginning to get a little scary with how well he knew how my mind ticked. Maybe I should leave a note for Presley to schedule some sessions with him later. He might have caught my screw is loose syndrome. I smile, shaking my head.

"Nah, brother. Everything's fine. Just trying to shake off the bad shit, before the even worse shit hits us."

The look on his face is one of disbelief, but he doesn't press the matter any further. I notice Raze moving to the center of the room, as a loud whistle of attention rips from between Hero's fingers in his mouth.

"I want to say a few words, before The Zezza's get here," he starts. "Over twenty years, I have been a Heaven's Reject. Not all of those years were easy, but we made it through them together. I could stand up here, and give you all an inspiring coach like speech, but we all know why we are here. When we take our oath and wear this patch," he says holding up a vest with our crest and colors proudly on display. "We pledge ourselves to protect our club, our brothers, and our families. That's where we find ourselves today. I want to thank each and every one of you for being here by my side, yet again."

Raze looks around the room, making eye contact with every single man standing with him. His brothers in blue and black and in arms. Behind him we are unified, ready to fight for our lives.

"Today we face an enemy like no other. But in life and death, we are one. Together, we leave this club-house to meet our maker. And together, we will rise or fall."

The men erupt in loud cheers and claps. The tension filling the room is cut in half, and an odd sensation of calm takes over. Brother after brother line up to shake Raze's hand, reaffirming their commitment to this club, until the sound of our trip wire for the front entrance wails. We all look to each other, knowing what that means.

"Showtime, motherfuckers!" one of my brothers screams out, as we all start for the door.

Chapter 25

PRESLEY

IN THE EARLY MORNING HOURS, a woman enters my room. Her raven hair blends into the darkness of the room making her seem almost ethereal in the softening dawn lights, peeking through the window. Hues of orange and pink ring her body, as if she's wrapped in a dawn halo. The softness of her footfalls doesn't make a noise, as she approaches me. She leans down, and whispers something in the same foreign language as my guards.

"I don't understand," I say to her.

"Come," she says with a heavy accent. Her small hands untie the bindings away from my wrists and feet that held me hostage in my bed. I slide my feet off the bed. The coolness of the floor shocks my system against my bare soles. The woman reaches for my hands, and I catch a glimpse of her brown eyes.

Sadness and pity fill them, obviously directed at my status here.

Is she a prisoner here as well?

I push to my feet, stumbling as I find my footing, and pad along after her outside the door. The guards that normally flank my doors are gone. The door grows smaller and smaller with the distance she pulls me away.

"Where are you taking me?" I whisper to her, but she doesn't respond. She soon stops us outside of a door, and uses a key to unlock it. She gestures for me to go in first. I hesitate for fear this is just another trap of Gio's to get me to break. She gestures again, but this time she smiles. Do I go in? She doesn't seem as if she's a threat to me with her small stature and gentle nature, but this could be a façade to make me feel safe.

"Please," she urges. What do I have to lose if I do as she asks? It's not as if my life could be saved at this point. I seriously doubt that this woman would be the means of my escape. I step into the room, and I hear the click of the light switch behind me. The room illuminates, and my eyes grow wide. I'm in a bathroom. She locks the door behind me, and steps around me, gesturing to the shower that sits in the corner of the room across from the toilet.

"Please," she urges again.

"You want me to take a shower?" I ask, confusion clear as day on my face. What's the point of cleaning up when I'm just going to die later? This makes absolutely no sense. The woman nods her head, stepping forward into the stall and turning on the shower. A stream of water bursts from the nozzle. Steam soon begins to fill the room.

"You clean," she orders a little more forcibly this time. Her hands start for the dress I have worn for the past several days. It sticks to my skin from the blood and sweat, and it hurts, as she peels it away from my body. She looks over me with even more pity, before ushering me into the shower. The hot spray stings as soon as it hits the open wounds on my face. I hiss at the sensation, turning away from it. My eyes fall down my body. Cuts and bruises mark just about every limb of my body. Streaks of dried blood cascade down my body from the bra and panties I still have on. I look like someone's personal punching bag. I reach up to touch my face with my hands, only finding more cuts and extreme swelling on my cheek from Gio's attack for my disobedience yesterday.

I try to relax, but the woman's hands shock me as she grabs my hair, pulling the remnants free from my last night with V. Before I can protest, she pulls a bottle from a small cabinet to the left of the shower and places the contents on my hair. The soft fragrance is pleasing and calming. She makes quick work of washing my hair, before pulling me out of the shower. I shiver, as she gives me a soft cotton towel to dry off with. She fumbles with my hair, piling the wet glob of tangles in a bun high on my head, which she secures with a rubber band.

The cabinet re-opens and a shirt and pair of sweatpants come out of it. She helps me into the clothes quickly, and pulls me back to the door again. The point of all of this is still foreign to me, but as soon as the door opens revealing Gio and his goons on the other side of it, I know. This was the bath before the blood bath. He was washing away the evidence of my time here.

"Good morning, Presley," he chuckles. "It's time we go to see your family."

He produces a black bag, shoving it over my head.

"Take her to the car," he orders. Two pair of hands grabs me and jerks me forward. I stumble as they pull me, until I can feel warm pavement underneath them. The familiar click of a car door comes from my left. One of the men grabs my head and shoves me inside. I land roughly against the smooth interior of the car, and the door is slammed with a loud bang, sealing me inside. Several minutes go by, before I hear the door opening again. The car dips as several people enter. I scuttle as far as I can away from them despite not knowing where I am exactly in this car.

The front door clicks open, and another dip tells me the driver has entered the car. The ignition dings as the jingling keys slide into it. A soft hum fills the car, as the engine starts. I commit the sounds and feelings around me, as the car takes off. The sounds of rocks crunching under the weight of the tires, the turns we take, and even the bumps we hit. Anything I could use to identify where I am should I survive this after all. Light passes through the black bag on my head the longer we drive.

The dark, monotonous voices of men converse around me. I pick Gio's voice out of the conversation and try to listen in when he decides to speak English.

"My wife," he chuckles. "She's soft-hearted. I tried to tell her there was no point in cleaning the girl up."

The men around me laugh at his words. The gentle woman was his wife? How could she be married to a monster like that? Was this forced upon her, or did she agree to this willingly? I had read case studies about women like her in college. Stockholm syndrome was the medical term for falling in love with your captors out for survival. Was that what happened to her? My heart aches for her, a complete stranger for being in his kind of world. I hope she could escape someday if that was the case.

The car jolts as it comes to halt. Are we here? Are we at the clubhouse?

"Search everywhere. Every outbuilding. Every room. If you find someone, kill them unless they're the girl," Gio's voice orders. The car doors open, and I can feel several exit the car.

We wait in silence. I listen for the familiar sounds of the area around the clubhouse, and it only confirms that we are in fact here. The exchange that I didn't want. The deal my brother made against my wishes, sacrificing one sister for another.

Please have a plan, Mikey. Please let what's on the surface not be as it seems. Ginny deserves to live.

"Clear, boss," a muffled male voice rings out from outside the car.

"Let's do this," Gio's declares, as a hand grabs me. A scream slips from my lips, as they drag me out of the car. My knees hit the dirt hard. What was another bruise to the collection he had already accumulated on me. "Say nothing," he beckons me from above, as I'm thrust from the ground and tugged. He shoves me down again. This time removing the hood from my head. My eyes burn from the sun beaming down, but they adjust quickly.

My brother, and so many of his club members are

lined up single file all along the front of the club-house. So many of the faces with him are unfamiliar. These men have come here on my behalf. Men who don't have any idea who I am, but as soon as my brother asked, they came for him. V stands to his left with Hero flanking the other side. His eyes connect with mine.

"You son of a bitch," V's voice yells out.

His fists curl at his chest, as he sees the damage that they've done to me with my time with them. He starts to charge toward me, but Raze shoots his arm out to stop him. This was going to be a delicate balancing act, and his rage-fueled reactions were not going to make this situation any easier.

"Enough, V. Back down."

"You should have better control of your dogs, Michael," Gio exchanges. "Show me the girl."

The line of men shuffles around, and an opening forms next to Hero, as Slider brings out Ginny. Her body is limp against his. Ginny's slumped form kneels down in front of them with her dark hair covering her face completely.

They're doing this. They're going to trade me for her. This is not what I wanted.

I look for Ratchet, not finding him in the crowd. Oh god. He was shot in my kidnapping. Did he die?

Is this why they have no qualms in trading her for me? Because her brother was no longer a problem?

Please god no.

"I held up my bargain. The clubhouse is empty. We're unarmed. Give me Presley."

"Tut, tut," he bellows. "In good time, Michael. I have a business proposition first."

"Not interested. The deal was for Ginny and Presley's trade. Not a fucking business deal."

Gio paces behind me. He's pissed that my brother won't hear him out. His feet shuffle quickly behind me, as I feel the warm metal of a gun being placed to my head.

"You will listen to what I have to say, or I'll blow her brains out right here on your property."

V starts to charge again, but this time one the man to his left grabs ahold of him, securing him in a bear hug. "No" I mouth to him. This isn't helping at all.

"Just get on with it, and take that fucking gun away from her head," Mikey demands.

"I'll think I'll leave it just where it is."

"Just get on with it," V interjects.

"I want your connections to the skin trade."

Mikey's entire body flinches. My father was the one who was involved in that. Not my brother. Gio is fucking crazy.

"Why the fuck would you think I had access to that shit? We don't deal in girls."

Gio clicks the hammer back on the gun, driving home his point to my brother. The sound of the car door opening sends my head spinning back. The older man from the call steps out.

"Motherfucker," a voice calls out, from the club's side of the fight.

"You're supposed to be dead," Mikey coolly states. His face flashes with concern. Who is this man?

"You will show my father respect," Gio orders to my brother.

He's the leader? Fuck, this is so bad.

"What is that old saying?" the old man says. "Ah, yes. The news of my death was greatly exaggerated, but back to business. What my son is alluding to you is that you'll be re-opening your pussy transport business again. For me. Thanks to you, my family has acquired your old pal Rex's inventory."

"You're already doing it right now with acquiring the girl for me. What's one step further?" Gio interjects.

Hero and V look to Raze, seeking answers to the impossible question laid before him. Gio's plan is all out on the table now. While Ginny was his main concern, Gio found another way to manipulate the club. My capture opened up a new business venture for him, because he knows my brother would do just about anything to get me back.

"And if I agree?" Mikey questions. "What's in it for me?"

"I'll equip you, and of course, your sister will walk free, as soon as we conclude our little business transaction."

"She's off limits, and that extends to the rest of the women and children. They will not be harmed."

"Deal," Gio casually agrees. "Not one little hair on their heads will be harmed. Do we have an agreement?"

"Yes."

"No!" I scream out. "Don't be like our father. Just let them kill me. Please don't do this."

Gio strikes the gun against my head, sending me spiraling to the ground. My brother roars at his assault on me.

"Let's get this over with," he orders. My brother roughly grabs Ginny by the arm and leads her toward the dividing line between the two groups. He tosses her to the ground like a discard toy, and walks away from her. Gio drags me off the ground, mimicking my brother's action. He tosses me to the ground, and I reach out to touch Ginny's outstretched hands. She trembles under my touch.

Gio kneels down next to Ginny with the gun still in his hand. "You've been a tough girl to find, Veve." His hand moves her hair away from her face in one movement. Her eyes peer up connecting with mine, and I nearly gasp.

Gio's eyes flash with rage when he realizes the same thing. That's not Ginny.

"Who the fuck is this?" he roars. "This isn't the girl."

"Run, Presley," V calls out. My feet scramble below me, but Gio catches me, before I can even take off. Within half a second, his arm is around my neck and the gun is pressed against my temple. It shakes under his grip.

"Say goodbye to your brother," he says into my ear.

"I love you, both," I scream, as a shot rings out. A sense of peace flows over me, as my body falls forward.

Chapter 26

VOODOO

THE MOMENT that bastard pulls her from the car, and he rips that hood off her, I fucking lose. Her face is barely recognizable from the swelling along the right side of her jaw. Both of her eyes are black as the damn night. The only thing left untouched on her face was her nose. How he hadn't broken that in the process I will never know.

Raze warns me to back down, and every fucking fiber in my body wants to tell him to go fuck himself. She's hurt. How can I stand here watching him toss her around like a goddamn rag doll? My heart is beating so hard that it's a wonder that I haven't had an aneurism or a heart attack.

I vow that for every mark on her body, he will receive the same thing. A cut for a cut. Gio Zezza would not leave this place alive if I had anything to do with it.

Then he caught on. Gio takes one look at our other version of Ginny, and realizes the deception. We knew going into this that we couldn't give him Ginny. Not a fucking chance, but we had to give him something. We turned to our club girls, asking for their help. Not demanding. This was a dangerous plan. It came with its own risks and that was something we couldn't just blindly order one of the girls to do. Misty volunteered. Her build was close enough to Ginny's. Add in a little hair dye, and you have a good enough lookalike from afar. We instructed her to keep her face down, and to not say a word. She followed every rule that we gave her to a tee, but it wasn't enough.

We had tried and failed.

But I wouldn't.

This was not how her story was going to end.

The shot that stops my heart rings out. I watch in horror as she and Gio fall to the ground. And then it happens. Police cars come flying in the parking lot followed by dozens of men in bullet proof vests, guns drawn. They circle us and The Zezza's. The look on their faces tells me all I need to know.

Game fucking over, Gio.

That is if he is still alive.

Good thing I had negotiated a dead or alive clause.

A chopper skims over the top of the clubhouse, kicking up dust all over the parking lot. The air off of its blades, whips through us like a damn tornado. Every pair of eyes are wide in shock, except for mine. Plan B just arrived with the goddamn Calvary. Just in time.

The plume of dust from the chopper blocks Presley and Misty from my view, except for the outline of bodies dotting the ground.

Please don't let it be her form lying on the ground. Not after all of this.

I start for her, but a swarm of FBI agents surround us. One horse collars me, dragging me down to the ground. I fight against his grip.

"Get off of me. I have to see if she's okay!"

He shoves his knee against the back of my head, pinning me to the ground. My chest heaves, as I still try to fight. The agent puts even more pressure on me, and I know I'm trapped.

"Get on the ground," they all scream at us. Raze looks back down at me, knowing what I have done. My brothers take to their bellies in the dirt with their hands on the back of their heads. The armed agents check us one by one for weapons roughly. They find nothing. Just like in the clubhouse. I had made sure of that. "Woah. Easy killer," I tell the agent frisking me. She must have liked what she found because I'm pretty sure she owes me dinner, after where her hand was just searching. I'd give her a solid B plus for enthusiasm if I was grading her frisking performance.

Raze rotates his head toward me.

"This you?" he asks. The agent searching him presses his head into the dirt, causing him to growl back.

"Yeah," I admit to him, as the officers move down the line. "Plan B in case shit went south."

"This going to work out in our favor?"

"It should."

"Explain yourself."

I exhale, and lay it all out for him.

"I knew we were outnumbered. So, I did the one thing that no one would ever expect, I called the FBI. They wanted The Zezza's, and I knew exactly where they would be. It was a dark horse long shot to protect as many of us as I could."

"You protected us."

"Yes. In exchange for them," I say, while I nod towards them. "They wanted Gio, and I gave him up to keep us safe. The club. Ginny. Presley. All of you."

He's angry. Just like I thought he would be. I had defied his orders and gone rogue. But that decision just saved our lives. I just had to hope that when the dust literally settled, that Presley was still there.

The clubhouse door kicks open behind us as an officer drags Ratchet out. He looks up noticing the chopper hovering above, and his eyes immediately find me.

"What did you do, asshole?" he calls out, as they shove him down.

"What I had to do," I answer.

The blades of the chopper echo off the mountains behind us, drowning out most of the sounds from the other side where Presley and The Zezza's lie.

"Officer," I yell. "The women. Are they okay?"

None of them fucking moves. Presley and Misty aren't who they're after. That's not the deal that I made. We're all after thoughts, until they secure who they came for.

The sound of the chopper above starts to get quieter, as it hovers away from the clubhouse. I watch as it lands in an open section of our property, kicking up more dust as it lands. Two men exit in the distance, walking towards the scene in front of us. They look over at us, before diverting their attention to The Zezza's.

My gaze moves instantly to the spot where Presley should be, as the dust begins to settle.

I will sell all my comic books and action figures if

she's there. I make promise after promise to the man upstairs, hoping that he's listening. I would give up everything I own to just see her breathing.

The air finally clears enough. Misty sits slumped over by an agent who is talking to her. Another agent kneels on the ground next to a too still Presley.

"I'm sorry to do this, dude, but you need to get your ass off of me." I twist my body, rolling the agent off of me and releasing his hold on my neck. I'm on my feet in a few short seconds. I scrabble and skid trying to get to her. Ignoring the fact that half a dozen guns and men are chasing after me. I skid, as I get close enough and slide in next to her body. The agents near her draw their weapons on me, screaming at me to get down. They can shoot me for all I care. It won't stop me from checking on her.

"Let him be," a voice orders the agent.

"Presley," I yell grabbing for her. Her body is limp, as I roll her over onto her back in my lap. The damage to her body is much worse close up. I rake her body, looking for wounds from the shot, but find none. She wasn't hit. "Baby, please wake up." Her lashes flutter.

"That's it. Come back to me," I beg. I pull her upper body into a deep embrace, and I cry like a bitch against her shoulder. It's when I feel her hand splaying across my back that I realize that she's awake.

"V?" she whispers in a hoarse voice.

"It's me, Presley. It's me."

She pulls me in as tight as she can, sobbing.

She's okay and in my arms again. I fucking did it.

For one fleeting second, I look to where Gio lies with a bullet wound right in the middle of his forehead thanks to Ratchet's crack shot from one of the hidden rooms. You would have had to know this entire clubhouse from floor to ceiling to spot the false wall, where he sat armed and ready for the right moment to take the shot. May he rot in fucking hell.

Presley shakes, as she pulls away from me. She's weak.

"I'm so fucking sorry," I cry.

"Sssh," she hushes me. "I'm okay."

I sit there in the center of everything just holding her. Not caring about anything else, but the fact that she's breathing. The time passes slowly around us. It's like watching a video in slow motion. Men move around us in handcuffs, as The Zezza's are systemically rounded up, and shoved into the vans that arrived sometime after the raid began.

Nothing in this moment is more important than the woman in my arms. She is the moon to my stars. The Khalessi to my Khal. I could name about a million other pop culture couple references, but none of them would compare to this moment. It's just the two of us in a firestorm of guns, villains, and heroes holding onto each other for dear life. It's the perfect ending to a sordid and dangerous tale.

Well, until it isn't.

The agents gave me my time with Presley, but that's coming to an end. I spy them closing in on me, and I know my freedom is coming to an end. "Whatever happens," I whisper to her. "Know that I love you." My lips touch hers for the first time in days, before the agents rip me away from her.

I don't even struggle as they do.

"Wait!" she screams. "Where are you going with him? You can't do this!"

She tries to push to her feet, but she's too weak to fight.

"Just remember what I told you," I utter, as they continue to drag me away.

The agents don't stop, and neither does Presley's protests for them to stop. I see my brothers now standing with agents all around them. One of the men who exited the chopper stands near Raze, as the agents deposit me in front of him.

"Mr. Martin, I presume," he asks. His sunglasses conceal his eyes, but I can feel them on me.

"Martinez," I greet him. "Nice to put a face to the voice."

"I have to say when you called, I only expected Gio and just a few of his men. I never thought that I'd be walking out of here with Don Zezza, and so many of his men." Martinez looks around the scene, gesturing with his hands.

I shrug my shoulders. "I aim to please, I guess. Is our deal still intact?"

"You gave me what I wanted, so you'll get what we agreed to. Agent Billings," he says to the man on his left. "Take Mr. Martin into custody." The agent whips a pair of cuffs off of his belt, and slaps them tightly around my wrists. They click as he locks them hard enough around me to stop the blood from flowing into my wrists.

"I don't fucking think so," Raze roars. "You got what you came for. You don't need him."

Agent Martinez turns to my president about to reveal the last bit of my plan.

"Mr. Sanders, I would watch what you are about to say every carefully. Mr. Martin offered himself up to us as a part of this deal."

"Is this true?" Raze sternly inquires.

"Guilty as charged, Prez," I admit, raising my cuffed hands in front of me. "I knew they wouldn't come just for a random tip, so I gave them something to sweeten the deal. I gave them me. The man who has been hacking their systems for years, in exchange for a free pass for the club."

Raze glares at me, before his gaze softens ever so slightly in the realization that I had sacrificed myself for them all. One man for many. I was proud to do this for my brothers and for Presley.

"Keep her safe, Raze," I ask. "Please, keep her safe for me."

"You know I will."

He shoves Agent Billings out of the way, and brings me into the tightest bromance embrace I think that has ever happened in the history of the world. I wish someone would have taken a picture for black mail later, but it wasn't exactly the best time for that.

"Time's up, Martin," Billings declares, pulling me away from my club, towards the car. My brothers yell, as they pull me away. Not knowing that this was of my own making. Martinez says something to Raze, before he follows behind us.

Step by step, I look to Presley. A medic is checking her injuries, as I walk past her. She cries out for me, but I can't look back to her. If I do, this won't happen, and the club will take the brunt of this shit. That can't happen.

"Wait!" a voice calls out from behind me. I turn, seeing Slider jogging towards us, as Billings starts to shove me into the car. Martinez steps between us, as Slider skids to a stop.

"It wasn't him who hacked your systems," he expels with heaving breaths. "It was me."

"What the fuck?" I exclaim. "What the hell are you doing, dude?"

Slider shoots me a shut the fuck up glare.

"He was protecting me. I was hacking into the government databases. Not him."

"Is this true?" Martinez asks me.

"It is," Slider interjects. "I should be the one going to jail. Not him. He's innocent. I broke into your mainframe just this week looking into the Zezza file. You should find the trail hidden away in the code."

Jesus. Has he been watching me work?

Martinez and Billings look at each other, trying to figure out if this was another fucking game or if Slider was telling the truth. I try to mouth to him to shut up, but he shakes his head no. Why is he doing this? Just let me go down for the club. It was my bed, and I was going to fucking lie in it.

"Release him, and arrest this man," Martinez orders. "Didn't catch your name, son."

"No, Slider. Don't do this," I argue, as the cuffs come off of me and onto him.

"It's my time," he utters. "Can I have a minute alone with my brother?"

Martinez agrees after everything we just handed him and steps a few feet away with Billings watching us both. It was a courtesy I doubt many got from the FBI. Then again, not everyone drops half of their America's Most Wanted List in their lap at one time. What can I say? We're overachievers.

"Why are you doing this?" I ask him.

"Because for the first time in my life, I know what it means to have a family. You saved us all, and I will not let you go down like this. Now go get your girl." Slider smiles, before calling back Billings and Martinez.

They shove me back, as they shove him in the back of the squad car and shut the door. Billings hits the trunk a few times. The patrolman in the driver's seat puts the car into drive, taking my brother instead of me away. He turns away just as they reach the edge of the drive, and disappear down the road.

I sacrificed everything for my brothers, and in turn, Slider did that for me. I would be re-paying him the best way I knew how. By using the information that I had pulled from the federal server and stored on my secure server. He would still have to serve time, but I would make for damn sure he would be done within the year.

It was the least I could do for the man who just gave me my life back.

Chapter 27

PRESLEY

WITH V SAFE, I let the last bit of my strength fade away into a deeply exhausted expanse of nothingness. I barely remember the medics carrying me to the back of the ambulance on a gurney, or even my hospital stay. There were flashes of light, and brief whisperings of V's voice telling me to rest. My mind was a dreamless state. The nightmares of what I had dealt with at The Zezza's, faded with the pain medication that the doctor's pumped into my veins, as my body healed itself from the trauma I had endured.

For days, I slept in a peaceful, drug-induced coma, until it was finally time for me to go home, under V's watchful guard. Though we never spoke, I knew he was there. I could feel him holding my hand or talking to me about some stupid movie he wanted us to see just to pass the time. His voice was the only constant in the veil of darkness of my dreams. I clung to it.

The crack I had felt in my face that day had thankfully not needed surgery. Even as the wounds on my face healed, Gio had left his mark. A few tiny scars were left near my eye and chin. Reminders of what I had went through and of what I had survived. The rest of my body would heal the doctor had assured me when I was discharged. The only thing I had left to worry about was my mental health. So much had gone on during the last few weeks that my brain was almost mush. I added seeing a therapist of my own to my checklist once my body healed. It was time that my role in the office changed to that of a patient. But when I was ready to go back to work, I would know exactly how those who sat across from me felt because I had experienced it. If I could take away something from this time in my life, it would be that I would be a better therapist for it.

The entire car ride from the hospital my brother smiles, talking about his family, and how we would finally be getting our chance that we were denied as kids. He is animated as he talks, telling me about Roxie's new word. The way he talks about his family makes me happy. With time, I hope to love them just as much as he does. It was time The Sanders's siblings finally got to know each other again.

My body is still weak, as my brother wheels me into the clubhouse, and I get a standing ovation from his brothers. Because of the men that I had once despised so much, I was here. One day I would thank each and every one of them for standing here at my brother's side to protect me. I also needed to thank Misty and apologize to all of the club girls. For too many years, I had looked down upon them, but in Ginny's hour of need, Misty stepped up. Not something that I could easily forget again, even if I didn't agree with the way they chose to live their lives.

V is noticeably absent from the room, as I had suspected he would be. Our relationship wasn't exactly on clear terms. We had some things we needed to talk about in private, but first, I had to see Ginny.

Mikey takes me to her room and leaves us alone inside. Ginny looks so different sitting on her bed today. There's lightness around her that I had never seen before. This was a woman who had tasted freedom for the first time.

"You okay?" she asks, seeing the bandages around my arms and stitches in my face.

"I am, but I'm not here to talk about me."

She shifts on the bed, grabbing a stuffed tabby cat

off of her bed and pulling it into her arms to comfort her. She sniffs its fur and smiles.

Must have been a gift from someone special. Ratchet maybe?

"Cute kitty," I remark.

"It was a gift from Slider," she declares. "I told him about the little cat I used to take care of before my dad died, that lived under our house."

"That was a sweet gesture. So how are you really?"

"I'm okay for the first time in my life. My anxiety has been almost non-exist. It's like a weight has been lifted off of me."

"It's because you've put the demons of your past to rest," I smile.

"You mean Ratchet did," she reminds me of her brother's part in Gio's death.

"How is he?"

"He's hovering like usual," she teases. "I spent the night at his house for a few days. Asher is really good at video games. Me not so much."

She smiles wide, as she thinks of her newly expanded family. Having her brother around would be a good thing for her along with Ricca and Asher. They would be the ones who helped Ginny heal the most. She would finally have the family she deserved.

"What about you and Voodoo?" she asks, hugging the stuffed cat tighter in her arms.

"Things are complicated," I casually deflect. And that was an understatement. A part of me still wanted to hate him because he destroyed the trust that I had put into our relationship, but I couldn't. He and I definitely needed to work some serious things out. That was a given. As he stayed by my side in the hospital, I could hear the pain in his voice. It didn't take a doctorate in psychology to know that he would blame himself for my kidnapping. Despite the manner in which it happened, it was only a matter of time before they caught up with us. The important thing that we both had to remember was that we all survived, and that was because of him.

The moment the FBI showed up in a massive raid, I knew it was him. No one would suspect it because it meant putting everything on the line, including the club. In all of my years as a therapist, feats like this were achieved by someone who has nothing else left to give, but himself. He saved me, and everyone else in the process. He was the hero in all of this despite the fact he had started off a pseudo-villain.

Lord. I'm starting to sound like him with all of this bad guy vs good guy talk. I might need a limit to the number of his pop culture references in a single day. Who am I kidding? He would just find new ones that I wouldn't catch.

"I think you should give him another chance," Ginny offers up as advice. "He's not a bad guy."

"I know he's not, but he and I need to talk a few things out."

A knock comes to Ginny's door, and Mikey reappears. "You're rides here, Ginny."

"Ride?" I ask, turning my attention back to her.

"I'm going back into protective custody, until the trials are over. Agent Martinez doesn't want to take any chances. It will only be for a little while, then after the trial I'm coming back."

"And your brother isn't here to see you off?"

"I asked him not to be. He doesn't need to see me leave again, but Agent Martinez agreed to let me call him every day, if I wanted to. I just have to get through this, and then I'll really be free."

She slides from the bed still clutching the stuffed cat against her chest. Ginny wraps her arms around me in the wheelchair, hugging me. "Give him a chance," she whispers against my ear, before pulling away and walking out the door. I swell with pride seeing her so strong for the first time in her life. She was becoming the woman she was meant to be.

I wheel myself around in the chair toward the doorway. Mikey starts toward me to help, but I wave him off. My hands lower to the brakes on the wheels, and I press them down into the wheels. My brother leans down, seeing what I'm doing, gently removing each of my feet from the footrests and pops them up for me.

"You ready for this?" he asks, extending out his hand to me. I take it. His strong hand steadies me, as I pull myself to my feet for the first time in days. My legs shiver and shake, as they remind me that I'm still not one hundred percent just yet. I take a baby step forward and then another with Mikey following right along beside me. We pause outside of my room, and he reaches for the door.

"I'll be in my office if you need me," he says, reminding me that he will beat V's ass for hurting me in his own, more subdued kind of way. Just what a big brother should do for his little sister. I hold onto the doorframe, reaching up to kiss him on the cheek.

He opens the door for me, and once I'm inside, he closes it behind me. The first thing I notice about the room is that it's changed. The bedding. The furniture. Even the flat screen is different. Did he do this?

V steps out of the bathroom with a vase of flowers in his hand and stops on a dime.

"Hi," he mumbles.

"Hi."

He quickly walks to the new bedside table, and

places the beautiful bouquet of roses and lilies onto it. I take a small step towards him and stumble slightly. V rushes to my side, picking me up in his arms, and lying me down on the bed. He adjusts the pillows behind my back without a word, before spinning around and heading for the door.

"Wait," I call out to him, making him pause. He turns to face me again. The nervous V is back, and he's watching me like he's waiting for the other shoe to drop. "Don't leave."

"Are you sure?" he asks.

"Yes, we need to talk."

He casually walks toward the bed, trying not to show his nervousness. I stifle a smile when I think about how every man reacts the same way to those four little words coming from a woman's mouth. Granted that when most women say it that it means that there's an ass-chewing to follow. He sits down on the edge of the bed with his eyes cast down onto the floor. When he lifts them to meet my gaze, I can see the sadness behind his beautiful blue eyes.

"I'm sorry," he starts. "This is all my fault. If I had told you from the beginning that I was Beauregard this would have never happened."

"I'm not mad at you."

He flinches.

"That's not exactly what I thought you would say."

"I know, but it's the truth. That day when you told me what you had done, I was furious with you. You cut me deeply."

"I know I did," he says, not even trying to hide his guilt. "I was so fucking stupid."

"But I forgave you the minute you came for me in that parking lot. Every angry thought I had about you melted away because you were willingly to sacrifice yourself to save me and this club."

"Raze told you about what I did, didn't he?" he sheepishly asks.

"He did."

"So where do we go from here?"

"The first thing you can do is wipe that sorry look off of your face, and go get me some popcorn."

He cocks an eyebrow at me trying to figure out where I'm going with this.

"When you get back, you can pick out any stupid movie that you want."

"Any movie?" he teases with an eyebrow wiggle. "God, I love it when you talk dirty to me."

"Not those kinds of movies, Beau."

He pauses when I use his first name. A smile like I have never seen forms on his face.

"I never thought I would say this, but my name coming off of your lips sounds so damn good."

"I think I might be able to top that," I challenge him. "I love you, Beau."

"I love you, my Khalessi."

"Your what?" I laugh. "What the hell is a Khalessi?"

He smacks his hand against his face in shock. Was it another one of his movie references that I wasn't picking up on?

"We've got to fix this lack of pop culture education of yours, woman. You're as bad as Hero. It's *Game of Thrones*."

"No idea."

"I love you," he smiles back at me. This time leaving the pop culture reference off.

"I know," I fire back at him, surprising him for once with a pop culture reference of my own. He smiles wide.

He slides forward on the bed, pulling me into a gentle kiss. The connection between us growing stronger once more. At first, it was soft. Like kissing the clouds, but it grew bigger and more intense. It's a kiss for the ages, and one that I don't ever want him to stop. His hands fall to my shoulders, and I wince when he touches one of my still tender wounds.

"Shit," he mutters with his lips still pressed

against mine. He breaks the contact, checking my face for any visible signs of pain.

"I'm okay. I promise."

"You're really not. Nice try. Until you're fully healed, I'm putting myself on a self-proclaimed no-sex penalty."

"Fine," I huff. "But don't be surprised if I jump you in your sleep, once I can do that, I mean."

"Baby, I will welcome that kind of attack with open arms, but until then, how about that movie. I'm thinking a *Twilight Marathon*."

"Did you really just say what I think you did?"

"I did. Now you sit back and relax. I'll get the popcorn, and then I'll introduce you to the sparkling world of vampires and werewolves."

I roll my eyes and laugh. My life is about to be become a nuthouse of crazy, and I wouldn't have it any other way.

Chapter 28

THREE MONTHS LATER

VOODOO

IF YOU WOULD'VE ASKED me a year ago if this would have been my life, I would've laughed in your face. Not like a heehee or a haha. I'm talking about a spit flying from my mouth full on belly laugh of impossible realities kind of laugh. My life solely revolved around the club and my computers. Thinking back in comparison now, it was pretty pathetic. I was a biker with a nerdy side of crazy. I didn't realize how miserable I was in my fortress of solitude, until Presley.

She has changed my life in more ways than I could have imagined. We had our ups and downs over the last few months, but we'd finally found that sweet spot in our relationship where nothing could stop us. Well, maybe her brother, but he'd finally accepted that I was going to be a part of his family someday. I take a great deal of pleasure knowing that I can torture him with the thought of me marrying in The Sanders's clan. He pretends to hate the idea, but as long as his sister is happy, he is okay with me deep down. Well, until the day that I fuck up, and then the ass kicking threats will come back with a vengeance. Marriage just wasn't in our immediate future.

One of the many nights that Presley laid in my arms in post-coital bliss, we talked about marriage. It was something that we both wanted down the road, but we agreed that we didn't have any reason to rush to the alter. We were happy with where we are, and there wasn't any need to change it.

Finding our own house was the biggest priority. While living in the clubhouse was fine, I wanted a space of our own. A private getaway paradise for the two of us. I had a decent amount of money saved up from my years of bachelorhood, so all we had to do was find the right place.

As I left our bed this morning, I looked down on the woman who would someday bear my last name. Her beauty radiated more and more each day, as she healed her mental wounds. At her insistence, I helped her find a therapist she could talk to that was local, and it seemed to help. I knew that she would one day want to go back to work. She loved to help people, and I wouldn't stop her from doing it. Helping those who were lost was therapy for both her and the patient. Trust me, she had helped me without even putting me on that little couch and doing sexy things to me. Which ironically enough was the first thing on my to do list once she did go back to work. A naughty therapist and a horny patient scenario sounded pretty hot when I thought about it. And I did. A lot.

The club has settled into a peaceful exist with the Zezza's behind bars. Ratchet kept us all informed about how Ginny was doing, as the court date creeped closer. She was doing well in her new safe house, and she was looking forward to coming back. I checked on Slider as much as I could. He was doing okay in prison, something that I had made sure of personally. It was the least I could do for what he did for me. When his case came to court last month, I put the real hacking skills to work. The look on Agent Martinez's face, when I e-mailed him copies of the videos I had found featuring Agent Billings and a few female co-stars in a little film called *"Agent Hung: Sorority Sluts"* had to have been priceless. I was sad that I couldn't see it in person. Slider's deal of five years in maximum-security prison soon fell to one year in a minimum-security facility with the possibility of early parole in six months for good behavior. As soon as his sentence ended, I would be throwing him the biggest fucking patch party in the history of our club. His act of sacrifice earned him that honor and then some.

After a quick run of the upcoming security jobs at Church, I slipped back to our room only to find Presley already out of bed. I rip off my cut and t-shirt along with my boots, before hopping back into bed. If I played my cards right, and I usually did, I would be dragging her sexy ass right back into bed with me.

I must have dozed off because, when my eyes open again I can't believe what I'm seeing. Presley is wrapped from head to toe in a black spandex cat suit. It hugs her curves like a fucking second skin. My dick jerks with approval.

Is this real? Am I dreaming this? Please let this be real.

"Do you like it?" she coyly asks, knowing what my fucking answer will be.

"Meh, it's alright," I tease her back.

She walks towards me. Each and every movement in that outfit makes my cock grow harder. This woman is going to be the death of me, and she fucking knows it. She slinks over to my side of the bed, turning and putting her ass on display. I consider reaching out and taking a bite out of it, but she turns too quickly to put my plan into action.

"Are you wanting to dominate, babe? Because if you are, I will gladly submit to anything you have in mind, as long as you have that outfit on."

"Not exactly," she declares, sliding one of her legs over my hips followed by the other. She centers her core over the top of my groin, making sure she brushes against me. Tease. My woman is a fucking cock tease, and I love it. Her ass cheeks grind into my groin, as she gyrates above me.

"Taking a page out of *American Horror Story* then?"

"Wrong again," she smiles. "Think a little harder."

"Hmmm."

Her hand slides to the zipper at her neck. The sound of the zipper sliding down draws my attention directly to her chest. She grins, knowing how much watching her take charge turns me on. The leather gives way, exposing the edges of her perfect, pulp breasts that bounce as she pulls the zipper down just below her sternum. No bra. Would I find no panties too if she unzips even more? I sure fucking hope so because if she keeps this up, I will be blowing my load in about half a second. Her dressed up as my favorite female superhero is beyond my wildest dreams, and believe me, my dreams are pretty fucking wild.

"Any more ideas?"

"Oh, I have plenty of those," I laugh as I roll my hips, taking her with me. She settles beneath me like a perfect fit. My finger traces a winding path down the front of her exposed chest. Goosebumps begin to pop up all over her skin.

I lay a kiss on her mouth, before moving down her neck and between her breasts. She moans, as I shove over the sides of her top, and place my mouth around a pink nipple that is already hard for me. My tongue runs circles around it, before I switch to the other.

"You still haven't figure it out yet," she moans.

"So demanding Agent Romanov," I utter, with her nipple still inside of my mouth.

I can feel her smile beaming down on me, as I finally tell her the real answer to her question. I move to her other nipple, sucking it into my mouth as my hand finds the zipper, pulling it down her belly even farther, stopping just above her pussy on purpose.

"Do you like dressing up for me?"

"Yes," she giggles.

My hand slips below her navel and against her clean-shaven pussy that is already wet with arousal.

"So wet for me already."

I slide a finger into her core, and she writhes underneath me. Her body responds to my touch instantly. She's been thinking about this because her body is ready and willing without much foreplay. Maybe later I will ask her more about this idea because I have a few costume additions that I would love to see in rotation with this one. Her back arches, as I slip a finger inside. She grinds her clit against my hand, seeking her orgasm far too quickly.

"Who's being greedy now?"

"Me," she moans. "Just keep touching me like that."

I remove my hand and she gasps, throwing me a very serious glare of disapproval. I grin back in response.

"As much as I love seeing you dressed like this, it's gotta go. I have plans for this body, and the leather is in the way."

She shimmies out of the sleeves of her top, pushing them down to her hips, as I continue to unzip her. I slide down to the edge of the bed. She lifts her legs wrapped in black-heeled boots, and puts the stiletto heel into my shoulder. I lean forward, trailing kissing down the warm leather and gripping the zipper for them in my teeth. I give it a tug, and pull it down to her ankle.

Presley watches me with hooded eyes with her teeth firmly planted over her bottom lip.

Her boot falls free from her leg. I toss is over my

shoulder, and it lands with a heavy thud somewhere in the room. I repeat the action on the other foot. The second boot joins the first, and my attention shifts to the cat suit.

I finger the edge of the suit at her hips, slipping it over them and sliding them down her legs. Presley lays completely exposed to me with her legs slightly parted. Her pussy glistens with arousal, and she looks delicious enough to eat.

I wet my lips with my tongue and position myself between her legs. She opens wider, inviting me to taste her. My tongue finds her sweet bud and goes to work. She squeezes my head between her thighs, as her release begins to blossom, under my tongue. While I could let her come with my face shoved into her, fucking her with my mouth, I decide against it.

"What the fuck?" she rebukes the removal of my mouth. "Why did you stop?"

"Because my cock will own your orgasm today."

A flash of excitement crosses her eyes.

Her arousal covers my lips, and I lick away the sweet taste of her, taking it into my mouth. She's the sweetest fucking thing on this planet. There is nothing to compare to the way she tastes. She's sweet, savory, and all fucking *mine.*

"Get on your hands and knees," I gruffly demand.

She rolls onto her side. Her ass pops up almost immediately. She wants this as badly as I do.

I sidle up behind her, positioning my aching cock at her entrance, before sliding inside with ease. Her walls constrict around me, as I push my way inside of her. She spreads her legs further apart, as she adjusts to my length. Her pussy is so fucking tight. If I didn't have better control, I'd be gone in just a few thrusts with the vice-grip around my cock, while it's buried inside of her.

"Fuck me, Beau," she begs. "I'm so close already."

"Not yet," I demand. "I want more of you."

My hips grind into her tight pussy from behind, twisting with every thrust. She locks her feet around my knees, drawing me closer. My hands fall to her hips, pulling her against me harder, as I deepen my thrusts. A scream falls from her mouth.

"Holy shit!"

Normally, I would care about my brother's being able to hear us, but today is not one of those days. Fucking her perfect pussy, until she comes for me, is the only thing on my mind. Her pleasure then mine. She will always come first in more ways than one.

"I'm close, baby," I tell her, as the brink of my orgasm lingers just below the surface waiting to break free. One of my hands slides from her waist, finding her breast. I cup it with my finger twirling her nipple between my thumb and index finger.

Presley tries to issue me another demand, but her ability to think is slipping away. Her breathy gasps take over. Fucking her senseless will be my goal from now on. If she can form words by the time she comes, then I didn't do my job well enough.

Life goals and shit.

The friction of her tight pussy and fucking her from behind hits that sweet spot of intensity. It's the one slight movement that sets my world on fire. My orgasm hits hard. Rocketing my come inside of her, as my head falls back. Her pussy milks my cock, drawing every last drop out of me, when her release thunders after mine. We both fall over in a heap of tangled limbs and heaving chests. We lie there for a few minutes, before I hook an arm around her stomach and pull her against my front. She scoots her ass against my groin. My cock takes notice, but I try to hush him back to submission for a few minutes.

"You're so beautiful just after you come, baby," I whisper against her ear. "I'm a fucking lucky man to have you in my life."

She giggles.

"Just me?" she asks.

Why does this sound like a trick question? Is

Ashton Kutcher about to pop out of the closet with a camera screw on the new sex version of Punked?

I wonder if my ass would look good at this angle. Not the time to squirrel, brain. Pay attention.

"Uh, yeah. Who else would else would I be talking about?"

"How would you feel about sharing me?"

What the fuck? It's only been a few months, and she's already thinking about making this two-some include more people. I don't fucking think so. I raise up on my elbows, pulling her onto her back and looking down at her.

"I'm not sharing shit. You're mine," I growl. "And I'm yours."

"Easy killer," she teases. "It's just that it will be a bit problematic is all."

"Explain, woman," I demand. "My blood is still in my dick, and my brain is not exactly following where you are going with this."

"It's just that in a few months it won't just be the two of us."

I freeze. Did she? Are we? Oh shit.

"I'm pregnant."

"But I thought? The shot. Oh god," I stutter.

"It's not one-hundred percent effective, and with everything that has happened, well, it failed."

I think about it for a second, before I open my

mouth again. This beautiful woman has been through hell and back, and now she's about to give me the greatest gift a man can get. A child. A Robin to my Batman. How could I not be happy about this? I pull her lips to mine, and kiss her one last time. She cries happy tears, and I cry with her. There's only one problem with this joyous news.

Her brother.

And that ladies and gentlemen is how I'm going to die. Because as soon as Raze finds out, it's Duck Hunt Voodoo all over again.

Send help and ice.

———

Did you enjoy Voodoo and Presley's story?
Click here to access an exclusive bonus story.

Did you enjoy Angels and Ashes?

Read more from the Heaven's Rejects MC Series.

Heaven Sent

Angels and Ashes

Sins of the Father

Absolution

Lies and Illusions

Resolution

Song List

"Bad Romance" – Lady Gaga

"Head on Collision" – A New Found Glory

"I Drive Myself Crazy" – N'Sync

"Blame It on the Boom Boom" – Black Stone Cherry

"Edge of a Revolution" – Nickelback

"Psycho" – Puddle of Mudd

"Sick and Twisted Affair" – My Darkest Days

"Beautiful With You" - Halestorm

"What Hurts the Most" – Rascal Flatts

"All Night" – Big Boi

"Rx (Medicate)" – Theory of a Deadman

"Kindly Calm Me Down" – Meghan Trainor

"She Fucking Hates Me" – Puddle of Mudd

"I Just Had Sex" – The Lonely Island (Voodoo's Favorite)

Acknowledgements

My seventh book completed. Wow! It almost seems surreal to even write that out. When I started this journey in 2015, I honestly had no expectations to be where I am today.

My first book was a means of distraction, while mourning my father. The second was the same, but in a different way. With each new book, my heartache hurt less, and my mind grew clearer. The strength that I had thought was buried with my father began to return with each word that I put onto paper. Although books are meant to be an escape from reality, they are so much more for me. Each new adventure has helped me find myself again. Telling stories of love, loss, and redemption, and in doing that, to find that inner strength that I had lost on February 20th, 2015, as I watched my father slip from this world. A memory that will never disappear completely from my mind.

But here I am nearly three years later, and I'm still writing, and piecing my family back together again without Dad being here. His loss really put things in perspective for me. The days where he would call in the middle of a movie or while I was at work used to feel line an annoyance or a burden. Yet now, I wish I could relish in every single second of those times to just hear his voice again. It's those moments that we take for granted each and every day that still hurts the most, because I missed out having more time with him. One more memory that I can never get back.

It is with that in mind that I write this. Take every single chance you have in your life to spend time with your loved ones. Cherish them with every ounce of strength that you have, because you will never know how much you will regret it when they're gone. Love yourself, love others, and live your life to the fullest. Make a mark on the world that your children, grandchildren, and family can take on into this world, even after you're gone.

The most precious gift of all is to know love, experience it, and in the end, let it go for others to carry on for you.

It is with that in mind that I want to personally thank everyone who has been a part of this book, and in my life.

There are no words that I can say to show my gratitude for what you have done for me, over the course of the last few months. Jaime's determination to make her man, as perfect as she has envisioned him in her mind. From Nikki's push to finish this book (and let me tell you she shoved hard). To Josh, Chelsea, and Shauna bringing these characters to life. To Rebecca's artistic vision of the final cover design, and to Brenda's final polish. It is because of you that this book was even possible. Thank you all from the bottom of my heart for your dedication, support, and professionalism to bring Lies and Illusions full circle.

For the readers, bloggers, pimpers, and everyone else in between that helped me spread the word about this book, I want to thank from the bottom of my heart. You played a hand in getting me to where I am today, and without you, none of this would be possible.

But the person I need to most thank is my husband, Glen. Throughout everything in the last eight years of our marriage, he has been my rock, my shoulder to cry on, and my voice of reason. He held me together the best he could, until I was ready to start fighting again to see the light in the world. Without him, I would have never taken the leap of faith that I did and started write. It was him who pushed me to find something that made me happy again, and with him at my side, I was able to do just that. I love you from my bottom of my heart.

Meet Avelyn

Avelyn Paige is a USA Today and Wall Street Journal bestselling author who writes stories about dirty alpha males and the brave women who love them. She resides in a small town in Indiana with her husband and three fuzzy kids, Jezebel, Cleo, and Asa.

Avelyn spends her days working as a cancer research scientist and her nights sipping moonshine while writing. You can often find her curled up with a good book surrounded by her pets or watching one of her favorite superhero movies for the billionth time. Deadpool is currently her favorite.

Want to talk books? Join Avelyn's Facebook group to learn about new releases, future series, and to hang out with other readers.

ALSO BY AVELYN PAIGE

The Heaven's Rejects MC Series

Heaven Sent

Angels and Ashes

Sins of the Father

Absolution

Lies and Illusions

The Black Hoods MC

Dark Protector

Dark Secret

Dark Guardian

Dark Desires

Dark Destiny

Dark Redemption

Dark Salvation

Dark Seduction

The Bastard Boilers MC

Property of Azrael

The Dirty Bitches MC Series

<u>Dirty Bitches MC #1</u>

<u>Dirty Bitches MC #2</u>

<u>Dirty Bitches MC #3</u>

Other Books by Avelyn Paige

Girl in a Country Song

Cassie's Court

9 781968 808990